HOUSTON HOMICIDE

HOUSTON HOMICIDE

BILL CRIDER AND CLYDE WILSON

FIVE STAR

An imprint of Thomson Gale, a part of The Thomson Corporation

THOMSON

GALE™

Detroit • New York • San Francisco • New Haven, Conn. • Waterville, Maine • London

LIBRARY OF CONGRESS CATALOGING-IN-PUBLICATION DATA

Crider, Bill, 1941–
    Houston homicide / Bill Crider and Clyde Wilson. — 1st ed.
      p. cm.
    ISBN-13: 978-1-59414-603-9 (alk. paper)
    ISBN-10: 1-59414-603-9 (alk. paper)
    1. Detectives—Texas—Houston—Fiction. 2. Private investigators—Texas—Houston—Fiction. 3. Houston (Tex.)—History—20th century—Fiction. I. Wilson, Clyde A. II. Title.
PS3553.R497H68 2007
813'.54—dc22   2007031579

First Edition. First Printing: December 2007.

Published in 2007 in conjunction with Tekno Books and Ed Gorman.

Printed in the United States of America on permanent paper
10 9 8 7 6 5 4 3 2 1

HOUSTON HOMICIDE

PROLOGUE

France, December 1944

We were near the German border the day I got shot for the second time.

It was so cold that I couldn't feel my feet anymore, and the wind was finding every rip and tear in my ragged combat clothing. I was missing about half the middle finger of my right glove and starting to worry a bit about frostbite and hypothermia. The sky was a gunmetal gray, and we hadn't seen the sun for days. If I'd dropped off to sleep, I'd have dreamed either of hot coffee and a down comforter or of sleeping in the sun while stretched out on the beach on Galveston Island.

But I was too cold to sleep, which was just as well. As the leader of a machine-gun squad, I had to stay awake and reasonably alert. Our .30 caliber Browning 1919A4 gun was belt-fed and could lay down a heavy field of fire, and someone had to be responsible for directing it. That someone was me, but at the moment we didn't have any targets, and I wasn't particularly eager for any to appear. If we started firing, the German 60mm mortars would rain down shells on us, and by that time in the war I'd already seen more than enough dead bodies on both sides.

The Combat Commander, Captain Jimmy Smart, must not have felt the same way, however. I turned my head to see a member of the rifle squad blowing on his bare hands to warm them. Smart had apparently ordered him to fire on a lone German soldier who had wandered into sight.

"Don't shoot!" I screamed, but I had a scarf pulled across the lower half of my face, and it must have muffled my voice, for neither Smart nor the rifleman heard me. Or if they heard, they paid no attention.

The rifle cracked, and I saw the German soldier jerk to one side before he fell.

Almost immediately the mortars started booming. They fired eighteen rounds a minute and each round had a blast radius of around thirty-five feet, not that I was thinking about any of that, not with the whistling sounds of the incoming rounds and the explosions that churned up the earth and sent shell fragments flying. I was just trying to get to some kind of cover, but my legs were heavy with cold, and it was as if I were running in water up to my waist.

I saw Smart's arm disappear just below the elbow as a shell fragment tore it away. Blood spurted out of the stump. Smart threw back his head and screamed, though I couldn't hear him. I turned toward him to help, though there wasn't going to be much I could do.

As it turned out, I did exactly nothing, because another mortar round exploded not far away from me—certainly not far enough. I think I heard the explosion, but I've never been sure because the next thing I knew, something hit me in the right leg. It was like being kicked by a mule the size of Texas, and it knocked me flying.

I was unconscious before I hit the ground.

CHAPTER 1

Houston, Texas, July 1969

In Houston in July the weather is enough to make a man wonder why any of the early settlers had decided to stay there. The humidity wraps around you like a hot, wet blanket, and the sun sets you to steaming before you've been outside for two minutes.

But the heat and humidity don't bother me much, and in fact they're good for my bum leg. It aches now and then in the winter when a norther blows down from Canada, but most of the time even the winters are mild enough to make me almost forget the little pieces of steel that are still embedded in my upper thigh.

The only time the leg really bothers me is when I sit for too long behind my desk at the cop-shop. I think it's the air-conditioning in the building that causes the problem, but luckily Detective Sergeants in the Homicide Division don't often have to sit still for long stretches at a time.

I'd just finished filling out a report in triplicate and was contemplating the dark carbon-paper stains on the tips of my fingers when Mac Perkins came by and said, "Lieutenant Bolce wants to see you."

I didn't have to ask why. If Bolce wanted me, it was bound to be about a homicide. I wiped my fingertips on my pants, not that it did the stains any good. It didn't do much for my pants, either. I got up, ignoring the twinge in my leg, and walked down to Bolce's office.

Bolce's an old-timer, like me. He wore an old gray suit, a white shirt, and a thin navy-blue tie that was so far out of style that it was almost in. He had one of those bulldog faces, with jowls that hung down on either side, and sad, wise eyes that had seen a lot more dead bodies than anybody should ever have to look at.

"Come on in, Steve," he said, motioning me forward with his hand. "Close the door."

My name's not Steve. It's Ted. Not Theodore. Just Ted. Ted Stephens. For some reason, however, nobody's ever called me Ted, except in the army. It's always been Steve. Even my wife called me Steve, before she left. Now she doesn't call me at all.

I suppose that if my last name had been Fitzgerald, people would have called me Fitz, and if my last name had been Hertel, they'd have called me Hurt, or maybe Turtle. So things could have been worse.

I closed the door and sat down in the old scarred wooden chair opposite Bolce's battered desk. The varnish on the chair seat had been worn smoothly away by the butts of a lot of guys like me.

"Got a homicide on Canal and Berkley," Bolce said. His voice, a sort of husky growl, matched his face. "I want you to go over there and have a look around. Wetsel and McGuire are already working it, but I want to hear what you think about it."

"Wetsel won't like it," I said.

For some reason Wetsel and I didn't get along. I'd never been sure just why, aside from the fact that he was a complete jerk.

Bolce waved a hand in front of his face as if swatting at a fly. "I don't give a damn what Wetsel likes or doesn't like."

I knew he meant it. Bolce did what he thought was best for the Homicide Division, and to hell with anybody's hurt feelings.

"Well?" Bolce said. "What are you waiting for? Get on out there. I don't like the way this one's shaping up."

I didn't ask him for any details because I knew he wouldn't give them to me. That wasn't his way. He thought that even a bare recitation of the facts might influence an investigator, and he wanted us all to keep our minds open.

Wetsel couldn't do that. There were times, and they were all too frequent, when his mind would close up like an oyster. No matter what the facts seemed to be, he'd go with whatever answer he'd already settled on and to hell with the evidence. If he'd concocted a theory about a case, he'd stick with it till the last dog died.

I left Bolce's office and got one of the black Fords they gave us to drive. It wasn't as bad as some I'd been in, but there were a couple of stained fast-food wrappers and a paper cup on the floor of the passenger side, and the interior smelled like hamburgers and greasy fries.

The Ford's air conditioner was working, which was a good sign, but I didn't turn it on. I rolled down the window and let the hot, humid air blow on me as I drove along. I could smell the chemical plants all the way from Deer Park, and there was a whiff of the Ship Channel in the air as well. The smell didn't bother me. In a weird kind of way, I even liked it.

A young woman walked along the sidewalk. She wore a long, billowy red dress that didn't quite hang low enough to hide her bare feet, and she had a baby in some kind of carrier that she wore in front. She had on granny glasses with purple lenses, and her long, straight hair hung halfway down her back. When I passed by, she smiled and waved, making a "V" of her first two fingers. The baby smiled, too. The heat and humidity didn't seem to be bothering them.

My shirt was sticking to me by the time I got to the corner of Canal and Berkley, and I loosened my tie. The whole world, except for the Houston Police Department, had followed the hippies' lead and gone casual. Not us. We still had to wear jackets and ties. Some guys still wore hats. I'd given that up a year or two earlier.

I drove along under the wide branches of oak trees that shaded the lawns and sidewalks. It was around eleven in the morning, so the neighborhood traffic wasn't too bad. Everybody going to an office was already there; it wasn't time for lunch, and nobody with any sense was going to be out shopping on a day like this one.

The neighborhood I was headed toward wasn't River Oaks, but it wasn't bad. The lots were bigger than average, and there were broad, well-kept lawns. The streets were wide and shady, and the houses were the kind the schoolteachers and cops couldn't afford.

The intersection near the houses where the homicides had occurred was crowded when I got there. A couple of blue-and-whites sat by the curb, and the Medical Examiner's van had pulled in behind them. Wetsel and McGuire's car, another black Ford like the one I was driving, was in front of them.

The news hounds' cars were parked haphazardly along the curb and in the street. I hoped there wasn't an emergency that would require fire trucks or an ambulance to come rushing down the street.

I found a spot behind the M.E.'s van and got out. Some of the neighbors were standing in their yards, craning their necks, trying to get a fix on the latest arrival. A couple of reporters I knew for the *Chronicle* and *Post* spotted me and started in my direction.

I ducked under the yellow crime scene tape to avoid them, and they both started yelling questions at me.

"I just got here, fellas," I said. "I don't know any more about this than you do."

It was the truth, but of course they didn't believe me. For some reason, they never do.

The yard had been recently trimmed, and a crepe myrtle tree had shed some of its fuchsia blossoms on the grass. The house looked well cared for. It was a ranch-style home and the wooden sections had a coat of white paint that looked as if it had been put on not too long before. The cornice boards were all intact, with none of the rot you see all too often in Houston. The flower beds along the front were carefully kept and bloomed with blue periwinkles. A banana tree grew at one corner of the house, and its broad green leaves stirred around a bit in the muggy air. It was a nice neighborhood, a place where you didn't expect bad things to happen, unless you were a cop. Then you knew that bad things could happen just about anywhere.

I showed my shield to the uniforms at the door and went inside.

The air-conditioning was on, as it nearly always is in houses in Houston in the summer. But even with air-conditioning, some odors linger. I could smell the odor of last night's fried chicken, but floating under that was the muted scent of something more sinister. Gunpowder.

A couple of plainclothes cops stood on the other side of the living room, talking with their heads together. I cleared my throat, and one of them turned around. Wetsel.

He was dressed in what he considered the latest style. I wasn't sure if he was right, since I didn't keep up with that sort of thing, but it was important to Wetsel. Some people said that he paid more attention to his wardrobe than he did to his cases. His pants were flared, his shirt was blue, and his tie was paisley. His hair was a little too long on the sides and back, probably in an attempt to make up for the fact that it was almost non-existent anywhere else.

He didn't bother to look me over with his hard little black eyes. He didn't want to waste any time letting me know how glad he was to see me.

"What the hell are you doing here?" he said. "This is my case." He corrected himself. "Mine and McGuire's."

That was typical of Wetsel. Every case was his, at least as long as things were going well. You could bet your last dime that if the case was solved, he'd get the credit, and McGuire would be just a footnote. But if things went south on him, Wetsel could do the fastest one-eighty you'd ever seen, and suddenly McGuire would have been in charge from the get-go. If there was a screw-up, Wetsel never took the blame.

"Bolce sent me," I said.

"Fuck Bolce."

"Good idea. Why don't you call him and share it with him."

"Fuck you, too, Steve."

Wetsel was feisty. I had to give him that. He was only about five-seven or -eight, while I was a couple of inches over six feet. He was stocky, with wide, powerful shoulders and a belly as hard and flat as a board fence. But I was in pretty good shape myself, for a guy my age, and I had the reach on him. I figured that if we ever actually got into a fight, I could take him in under a minute as long as my leg didn't give me any trouble. But if Wetsel was scared of me, he never showed it.

"I didn't ask Bolce to send me here," I said. "I just do what I'm told, same as you."

"Yeah, right," Wetsel said.

He gave me a disgusted look and walked past me and through the front door into the yard.

"What a sweetheart," I said.

"Miss Congeniality," McGuire said, and I grinned.

McGuire was about my age, eight or ten years older than Wetsel, but he was one of those guys who looked thirty-five when he graduated from high school and then looked thirty-five from then on. I figured he'd still look thirty-five when he died. His face was smooth and unlined, his chin was firm, and he had the eager, go-getting look of a used-car salesman. He took a pack of Camels out of his shirt pocket, shook one out, and offered it to me.

"No, thanks," I said. "I quit."

"So did I. Twenty or thirty times."

He tapped the cigarette against his watch crystal, stuck it in his mouth, and lit it with the flame of an old Zippo.

"What have you got here?" I asked.

McGuire exhaled a cloud of smoke and squinted at me through it. "Three bodies," he said. "A man and a woman, man and wife, both in the same bed. And an older woman in another room. Mother of the man. Each one got two bullets in the head."

There was a kid's book lying on the coffee table nearby, something by Dr. Seuss. McGuire saw me looking at it. He was a lot sharper than Wetsel. He said, "Three kids. Two boys and a girl. The girl's the youngest, probably about two. The oldest boy's around five or six. They slept through the whole thing. CPS has already been here, so the kids are being taken care of."

I imagined that the kids were scared and worried. This was something that would affect them for the rest of their lives. They were still alive, but they were as much victims as the people who were dead.

"So the kids lost their parents and grandmother?"

"No. The uniformed cops talked to the neighbors. Their story is that the children's father is a son of the man who was shot. He and his wife died in a car wreck a year ago."

"You have the victims' names and a positive ID?"

"Nothing positive yet, but from what the neighbors told the uniforms, it's likely that the couple are Mr. and Mrs. Ralph Parker. The other woman's a Mrs. Parker, too. Ralph's mother, like I said. She lived here in the house."

I thought the information over, but there wasn't anything really unusual in it. I said, "I guess I'd better see the bedrooms."

I started to move forward, but McGuire put up his hand. He was holding his cigarette between his first and second fingers, and smoke wafted away from the tip.

"What did Bolce send you for?" he said. "I know you and Wetsel don't get along, and I don't blame you for clamming up on him. He's an asshole, but he's my partner, and I'm stuck with him."

McGuire had a reputation as a good investigator, and even though Wetsel tried to blame him for most of their failures and mistakes, everybody in Homicide knew the truth of the situation.

"I don't really know why Bolce sent me," I said. "Maybe he just doesn't trust Wetsel not to come up with some screwy theory and ignore some of the hard evidence."

McGuire inhaled and blew smoke. "I can usually guide him in the right direction."

"But not always."

McGuire shrugged. "Hell, no."

"Then maybe that's why I'm here. Let's go in the bedrooms."

"It's kinda messy."

"Yeah," I said. "I'll try not to puke on your shoes."

"You know what, Steve?" McGuire said. "You're kind of an asshole yourself."

I gave him a grin. "So they tell me."

CHAPTER 2

The Medical Examiner was in the first bedroom. He nodded when he saw me at the door, and I nodded back. His name was Franklin, but his nickname was Ichabod, from the character in the story about Sleepy Hollow. He was even taller than I am and he weighed a lot less, being one of those guys who's all knees and elbows and whose suit hung on him like it would have on a scarecrow made out of broom handles.

The bodies lay on their backs on the bed. Blood had soaked into the pillows, and the smell of gunpowder was stronger here. There were other smells, too, much less pleasant.

"Ralph Parker, age forty-six," McGuire said. "And his wife Dorothy. Age forty-five."

"Find any brass?" I asked, now that the formal introductions were over.

"No brass," McGuire said.

"Automatic, then?"

Franklin straightened up and looked around. His face was sharp as an axe blade.

"Maybe," he said. "Silencer would explain why the kids didn't hear anything. But kids are sound sleepers, so the shooter might have used a revolver and picked up the brass."

"How many shots?"

"Four. Two each. One in the head, one in the chest."

"Any guess on the caliber?"

"The size of the wounds, I'd say it was nine millimeter, b

don't quote me on that."

"You know I never quote anybody except under oath."

"Right."

"Had the bodies been moved?"

"Post-mortem lividity would indicate that they haven't. They died right here in their bed."

I looked around the room. An expensive-looking jewelry box sat on top of the dresser. A man's clothes were laid out across the back of an old overstuffed chair. On the nightstand by the bed were a clock radio and a glass half full of water. There was fingerprint dust all over everything, but as far as I could tell nothing had been disturbed in any other way. This obviously wasn't a burglary gone wrong.

"Any prints?"

"Plenty. People live here, after all. But we don't know whose. The shooter might have worn gloves."

"How did he get in?" I asked.

"We don't know for sure," McGuire said. "Maybe the window. Just stepped right in and pulled the trigger."

I looked at the window, which was open. But the air conditioner was on. The two things didn't go together.

"Maybe they had the windows open at night," McGuire said. "Maybe they liked fresh air."

He said the last ironically, as if to imply that the phrase fresh air was an oxymoron in Houston.

"Nobody leaves the windows open and the air conditioner running," I said.

McGuire shrugged. "You never know what people might do."

I looked through the window and saw someone moving around outside, probably one of the crime scene investigators.

"Footprints?"

"Nothing so far."

"I need to see the other room."

"Help yourself. Barlow's in there, along with the evidence team."

I walked down the hall to the second bedroom. From the doorway I could see that a woman lay sideways across the bed as if she'd started to get up and fallen backward.

I didn't know the two evidence techs who were spreading fingerprint powder around, but I did know Angela Barlow, the crime scene investigator. She'd been on the force for about fifteen years and had a reputation as somebody who knew her business.

When I cleared my throat, she turned from her examination of the dresser and said, "Hello, Steve. What brings you here? I thought this squeal belonged to Wetsel and McGuire."

"Bolce asked me to have a look. Just to keep me busy."

"Sure," Barlow said.

She was short and soft-looking, with an impish grin, but she was far from soft. And she wasn't impish. I'd heard how she'd decked a civilian who'd tried to put the moves on her by landing a well-placed knee in his testicles. While he lay on the floor, she walked over to him and stomped his right hand.

"Never touch me there again," she'd said, but it was doubtful he'd heard her over the sound of his own groans.

"What do you have in here?" I said.

"Mr. Parker's mother. About sixty-five or -six, young for her age. Shot twice. One in the head and one in the chest."

"And that's it?"

"That's it. You can see for yourself. No sign of a struggle, nothing moved around. It was quick and clean. Two shots, in and out. Bang bang."

"He did the couple first?"

"Probably. She heard something, started to get out of bed. Then he popped her. She probably died instantly."

So had the others, I thought. The whole thing might not have taken more than a couple of minutes, and three lives were snuffed out just like that.

I went into the kitchen. McGuire was there, smoking a cigarette. I pointed to the telephone that sat on one end of the sink counter.

"I need to use that," I said.

McGuire blew smoke out his nose. "Hasn't been dusted yet."

"You really think the killer used the phone in here?"

"You never know."

I pointed out that he was smoking. "Taint the scene that way," I said.

"The killer didn't come in here."

"That's right." I pointed to the phone.

He shrugged. "Be my guest."

He didn't ask if it was a private call. He just turned and went out the door into the yard.

I picked up the telephone receiver and dialed Bolce's number. When he came on the line, I told him all I knew so far.

"That's not much," he said.

"Yeah. The killer neglected to leave his social security number."

"Don't get sarcastic. I want you to talk to the neighbors."

"I think Wetsel and McGuire will want to do the interviews. They won't want me to interfere. They'll think I don't trust them to do their job."

"Well, do you trust them?"

I didn't respond.

"Never mind," Bolce said. "I'll handle Wetsel and McGuire. You talk to the neighbors."

There was no use in arguing with him.

"All right," I said, and I hung up the phone.

The neighbors on one side were Dr. and Mrs. Reitman. They

both appeared to be in their fifties.

Dr. Reitman was mostly bald, with only a fringe of black hair around the sides of his head and a little stubble on top. He had watery blue eyes that were magnified by the thick lenses of his glasses.

His wife was a stout woman with iron-gray hair that she wore rolled into a knot on the back of her head.

"They're dead, aren't they?" she said.

We were sitting in the kitchen of their house at a round oak table that they must have found at a flea market and refinished themselves. It was better-made than most furniture you could buy these days, and the four oak chairs around it were as sturdy as concrete blocks. The kitchen appliances were all Harvest Gold, a popular color that I'd never been fond of. We each had a cup of freshly perked coffee in front of us, and the smell of it filled the room. I'd tasted mine already. It was strong and black with just a hint of cinnamon.

"We'd really like to know," Mrs. Reitman said. She was holding a wadded tissue in her left hand. "There's been nothing on the radio or television, and the uniformed officers who talked to us wouldn't say, but I know they're dead. I can feel it."

The air conditioner was on here, and the house was cool. Sunlight came in through the window over the sink, and in the tree just outside the window hung a hummingbird feeder filled with red liquid. Two hummingbirds hovered around it, their wings vibrating so fast that I couldn't really see them, just the disturbance in the air that suggested they were there.

I took another sip of coffee and set the cup back in the saucer without a clink. The cups were a little more delicate than I was used to.

"Well?" Mrs. Reitman said.

"They're dead," I told her.

I thought she might start crying then, but she didn't.

"The children?"

"They're fine," I said. "They slept through the whole thing. They're under the care of Child Protective Services for the time being."

Two big tears leaked out of her eyes and ran down her cheeks.

"Thank God for that," she said. "Are you a believer, Mr. Stephens?"

It wasn't a question I got asked a lot. I said, "I think you could say that."

"That's fine. I'm a lay minister in the Methodist Church, myself. Would you join us in a prayer for the souls of the departed?"

I felt a little strange about it, but I said that I would, and she took my right hand. Dr. Reitman, who so far had said nothing except to introduce himself, took my left. Mrs. Reitman began to pray, asking God for mercy on the souls of the Parkers and comfort for those who were left behind. When she said "amen," she and her husband released my hands.

She dabbed at her eyes with the tissue in her left hand and said, "What do you want to know?"

My approach isn't so much to ask questions as it is simply to let people start talking. Sometimes they'll tell me more that way than if I prod them. And if they don't, I always have a list of stock questions I can ask.

"Just tell me what you know," I said.

"We heard the shots sometime early this morning," she said. "We couldn't tell where they'd come from, but we called the police. A cruiser went through the neighborhood, and when nothing seemed wrong, it went away."

"How many shots?" I asked.

"I'm not sure. Our house is closed up at night, and so is the Parkers'. But we're both very light sleepers, and we came awake at the same time. I'm sure that if our windows had been open,

22

we would have heard things more clearly."

I thought about that open window in the Parkers' bedroom.

"Who called the police this morning?"

"I did. I always see Dorothy—that's Mr. Parker's mother— when I go out to get the paper in the morning."

"Wait a second," I said. "I thought Dorothy was the wife's name."

"Oh. Yes. It is. They were both named Dorothy. I always thought that was a little strange."

"Just a coincidence," I said.

Some cops don't believe in coincidence. That's because they haven't been on the job long. After a while, you find out that coincidences happen all the time.

"I'm sorry I interrupted you," I said. "Go on, please."

"Well," Mrs. Reitman said, "Dorothy likes . . . liked . . . to walk around outside in the mornings while it's a little cooler. So do I, and we'd usually have a little chat. When she didn't show up, I called again and told someone about the shots. I said I thought there had been foul play. The police knocked on the door and eventually went inside."

"Tell me about the family," I said. "Start with the one you knew best. Dorothy."

"Dorothy and I were friends. We talked in the mornings, and now and then she'd come over for coffee in the afternoon. But that's not what you want to know, is it?"

"Whatever you want to tell me will be fine," I said.

"Well, her last name's been changed a few times. She was married for a while to a man called Aaron Winetroub. Have you heard of him?"

I'd heard of him, all right. Winetroub had been a friend of Meyer Lansky, the Little Man. Not a millimeter over five feet tall, Lansky had risen to great heights in the underworld. He'd been pals with Bugsy Siegel and Lucky Luciano, and he'd helped turn criminal enterprise into big business in both the U.S. and Cuba. Rumor had it that in the last few years he'd moved into drug smuggling and prostitution, meanwhile investing money in legal enterprises like golf courses and hotels. No one knew how much money he was worth, but it was rumored to be in the hundreds of millions of dollars. I didn't doubt it.

Winetroub wasn't in the same league with Lansky, and he didn't have a lot of the same friends and business associates, but he'd made a lot of money at the tables in Vegas and other places. He'd probably lost a lot, too.

"We never met him," Mrs. Reitman said when I told her that I was familiar with Winetroub and his background. "When he died a few years ago, Dorothy inherited a lot of money. I don't know how much, and she didn't flaunt it like a lot of people would have." She looked at my cup. "More coffee?"

"Please," I said.

She took the cup and got up from the table. While she was pouring me some more coffee, her husband touched my arm and spoke for the first time. He said, "My first name is Isaac. Would you please address me that way?"

"Sure, Isaac."

"Good. I'm not comfortable with titles when talking as a friend."

I wasn't sure when he'd decided that I was his friend, but I didn't think this would be a good time to ask.

"Mrs. Parker . . . Dorothy," he said. "She took her first husband's name back after Winetroub died. She went through the courts to make it legal. I thought that was odd. And she never spoke about Winetroub to us except once when we first met her."

"I'm sure she had her reasons for not talking about him," Mrs. Reitman said, setting my coffee cup in front of me.

I could see steam rising off the surface of the coffee, which was fine. I liked it hot.

"Don't burn your tongue," Mrs. Reitman said.

"Don't worry," I said. "I won't."

"We never met her first husband, either," Isaac said. "She was my patient, and while I can't discuss her medical records with you, I can give you an opinion if you want one."

I took a sip of coffee. It didn't burn my tongue.

"I'll take whatever I can get," I said when I'd put the cup back down.

"Then I'll tell you that I believe the woman was under a lot of stress," Isaac said.

"Ha," his wife said. "And who wouldn't be? Her grandson had threatened to kill her."

"And the rest of the family, too," Isaac said. "She said that he was involved in drug deals, like too many young people are these days, with their long hair and their hippie clothes."

"What's the grandson's name?"

"Stanford Parker," Isaac told me.

"Did you tell this to the other policeman who was here?" I asked.

"Yes," Mrs. Reitman said. "He seemed happy to know about it."

I was afraid that would be the answer. If I knew Wetsel, and I did, the valves of his attention had closed. He'd already have convicted the grandson in his own mind and sentenced him to spend the rest of his life on Death Row up in Huntsville. The arrest and trial would be merely a formality as far as Wetsel would be concerned.

"Did the family have any other enemies that you know about?" I asked.

"The husband, Ralph, was a lawyer," Mrs. Reitman said, as if that explained a lot.

"He might have made enemies in his work," Isaac said to

clarify things for me. "I know that many lawyers do."

I couldn't argue with that, but most lawyers' clients don't sneak into their homes in the middle of the night and execute them.

We talked for a while longer while I finished my coffee, but I didn't get any more useful information. I thanked them for their coffee and their time and went to the house on the other side of the Parker residence to see if I could learn anything.

As it turned out, I didn't learn anything at all.

Wetsel was already there.

CHAPTER 3

Sometimes I thought that maybe it was my problem with cop bars that had turned Wetsel against me. Wetsel was the kind of guy who liked to hang out when he was off duty, and the places he preferred were the ones where other cops went to do their off-duty drinking. He'd asked me to go with him a couple of times, years before, but I'd always turned him down.

It's not that I don't drink. I'll have an occasional bourbon and water, or maybe a glass of wine with a meal, but that's about it.

And it's not that I don't like hanging out. I do that now and then, too, usually with Clive Watson, a friend of mine who's a private investigator. But when we go out, we go to a place where we can get decent food, which is something that's usually in short supply at cop bars.

Maybe Wetsel resented the fact that I'd rather hang out with a P.I. than with him. Private eyes weren't always held in high esteem in the department.

At any rate, for whatever reason, Wetsel and I weren't destined to be the best of pals.

I rang the bell at the house on the other side of the Parkers' place, and Wetsel came to the door.

"I got this," he said, opening the door only about halfway when he saw who was there. "You can leave right now."

I could have told him to go piss up a rope, or I could have called Bolce, but I didn't do either one. I didn't see any percent-

27

age in starting something that might turn nasty in front of civilians. So I just tipped Wetsel a little half-salute with my forefinger and got out of there.

Since it was nearly noon, I drove out on the Katy Freeway to Sam's Deli for a hamburger. No lettuce or tomatoes, which are hard for me to digest. Just meat, bread, pickles, and a smile from Henry, who runs the place.

Whenever I go there, I'm reminded of an old radio show called *Duffy's Tavern*. It always began with the manager answering the phone and saying, "This is Archie the manager speaking. Duffy ain't here."

Sam was never at his deli, either. He'd long ago turned it over to his brother, Henry, and gone somewhere to count his money.

I parked and went inside to be greeted with the smell of frying hamburgers, onion rings, and pastrami.

"How's tricks?" Henry said from behind the counter when I walked through the door.

If I'd told Henry the truth about how things were, he'd have stopped smiling, and the clientele would have been alarmed, so I just said what I always did.

"Same old, same old, Henry. And how are things with you?"

"Just great," Henry said, like always.

Henry was a guy who never seemed to have a worry in the world. He always wore a smile on his seamed face, and I hoped he would never have to see three people shot dead in their beds.

"You want the usual?" he asked, and I nodded.

The clean linoleum floor was patterned with black and white squares. I walked to a vacant table by the window and sat down. I could see the cars and eighteen-wheelers rushing up and down the freeway, all of them exceeding the speed limit, but it was cool inside the deli, and I couldn't smell the exhaust fumes that hovered above the cars and trucks, making the air seem wavery and strange.

Henry had a little radio behind the counter, and some singer was claiming that "everything is beautiful, in its own way." It was nice to know that somebody thought so.

I looked around the deli. Nobody I knew was there. The man at the next table had hair longer than most women would have worn only a few years before. I ran a hand across my own brush-cut blond hair and wondered if I looked as odd to him as he did to me.

The woman with him looked as if she might be on her way to audition for a role in a movie about nineteenth-century European gypsies. Styles had certainly changed since I'd almost gotten my leg blown off in France all those years ago. Thinking about it, I got a little tingle in my thigh, and I rubbed it with my open palm.

Henry brought me my burger, and we talked for a second before I ate it. When I was finished, I paid him at the cash register and drove back to the station.

There was a note in my box saying that Bolce wanted to see me as soon as I came in. I went to his office, closed the door without being told, and sat down.

"So," Bolce said, leaning forward. He laced his fingers together and leaned his forearms on the desk. "What did you find out?"

I filled him in on what I'd learned from the Reitmans and told him that Wetsel hadn't wanted me to talk to the other neighbors.

"I can go back if you think I need to," I said.

"We'll see. For now, I think Wetsel's found out some of the same things you did."

"Did they tell him about the son's threats?"

Bolce sighed. "They did. He's convinced that the son's the perp."

It figured.

Bolce noticed my sour expression and said, "You have to look at it from Wetsel's point of view. When something like this happens, there's usually a family member involved. And the son has a motive."

"If you want to call it that. But putting that aside, what about evidence?"

"Wetsel doesn't always worry a lot about evidence. He wants to pick up the son and sweat him for a while."

I didn't say anything.

"I told him to forget it," Bolce said.

That cheered me up a little. "He didn't like that, I'll bet."

"Not much, but the son will keep. He won't be going anywhere until after the funeral, if then. The kids are with the CPS, so they're not in any danger from him, if they ever were." Bolce unlaced his fingers and leaned back in his chair. "I want you to do a background check on the son. For that matter, go ahead and check out the whole family."

"Me? Why? This is Wetsel's case, his and McGuire's. They don't want me nosing around."

"To hell with that. Wetsel's already got his mind made up, so he's going to slant his investigation one way and one way only. That's not an option here. We have to do a thorough job."

"We always do," I said.

"We try," Bolce said. "But Wetsel's too set on one theory. This one smells funny to me, and I don't want him to screw it up. I have another lay-down case I'll put him and McGuire on to get them out of the way."

A "lay-down case" was one where there was no real question of who was guilty. The killer had been caught with the gun in his hand, or he'd given an iron-clad confession.

"Wetsel won't like it," I said.

"If he doesn't like it, let him request a transfer to vice," Bolce said. He stood up as a way of dismissing me. "You get busy on the Parker case. It's yours now."

I didn't argue with him. I just said, "Yes, sir," and got out of there.

There wasn't much more I could do that day, so I spent the rest of the afternoon catching up on my paperwork, trying to clear my desk for the new investigation.

After work, I went home, grilled a steak, and ate alone, which is pretty much what I'd been doing since my wife had moved out and filed for divorce. Somehow she'd gotten the idea that I was having an affair. I still had no idea who'd put the idea in her head or where it had come from. I'd tried any number of times to explain to her that I loved her, that I'd never run around on her, that I couldn't stand the thought of living without her.

She didn't listen. The more I protested my innocence, the more convinced she was that I was lying.

"You always lie, Steve. That's what cops do. They cover up and lie," she said in one of our last fights.

"You know better than that, Sarah," I told her. "I've never lied to you, not once in twenty-three years."

"You're lying right now, you son of a bitch," she said.

Sarah was a religious woman, and she never cussed, not unless she was in a rage, and at the moment her blue eyes were throwing sparks like the end of a broken power line in a mud puddle. She was a redhead and had the temper to go with the hair, and even when she was angry with me, she was still the most beautiful woman I'd ever known.

"Who's put this crazy notion in your head?" I said. "I can't believe this is happening to us."

31

"Believe it," she said, and ran out of the room before she started crying.

She left two days later. That was a month ago, and I hadn't seen her since. She wouldn't return my phone calls, and she wouldn't even tell me where she was staying, though I'd managed to find out by my own devious methods. It didn't do me any good. She wouldn't answer the door when I went by.

If I'd been a drinking man, I'd have drowned my sorrows in some bourbon, but instead I cleaned up the kitchen and watched a re-run of *Hawaii Five-O*. That Steve McGarrett had it made, I thought. Blue water all around, and a bunch of crimes that could be solved in one hour, counting commercials.

On the news I saw that the Apollo 11 had lifted off for the moon. I hoped the crew would make it safely. I'd thought about the possibility of men landing on the moon since I was a little kid, and it was hard to believe that now they were actually going.

I went to bed and hoped I'd dream about Hawaii and hula girls, or about flying to the moon.

I didn't. I dreamed about Sarah, instead.

CHAPTER 4

The next day, I went to the Evidence Room to see what the crime scene analysts had brought in from the Parker house. I was mainly interested in any documents that had been found, and after I signed in, I was shown two boxes full of them.

"Is that all?" I asked.

Rod Franklin was in charge that day. He's big and mean, and he's not on the streets because he'd knocked three teeth out of a teenager who'd called him a pig.

"It's all they've brought in so far," he said. "You can check back tomorrow if you don't find what you want."

I signed for the two boxes and put them on a big table that was there for that purpose. I started going through them, putting the ones I'd looked at in a neat stack beside the boxes.

I was looking for a will, and it didn't take me long to find two of them, right under some birth certificates, passports, and deeds.

There were two wills, one for Parker and one for his wife. They were only five months old. I read through them quickly. The Parkers had been richer than I'd have guessed, even though they lived in a nice neighborhood.

Parker had left everything to his wife, assuming, I suppose, that he would die first. If she predeceased him, however, the money was to be divided among family members. But not evenly. He had left five thousand dollars to his son, Stanford. That was the small bequest, though it wasn't small to me. The rest of the money went to the Parkers' daughter, Amy, and the three grandchildren. I hadn't even known about Amy, but she stood to inherit a cool million dollars. That was an amount big enough to get anybody's attention, but it was only the beginning. The grandchildren would inherit even more: three million bucks to be divided among them.

It was an awful lot of money. I'd never live long enough to earn that much on my cop's salary. But that was only the beginning.

It took me a little more digging, but I found the older Dorothy's will, too. It had been executed on the same day as the other two. In it, she left everything she owned, including nearly six million in cash, to her great-grandchildren.

I'd thought three million was a lot of money. We were up to ten million now. There were plenty of people in Houston who'd kill you for a hundred dollars, or even ten bucks. But nine million? They'd be lining up around the block.

The thing of it was, however, that the son couldn't touch it. All he got out of the deaths was a relatively measly five thousand.

After I got over my amazement at the amounts of money I was dealing with, I continued to go through the papers. The next interesting thing I found was a copy of a deed for a home that the older Dorothy still owned in Las Vegas. She'd inherited it from Aaron Winetroub. There was a lease agreement showing that the house was rented to a man named Hal Grubble, but I didn't find any rent receipts.

The bank records were down a little deeper in the boxes, and I looked through them to see if there were any regular deposits that might have represented rent money. I didn't find any.

I went through the rest of the papers, but I didn't find anything else of interest. I put them all back in the boxes and took the boxes to Franklin, making sure he recorded their return.

He did, and we talked about the Apollo astronauts for a few

minutes. Then I went up to my office.

I didn't have any messages, so I called Clay Lang, a civil lawyer I knew, and asked him what he knew about Ralph Parker.

"He's dead," Clay said.

Just what I needed, a little lawyer humor.

"I'm glad to know you read the papers," I said. "I was hoping you could tell me a little more about him than that."

"He's a plaintiff's attorney," Clay said, sounding a little hurt that I hadn't appreciated his joke. "Works on all kinds of claims. You get hurt on the job, he was a go-to guy. Or if you got hurt in a car wreck."

"Ambulance chaser," I said.

"Nope. He was classier than that, and strictly on the up-and-up."

That was something I'd have to check on. Not that I wouldn't take a lawyer's word for it.

"By the way, Steve," Clay continued, "my wife's cousin is in town. She's been living in Florida for the last few years, but her husband died of cancer six months ago, and she's looking to move back to Houston. Why don't you come out to the house for dinner some night and meet her."

Clay's heart was in the right place, I guess, and he probably didn't know that he was about the fiftieth person who'd tried to fix me up with somebody since Sarah had left. But I didn't want to be fixed up.

"I'll be busy with the Parker case for a while," I said. "Maybe later."

"Sure," Clay said, but I could tell he knew better. That was fine with me.

I hung up the phone and thought about the next step. It was time to pay a visit to the courthouse.

Naturally it was raining. A shower had come in from the

Gulf, and drops as big as dimes were pelting down. The Ford's wiper blades had trouble keeping the windshield clear, and when I got out, I stepped in a puddle that was higher than the top of my shoes. I sloshed to the courthouse through the downpour, wishing I had an umbrella, or even a hat.

Harris County has more than one courthouse. The one I was headed for, where the trial records were kept, was finished in 1910 but dedicated in 1911, so people get a little confused about exactly how old it is. The new courthouse, which was finished in 1953, doesn't have any of the character of the older one. Of course if you like character, the nineteenth century courthouse is still standing, but it's more of a museum now than anything else.

I went up the concrete steps as fast as I could. I don't run very well in damp weather, thanks to my bad leg. When I got to the high roof of the porch, I stopped and tried to brush water out of my hair with one hand and off my clothing with the other. I didn't do much good with either hand, so I went inside, still dripping, and headed for the room where the cases would be on file.

The clerk cocked an eyebrow at me, so I told her that I'd lost my umbrella.

"That happens a lot," she said, and went to get what I asked for.

When she returned, I knew I was going to be in the courthouse for a long time. Parker had been involved in a lot of cases, and I'd have to look at each one to determine if there might be some motive for murder hidden in it. It was boring work, the kind of thing that a cop like Wetsel hated, which was one reason he so often took the most obvious answer and ran with it.

I didn't like the work, either, but it was something that had to be done if you were going to do the job right. I believe in doing the job right, even if it takes a little longer.

Or a lot longer. I was still going through the cases when the courthouse closed for the day.

The rain had stopped earlier in the afternoon. Steam rose off the pavement, and the air was heavy with humidity, but it smelled fresh and clean for the first time in a while. I knew the smell wouldn't last long.

My house was just as lonely that night as it had been every night for the last month. I had a frozen TV dinner that tasted like cardboard. I stayed up to see Johnny Carson's monologue and then went to bed.

I spent most of the next day in the courthouse, and after all my searching I came up with only two lawsuits that might possibly have a bearing on the homicides. Both were still pending, and both were replete with denials by the attorneys for the civil defendants.

Each of the cases involved a small company that was being sued for an amount that would surely put it out of business forever if Parker won the case for his client. The owners of those companies might well want Ralph Parker out of the way badly enough to have him killed, so those were the cases that I'd have to check out further. I got copies of the two cases made and took them back to my office, where I could read them more carefully. I was just getting into them when Bolce called me to his office.

"The Parker funeral's tomorrow afternoon," he said. "I want you to go."

I told him that I'd already planned to, mainly to get a look at Stanford Parker. I asked where the funeral would be.

He gave me the name of the church and said that burial would be in a cemetery called the Garden of Memory.

"That's the one down south off the Gulf Freeway. I can

remember when cemeteries didn't have names like that."

I could remember, too, but I didn't mention that to Bolce. I just told him that I'd be there.

The Garden of Memory was well-financed and well-maintained. The grass was green, the trees were trimmed, and there were flowers on every grave. Nobody asked or cared whether they were put there by members of the families of the deceased or just by some sweaty guy who worked for the funeral home. It was the appearance that mattered.

There had been nothing out of the ordinary at the church, though a funeral for three murder victims was unusual enough in itself. I'd had a look at the son, but I wanted to see if he showed up at the gravesides.

I'd gotten out of the church quickly and gotten a good head start on the funeral procession. As the cars arrived, I stood under an oak tree and watched.

It had rained earlier in the day, and the sky was still covered with thick clouds. Water dripped and ticked in the leaves of the oak tree, and occasionally a drop would hit me on the head or shoulders. The salty smell of the Gulf air mingled with exhaust fumes from the freeway.

The Reitmans saw me under the tree and came over to join me. Mrs. Reitman pointed out Stanford Parker.

"Not a tear in his eye," she said. "Not a one in the church, either. It's not natural."

"I thought he had a sister," I said. "I didn't see her at the church."

"She's didn't come. She had to go to the hospital after she heard the news. I don't know what's the matter, but I'm sure she's showing more grief than her brother."

Mrs. Reitman looked scornfully in Parker's direction.

Stanford Parker was tall and thin, bushy sideburns and black hair that fell almost to his shoulders. His dark gray suit didn't fit and looked like something he'd had around for years without trying on. He stood off to one side, and no one approached him. He stared straight ahead, not making eye contact with anyone. After the preacher said his piece and commended the bodies to the earth, Parker turned and walked off. I watched as he got into his car and drove away, trailing exhaust smoke.

"No respect," Mrs. Reitman whispered. "What kind of man shows no respect for the dead?"

Isaac Reitman tugged at my sleeve. I looked at him, and he jerked his head to indicate that he wanted me to follow him. We left his wife and walked a short distance away.

"I've remembered something that might be important," he said, and proceeded to tell me that the elder Mrs. Parker had a house in Las Vegas that she'd rented to a man named Grubble.

I told him that I knew that already because I'd discovered the lease agreement.

"But did you know that she planned to marry this Grubble?" Isaac said.

I certainly hadn't, and I thought that might explain why I'd found no rent receipts or deposits. Grubble was freeloading.

"Well, it's true," Isaac said. "As it happens, my cousin is a lawyer. His name is Marcus Payne, and he knew the Parkers through me. Dorothy was planning to write a new will, and she didn't want to use her son to draw it up." He paused. "So she asked me to set up an appointment with Marcus. I was glad to do it."

I didn't see how this would have much bearing on the murder, but I didn't interrupt. I'm always willing to listen when someone starts talking about a case.

"This was only a few days ago," Isaac said. "Marcus hasn't done the will yet, and he was worried about it. He called me to discuss it."

This was getting more interesting. I asked what there had been to discuss.

"Dorothy talked to Marcus about Grubble, and Marcus said she was going to make him her beneficiary. Leave everything to him, not just the house. Grubble's a young man, only thirty-two, and Marcus thought he might be after Dorothy's money. She was an attractive woman, but she was . . . older. You know what I mean, I'm sure."

I knew. I said, "She didn't leave the money to Grubble, though. Not if the will hasn't been drawn up."

"True, but Grubble didn't know that. From some of the things Dorothy said to Marcus, he gathered that she'd hinted to Grubble that the will had been executed and that he'd be the beneficiary. Marcus said that was her way of making sure Grubble didn't lose interest in her."

Well, six million dollars would have kept my interest, all right.

And it would also be a powerful motive for murder.

Back downtown, I told Bolce what I'd learned. He thought it over and said, "I'm going to have to tell all this to the Captain, but I don't want it to go any further. You can write your report, but don't let anybody see it except me. The Captain's already told me he's going to sit on it."

"What about Wetsel and the throw-down case you put him on?"

"He and McGuire wrapped it. It was too easy. I should have given him a tougher one."

I'd been afraid of something like that.

"This is your case now, anyway," Bolce said. "It's not that we don't trust Wetsel, but you know how he is. He's already decided that the son is guilty, and he won't be happy until we've arrested him and sweated a confession out of him. But that's not going to happen."

I started to say something, but Bolce held up his hand.

"I'll take care of Wetsel. He and McGuire can help out. They can do some interviews, maybe even with Stanford Parker, but they're not going to arrest him. I want you to handle everything else."

Bolce was acting like Wetsel. His mind was made up, and nothing I could say would change it. I told him I'd do my best, and he let me go.

Just before I left for the day, McGuire came by my office. He stopped just inside and lit a cigarette.

"Still not smoking?" he said.

"You're not helping any."

"Yeah." He inhaled and let the smoke dribble slowly out of his mouth. Then he said, "I thought you'd like to know that Wetsel and I are still on the Parker case."

"So I've heard. So am I, but I promise not to get in your way."

"Yeah," McGuire said. "I'll see you around, Steve."

He left without asking anything else. Like I said, McGuire's smarter than his partner.

CHAPTER 5

I was about to walk out the door when the phone rang. I thought about letting it go, but I was afraid I might miss something important about the case.

The call wasn't about the case, however. It was from my P.I. friend, Clive Watson. He wanted me to go to dinner with him. Since I wasn't looking forward to going home to an empty house, I said I'd meet him at the Fish House, a place we both liked.

Rush hour traffic in Houston is enough to turn saints into sinners, and there were times when I wished I were working in the traffic division, so I could give a citation to everybody in the city. But I wasn't in that division, and I couldn't give any citations. So I gritted my teeth and endured the endless crawling along.

When I finally got to the Fish House, I found Clive sitting in our usual booth. He was having a gin and tonic with three big lime slices. He was also smoking a cigarette. He was a chain smoker, which meant, as he put it, that he would "smoke chains if I could light 'em."

"You might as well have a limeade as that thing," I said, indicating his drink as I slid into the booth opposite him.

"Wouldn't have the same appeal," he said, raising the glass to me.

The waitress came over, and I asked for bourbon and water. After she brought it and I'd had a couple of sips, I could feel the tension that the traffic had caused start to slip away. I looked at the menu and ordered fried fish. Clyde had his grilled. He'd had some intestinal surgery a few years back and couldn't eat fried food anymore, which was too bad. I knew how much he enjoyed it.

Clive was no longer a young man. In fact, compared to him, I'm young. He was at least eighty, maybe a year or two older, but he still looked as if he could run a mile or more if he had to. The main sign of his age was his crew-cut hair, which was completely white. His wife, Anna, had died within the last year. I didn't want to mention her unless he did because he was still grieving for her. I knew a little bit about how he felt, as I'd more or less lost Sarah, even though she was still alive.

When our platters of fish arrived, Clive made the sign of the cross and bowed his head to say grace, the way he always did. I'd been a little self-conscious about that little habit of his when we'd first met, a long time ago, but now it was just routine. It might have bothered some of the other diners, but not me. I bowed and listened.

"Amen," Clive said when he was done. He crossed himself again, looked up, and asked me what I was working on.

I told him as briefly as I could. When I was finished, he said, "I might be able to help you check out the defendants in those lawsuits."

I didn't doubt it. He'd worked for most of the lawyers in town at one time or another and knew all the good ones.

"I don't want to put you to any trouble," I told him.

"Trouble? It won't be any trouble. Hell, I need something to keep me busy. Everybody seems to think I've retired. While I'm at it, I'll look into the companies, and I'll ask around about Parker's reputation."

I told him I'd appreciate it. He'd done me a few favors in the past, and I knew how valuable his help could be. With his connections, he'd be able to find out a lot more about Parker than I could, and he could do it more quickly.

"Good," he said. "Now let's talk about something else while we eat."

We dug into our fish, which was excellent, as always. At least mine was, and Clive seemed to be enjoying his, too. In fact, it was so good that for a while we didn't do any talking at all.

When we were well into the meal, Clive stopped eating for a second and said, "What do you hear from your wife?"

"Not a word. She won't answer the phone, and she won't see me in person. Our lawyers talk, and hers told mine that she hated me."

"I don't believe that," Clive said.

I didn't believe it, either.

"God meant for a man and wife to stay together for life," Clive said, and then he started to tear up.

I looked away while he got out a handkerchief and blew his nose. Then he told me for the hundredth time how much he'd loved Anna, what a good Christian she'd been, and how she'd been not just his wife but his best friend. He picked up his gin and tonic and saw that the glass was empty.

"I think I'll switch to bourbon," he said, and we both laughed, knowing that it would never happen. You can't drink bourbon with limes.

It was raining hard again the next morning. The wipers whipped back and forth across the windshield in a vain attempt to keep it clear, and water was running curb-deep in the streets by the time I got to the station. Houston is prone to flooding, and it doesn't take a lot of rain at one time to cause big problems. I was going to be inside most of the day, which was just as well. The water usually runs off pretty quickly after the rain stops, so I figured I'd be fine later in the day.

I sat at my desk and read through all my notes. While I was doing that McGuire came by again. He said, "There's one thing you ought to know. Wetsel wouldn't tell you, but I will."

I looked up at him. "So tell me."

"Wetsel's talked to Stanford Parker's girlfriend. She's alibiing him. She claims they spent the night of the murders together."

I hadn't found out about the girlfriend yet. I said, "But Wetsel didn't believe her."

"Hell, no."

"Do you?"

"I don't have an opinion," McGuire said, and left.

I added the alibi to my notes and typed up the report. When I took it to Bolce, he looked it over and said, "You have a lot of information here, Steve."

"Yeah. Some of it's from McGuire. Why didn't you tell me about what he'd found out from Parker's girlfriend?"

"I haven't seen Wetsel's report yet."

"Oh," I said, realizing that Wetsel was probably sitting on it to keep me in the dark. Thanks to McGuire, I was a little ahead of him, though.

"I'll let you know if Wetsel brings in any good information," Bolce said. "You have plenty here yourself, including what you got from McGuire. I'm surprised you haven't cracked the case already."

"It may take me another hour or two," I said.

"I can give you that long. Tell me what you're looking at. How many suspects do you have?"

"The son could've done it, but he has an alibi."

"Is it any good?"

"I don't know that yet."

"All right. Go on."

"The older woman's boyfriend could've done it," I said. "He certainly thought he had a motive. Or one of the defendants in the lawsuits could have done it. It could even have been a burglary gone bad, but I don't believe that for a minute."

Bolce didn't believe it either. He said, "I know you have a couple of other cases working. I'll assign them to somebody else. I want you to work this one exclusively. What's your first step?"

"I want to go to Las Vegas," I said. "I need to talk to Hal Grubble."

"Go," Bolce said.

Las Vegas and Houston might as well be on different continents, at least as far as the climate is concerned. When I got off the plane at the Las Vegas airport in the middle of the afternoon, I could almost feel the desert air sucking the moisture out of my skin. The inside of my nose and mouth felt suddenly dry, and the sun seemed twice as bright as it did on the Gulf Coast.

I'd called ahead to let the Las Vegas cops know I was coming in, and the homicide lieutenant I'd talked to said he'd send a couple of men to meet me. I spotted them as soon as I got inside the airport. Cops know cops. They spotted me just as easily, and I walked over to meet them, limping a little because I'd been cramped in the tiny airplane seat, and my leg was twinging.

Both the Vegas cops were big, but one of them was bigger than the other. He was the spokesman.

"Stephens?" he said.

"Ted Stephens. You can call me Steve," I said, setting down my bag and putting out my hand.

His hand swallowed mine, but he shook without trying to crush my bones. "I'm Charlie Bonner," he said. "This little guy with me is John Taylor."

Bonner had deep-set black eyes that looked down at me from under his thick black brows. There was a thin scar on his right cheek, and his nose had been broken at some time in the past. I wondered who was big enough to break it.

Taylor, who wouldn't have looked like a little guy if he'd been standing next to anyone other than Bonner, was the kind of person who had a perpetual smile, but it wasn't a real smile. It didn't touch his eyes, which were a very light blue, like chips of ice.

I shook hands with him and picked up my bag. Bonner asked me what I was working on.

"The Lieutenant didn't tell you?" I said.

"Lieutenant Colby just said we should meet you and help you out on whatever you needed."

"Okay," I said. "Here's the short version."

I told them about the homicides and about Grubble.

"We can check him out with our ID section. You got a date of birth, social security number, driver's license number, anything like that?"

"No. But there can't be that many Grubbles around. Besides, I know where he lives."

"Let's go, then," Bonner said.

People don't think about it much, if at all, but there's a lot more to Las Vegas than the Strip. People live and work there, after all, and there's a sizeable residential section.

We drove to the address on the lease agreement I'd found among Dorothy Parker's papers. The house wasn't as nice as the one in Houston, and there was no yard or trees. There aren't a lot of either of those things in Las Vegas. But there was a car parked in the driveway, a red Buick.

I jotted down the license number, and Taylor called it in on the radio to see if we could get a hit. We drove around with the air conditioner on while we waited for a response. Bonner told a few war stories, but Taylor just looked out the window. There wasn't much to see other than houses baking in the dry heat.

The radio squawked, and Bonner stopped talking while we listened. Grubble worked at the Lucky Star Casino, and it turned out that he had a police record, of sorts. He'd walked a bar tab at one of the casinos, and he'd once been picked up in Houston in a prostitution sting operation.

The bar tab wasn't a big deal. He'd paid up as soon as charges were filed, claiming that he'd been drunk and hadn't even known he'd skipped out without paying.

The prostitution arrest was a little more serious. He was so angry that he'd been tricked that he'd slapped the undercover policewoman he'd propositioned before she could get the cuffs on him. That little episode had cost him a thousand bucks.

"I thought the casinos ran a check on people before they hired them," I said.

Bonner nodded. "They do. A record like that's not bad enough to keep somebody from being hired, not in Vegas."

"We should check his work records," Taylor said. "See if he was at the casino on the night of your homicides."

I was surprised to hear him speak up, but it was a good suggestion. I'd been about to make it myself.

"I'd like to do one thing first," I said. "Can you take me to the courthouse?"

"Sure," Bonner said. "Why?"

"I want to look at the deeds," I said.

One thing that makes me different from cops like Wetsel is that I like to check every detail. I was sure that Mrs. Parker owned the house Grubble was living in. I'd seen a copy of the deed, after all. But a copy isn't the real thing, so it was something I wanted to verify.

And I got a little surprise. Dorothy Parker didn't own the house, after all. She'd sold it five days before the murder to a man named George Morgan. The notary seal on the deed showed that the transaction had been conducted in Houston, and the title policy had been issued by Great Western Title there. The lawyer of record was Clinton Von Bellow.

Damn, I thought as I looked over the deed. More players had entered the game.

CHAPTER 6

There was a pay phone in the courthouse, so I scraped up enough change to call Clive Watson long distance and ask if he'd ever heard of Von Bellow.

"Hell, yes, I've heard of him," Clive said. "He's my son-in-law."

Another coincidence, but maybe not such a big one. I can't keep up with all of Clive's offspring and in-laws. He has seven children, which makes it tough.

"He's connected with the case I'm working on," I said. "I'd like for you to check with him and find out about a man named George Morgan. Von Bellow did a real estate deal with him."

"I'll do it," Clive said. "You have a number where I can call you back?"

I didn't, so I said, "Don't call me. I'll call you."

"Where have I heard that before?" Clive said.

After we left the courthouse, Bonner headed for the Lucky Star. It was just off the Strip, not far from the Riviera, which was the only place in Las Vegas I'd ever stayed. But I'd been to Vegas only once before, back when I was married. I didn't want to think about that at the moment. I needed to keep my mind on business.

The people who ran the Lucky Star felt the same way: they had their minds on business. As soon as we walked in the door, we were among the slot machines, and the blackjack tables were only a few steps away. Although it was the middle of the day, there were plenty of players. Men and women sat in front of the slots as if hypnotized, putting in their coins and pulling the handles, waiting for the jackpot they were sure would be theirs on the next spin of the drums. Nearly everyone had a cigarette, and a haze of smoke filled the air. There was a lot of noise, but not much talk. People were too focused on their gambling to have conversations.

Even to get to the personnel office, we had to thread the maze that led us past more slots and gaming tables, but once we got where we were headed, the woman in the office gave us the information about Grubble quickly enough. According to the work records, Grubble had been in the casino, dealing blackjack on the five p.m. to one a.m. shift the night of the murders.

"So he's not your guy," Bonner said after we'd had a look at the worksheets.

"Unless the records were jiggered with," Taylor said.

The woman who'd given us the records heard him, but she didn't appear insulted. She said, "You can talk to Mr. Preston if you'd like to. He's the manager."

"Sounds like a good idea," I said, and she took us to his office.

It was nothing fancy, but the carpet was deep and the desk was solid oak with a polished top. Preston looked pretty solid himself as he sat behind the desk in his dark suit, white shirt, and conservative striped tie.

We introduced ourselves and told him what we were there for, and he asked us to have a seat.

"Hal Grubble is my nephew," Preston said after we were comfortable. "My sister's kid. I can vouch for his being here on the night you're asking about. We have surveillance tapes that cover the whole casino. You can have a look at them if you'd care to."

"Not right now," I said.

"We'll come back and check them," Bonner said. "If it turns out to be necessary."

"Maybe you'd like to talk to him," Preston said. "He goes on duty in about an hour, but he's in the building now."

I hadn't thought we'd get so lucky. I said, "I'd appreciate it if you could call him in."

Preston used the intercom to talk to someone, and in only a couple of minutes, Hal Grubble came into the office.

He wasn't exactly what I'd been expecting. He might have been thirty-two, but he looked no more than twenty-five. He was tall and well built, and he was handsome enough to be a movie star, with dark, curly hair that covered his ears, a petulant mouth, big blue eyes, and a finely shaped nose. He was wearing a flashy patterned shirt under his sports coat, and no tie. Instead he sported a heavy gold necklace. The only jarring note was that his sideburns looked like they belonged on a guy working in a filling station.

When I told him what we were there for, he readily admitted that he'd known Mrs. Parker, whom he called Dot.

"Man, she was something else," Grubble said, after sitting down and lighting a cigarette. "The hottest sixty-year-old I ever met. What a body. Bazooms out to here." He put his hands out in front of his chest to show us, in case we couldn't imagine it for ourselves. "No wrinkles, either. Maybe she'd had a face-lift. Anyway, I met her when I went to Galveston to visit my mother, and it was, like, instant attraction."

"So you got to know her pretty well," I said.

"Oh, yeah." Grubble grinned and tapped ashes into a glass ashtray on Preston's desk. "You could say that. I was there for two weeks, and we had sex just about every single day. I never saw a woman who liked it so much, even if she was sixty."

That was the second time he'd mentioned her age. I decided I wouldn't tell him that she'd been even older than he thought. Let him keep his illusions. After all, it didn't sound as if he had very many of them.

"We always went to a motel for the sex," he said. "She didn't want her son and daughter-in-law to know what was going on."

"What did you talk about?" I asked. "If you had time, I mean."

He wasn't offended by my crack. He said, "She told me all about her second husband. Aaron Winetroub. He was a big name around here for a long time. He owned the house I'm living in."

"About that house," I said.

"She said she'd give it to me if we got married. Hell, I told her from the beginning that I didn't want to marry her. I'm having too much fun to marry anybody. She's not the only woman in the world, you know what I mean?"

I knew what he meant, even if I didn't understand it. I was a one-woman man, myself, no matter what Sarah thought about me.

"You weren't paying any rent," I said.

Even that didn't faze him. "Nope." He ground out his cigarette and lit another one. "I was doing Dot a favor by staying in the house until she could sell it. Keeping it up, making sure nobody broke in. You know."

"Sure. Did you know that she'd been murdered?"

If I'd hoped to surprise him, I failed. He nodded and said, "Yeah. That was too bad. I really hated to hear it. Waste of a real woman, if you ask me."

Grubble stuck me as the type who figured the world pretty much revolved around him. He didn't mind living off a woman, and if she'd been killed, well, that was tough. But it wasn't going to keep him from having a good time.

"I don't suppose you have any idea who killed her," I said.

"Not a one. But I can tell you something you might not know about her."

"What's that?"

"She came out here once, stayed a week or so with me in the house. We hardly ever went out, except to eat or play a little blackjack. One night she had a little too much to drink, and she asked me to do something for her. A little favor, she called it."

"What kind of a favor?" I asked.

"She wanted me to find her a hit man," Grubble said. "Somebody to kill her grandson, a guy named Stanford Parker."

CHAPTER 7

I don't know what I'd been expecting to hear from Grubble, but it certainly wasn't that Dorothy Parker had tried to hire a hit man.

Without letting my surprise show, I said, "Why did she want her grandson killed?"

"I didn't really get into that with her," Grubble said. He combed his fingers through his hair, letting it fall artfully back in place. "She said something about how he was on drugs and had threatened to kill his parents."

"Did she say why he'd made that threat?"

"They'd been giving him money. I think they'd told him that they didn't like his lifestyle and that they were going to cut him off."

"So what did you tell her about the hit man?"

"Just what anybody else would've told her. That I didn't know anything about that kind of stuff and that it was something I didn't want to get involved in. I'm not saying I haven't been in a little scrape or two."

He paused and turned to grin at his uncle, who gave him an indulgent nod. Then he turned to face me again. "I mean, if you're cops, you know I've had a little trouble. But it sure didn't involve getting somebody whacked, you know what I mean? That's crazy stuff. I wouldn't touch it."

"What about the house, now that she's dead?" I asked.

"Hey, nobody's said anything to me about moving out. I'm

still taking care of the place. I'll stay until I get some kind of eviction notice. Then I'll leave."

He seemed awfully sure of himself, so I asked if he knew anything about Mrs. Parker's will.

He didn't quite meet my eyes. "Not a thing."

I thought that was the first lie he'd told. Except that it wasn't really a lie. He thought he knew something, but he was wrong. That was another little illusion I'd let him keep. He was probably going to get the eviction notice, even though he didn't know it. And he wouldn't be getting those millions he was probably already counting, either.

I thanked him and Preston, and stood up. Bonner and Taylor, who hadn't said a word during the entire interview, stood up as well. When we left the office, both Preston and Grubble were lighting cigarettes. The smell of the smoke reminded me of how good a cigarette could taste, but I pushed the thought out of my mind.

There was no need for me to stay in Las Vegas any longer, so Bonner and Taylor drove me back to the airport. While we were driving, I asked what they thought about Grubble and his story.

"He's a cold-blooded asshole," Bonner said.

Taylor just nodded.

"But I think he's telling the truth," Bonner said. "As much as I hate to say it. Except maybe about that will business. There's something going on there."

"Yeah," I said.

I told them what was going on, and Bonner laughed.

"Serves the bastard right," he said.

Taylor didn't say anything, just looked straight ahead with those icy eyes of his.

When I got home late that night, I went into the house half

expecting Sarah to be there. She wasn't, of course, and I wondered again who or what had turned her against me. How could she ever have thought I'd have an affair?

We'd met not long after I got home from the war, nursing my million dollar wound. I was stationed for a while at Fort Sam Houston in San Antonio, and one Saturday I'd visited the Alamo. Sarah was there, the prettiest redhead in Texas. She was wearing a big hat that partially shaded her face, but I could see a smattering of freckles under her green eyes.

While I was standing there admiring her, she walked right over to me. She asked me if I'd take a picture of her and her parents. They were all visiting from Houston and wanted the picture as a souvenir.

I was quick to take her up on the offer, and when I'd done my duty and was handing her the camera, I said, "There's a small fee, involved."

She looked at me with surprise and said, "A fee?"

"Sure. I want a copy of the picture."

She wrinkled her nose and grinned. "But I wouldn't know where to send it."

"I'm getting my discharge in a few days," I said. "And I'll be heading to Houston. It's my home, after all. So I can pick up the picture at your house."

Her grin got wider, and I could tell she thought it might not be such a bad idea. But she said, "I don't like to give my address to strangers."

I told her my name. "And I'm not so strange. Why don't you let your parents decide?"

They were still standing in front of the chapel, probably wondering what Sarah and I were talking about. But they found out soon enough. She did walk over with me, and when I told them a little about myself, they didn't seem to think it would be such a bad idea if I showed up at their house.

Two weeks later, I did, and six months after that, Sarah and I were married. We'd stayed that way for all the years since, and we still were, even though someone or something had poisoned her against me.

I promised myself for the hundredth time that I'd find out what was wrong and set it right, but first I had a murder case to solve.

Maybe it was wrong to put the case first, but it was my job, and I owed it to the people of Houston, who were paying my salary, after all, to give them my best.

I owed my best to Sarah, too, and I tossed and turned for an hour before I dropped off into a troubled sleep.

The next day I was a little tired from the trip and my bad night. And my leg hurt, but I went on in to work and gave Bolce an oral report on everything I'd learned. When I finished, I asked if Wetsel had accomplished anything while I was gone.

"I have his report on the interview with Stanford Parker's girlfriend," Bolce said, taking it out of a folder on his desk. He slid it across to me, and I skimmed through it.

It didn't take long. According to what the woman had told Wetsel, she and Parker had been together the day of the murders and all that night as well.

"This doesn't fit with Wetsel's theory about Stanford Parker," I said.

"You think that bothers Wetsel? He thinks the girl is lying, and he's still convinced that Parker's guilty."

I slid the report back across the desk. "What do you want me to do?"

"Stay on the case. Follow up on what you learned in Las Vegas and see where it takes you. Write up your report and bring it directly to me."

I told him I would and went back to my office to get started.

When I finished the report, I called Clive Watson to see what he'd found out for me about his son-in-law, Clinton Von Bellow.

Clive seemed glad to hear from me. He said, "I talked to Clint, and he told me that he doesn't know a thing about Dorothy Winetroub Parker or George Morgan. They just showed up in his office and asked him to prepare a deed and get a title policy on Mrs. Parker's house in Las Vegas."

I told Clive that people didn't just walk into a lawyer's office by accident.

"That's what I said to Clint. He says that a former client recommended him to Morgan, but he'd never met Morgan before. It was a straightforward deal. Clint just did the paperwork and helped them close at the title company. He remembers that Morgan got his loan through Rock Mortgage Company here in town. It's supposed to be a reputable firm."

I thanked Clive for the information, though I didn't think it was going to help me any.

"That's not all," Clive said.

I should have known he'd hold out the good stuff. I asked what else he had to tell me.

"I talked to a friend of mine about Aaron Winetroub," he said.

Clive had friends all over town, some of whom walked on the shady side of the law. In fact, he had better sources of information than most of the cops I knew, including me.

"Winetroub spent some time in Houston a good while back," Clive continued. "And he knew George Morgan."

"That's more like it," I said. "What else did you find out?"

"Winetroub and my friend Tony Antonelli were in business together," Clive said, and I knew he'd tell the story in his own way. Once he got started, there was no need to ask any more questions. But I did it anyway.

"Business?" I said. "What kind of business?"

"The illegal kind. This was a while back, and Tony's retired now, of course."

"Of course," I said.

"Right. Anyway, as I was trying to tell you, Tony and Wine-troub were in business. They were running a bookie operation, and those things need plenty of phone lines. George Morgan's the man who ran the lines for them. There was nothing unusual in that, according to Tony. Morgan ran the lines for nearly every book in Houston. He was the best in the business. Once Aaron and Tony wanted to open a book in the Bettis Building, and Morgan was the man they hired."

"The Bettis Building is right downtown," I said. "You're telling me there was a book running in there?"

"That's right. Morgan ran the phone lines in the elevator shaft so nobody would see them. They had ten or fifteen phones going all the time. They'd book bets on anything. Football, baseball, basketball, presidential elections, you name it. Biggest book in town."

I shook my head, then realized that Clive couldn't see me. "Hard to believe they got away with it," I said.

"Hell, half the vice squad was on their payroll. Well, two of the sergeants, anyway."

I didn't like hearing that, but I knew it was possible, even likely.

"Internal Affairs has probably gotten rid of those two by now," Clive said, but it wasn't much of a consolation even if it was true. Which was questionable.

"How did Morgan manage to run all those lines?" I asked. "He'd have to have access to phone company equipment, not to mention a way of tapping into their lines."

Clive laughed. "That's the good part. Morgan worked for the phone company. But he was making more money from Tony and Winetroub and the other bookies than he was at his regular job."

I didn't remember hearing about the break-up of a big book anytime recently. I asked Clive what had happened to Tony's set-up with Winetroub.

He laughed again, louder and longer this time.

"Tony told me that one day he was standing by the window of the Bettis Building, looking out, and he called Winetroub over to have a look. Down in the street, Sheriff Kerns and five or six deputies were getting out of their county cars. Tony and Wintroub didn't say a word to anybody. They just left the room, and went down the stairs and out of the building. That was pretty much the end of the book. Winetroub left town. Tony stayed around, but he'd go out to Las Vegas two or three times a month. Sometimes Morgan would go, too. They'd meet Wine-troub and party all weekend." Clive paused. "Dorothy Parker was with them, too."

I let all that sink in, but Clive still wasn't through. He said, "If you'll meet me for lunch at the Fish House, I'll tell you about those two lawsuits you asked about, the ones where Ralph Parker was serving as the plaintiff's attorney."

"I guess I'll be buying the lunch."

"Damned right," Clive said.

CHAPTER 8

After I hung up, I started writing everything down immediately, before it had a chance to get cold. When I finished, I read over my notes and tried to think of what to do next. The most likely possibility seemed to be George Morgan.

Clive wasn't the only one with contacts. I called a friend named Tom Laughlin at the telephone company, and he told me that Morgan had retired as a supervisor.

"George is living up at Lake Livingston, near Cold Springs," Tom said. "Last I heard he was in the real estate business up there."

"Do you remember the name of the company he works for?" I asked.

"He works for himself now. Got his own business. Big Tex Realty, he calls it."

I thanked Tom and considered whether I wanted to give Morgan a call. I don't like telephone interviews, since I prefer to be looking at the person I'm talking to. However, I could always ask Morgan to come in for a personal chat, so I called long distance information and got the Big Tex number.

When I dialed it, Morgan himself answered the phone on the first ring. He might have thought I was a hot prospect checking in, but if he was disappointed when I identified myself, he didn't let it show. He was very slick and very cooperative. He said he'd be glad to come in any time I wanted him to, and he mentioned how shocked he was when he'd read about Dorothy Parker's death in the paper.

"Dot was a fine woman," he said. "I liked her a lot."

"I understand you used to work for Tony Antonelli," I said.

Morgan paused, a little taken aback by my change of subject, then said, "I knew Tony, all right, but I never worked for him. You got some bad information somewhere. I worked for the phone company until a couple of years ago when I decided to go into business on my own."

"Maybe the work you did for Tony had something to do with telephones," I said.

"Well, I installed a lot of phones before I was promoted to supervisor," Morgan said, not giving anything away, not that I blamed him.

"But you knew him and Aaron Winetroub fairly well," I said.

"Yeah, sure, I knew Tony, but I didn't work for him. We were friends. Used to meet out in Vegas and party. Dot was there, too. What a woman."

"She was a little older than you," I said.

"Sure. But that didn't make any difference. She didn't look old. She really worked to take care of herself and that figure of hers. She was an exercise nut, but I think she'd had some help, if you know what I mean."

I asked him to spell it out.

"Well, you know how it is. She looked twenty years younger than she was. Hell, twenty-five years younger. There's no way she could have looked that good without some surgical assistance. I think she'd had some work on her boobs, and she must've had a face-lift, too. None of it was obvious, though. She was one beautiful chick."

She wasn't beautiful anymore, not with a bullet hole in her head, I thought. Morgan must have picked up on what I was thinking. He said, "Damn shame for her to go out like she did. I hope you catch the son of a bitch that did it."

"I will," I said. I didn't doubt it for a minute. "What about your business dealings with her? I know you bought a house from her in Las Vegas."

"Yeah. Nice place. She came to me and asked if I'd be interested, since I was in real estate now. I'd seen the house when I was out there, but I still checked it out before I bought it. Business is business, you know?"

I told him that I knew.

"Right. Well, she was pricing it low, so I bought it for resale. Some guy named Grubble's living there, I think. Dot was letting him stay in the house without paying her any rent, but she was going to make him get out after I bought it. I told her there was no rush. It was all right by me if he stayed until I got ready to sell."

"You ever meet him?" I said.

"No. Didn't care to. From what Dot told me about him, he wasn't worth knowing. I don't know what she saw in him. What's that old song? 'Just a Gigolo'? I guess that's about what he was."

That was probably true enough. "But you trust him to live there?"

"He was taking care of the place just fine, according to Dorothy. And I'll be putting the house on the market soon. Then he'll be gone."

Good riddance, too, I thought. Then I asked Morgan where he'd been the night of the murders.

"Am I a suspect?" he said.

That's what everyone wants to know, but not all of them will come right out and ask. I gave him the usual answer. "No. I'm sure you're in the clear. It's just that I have to cover all the bases."

"I guess I can understand that," he said after a slight hesitation. "What day was it that you wanted to know about again?"

I told him, and he said, "I'm pretty well covered, then. My wife, Linda, and I had dinner that night at Las Chicas. That's a Mexican restaurant in Cold Springs. We went with Ira and Sue Charles. Ira's a pharmacist at Walgreen's. After dinner, Ira and I took Linda and Sue home, and we went to a fishing camp we have on a little creek that feeds into Lake Livingston. We wanted to catch some catfish, so we set out some trotlines. We stayed out there until about two o'clock, and when we got home, it was probably closer to three. I didn't bother to check. I just went to bed and slept a couple of hours. I got up and went back to the creek around seven to check the lines. There was one really nice cat on there, went nearly twenty pounds."

If he was telling the truth, and I didn't have any reason to doubt him at the moment, he was in the clear on the murders. But I asked him for the Charleses' phone number just the same.

"Gonna check up on me, huh?"

"Part of the job," I said.

"I don't blame you." He gave me the number. "And if you're ever looking for any nice lakefront property up this way, you give me a call. I can fix you up with something you'll be real proud of. I might even show you my favorite catfishing spot."

I told him I'd keep that in mind and pushed down the hook on the phone. After a second or two, I let it go and dialed the Charleses' home. I got the wife, Sue, who verified what Morgan had told me, except the last part. She had no way of knowing about that for sure, though she did know about the big catfish. It seemed that Morgan wasn't really a suspect, though I never wrote anybody off completely.

I hung up the phone and looked at my watch. It was almost noon. Time to buy lunch for Clive Watson.

The day was gloomy and gray, as if the clouds were right down on the ground with us, and there was a fine mist in the air like smoke. It hung on my clothes and in my hair, and the air-conditioning in the car turned me clammy before it dried me off.

I drove to the Fish House through the noon traffic. Weather conditions meant nothing to Houston drivers, who would push the speed limit in a flood or a hurricane. I gripped the steering wheel and prayed that the slick roads wouldn't cause too many accidents. Especially not in my lane.

When I pulled into the parking lot at the Fish House, I relaxed a little, but not completely. Houstonians have been known to drive over the highway speed limit even in parking lots.

I got out of the car and walked across the lot to the restaurant door. The asphalt had an iridescent sheen as the oils on its surface mixed with the mist that settled there.

Inside the restaurant, I wiped my face with my handkerchief and looked around. Sure enough, Clive was already there, sitting in his usual place with a gin and tonic full of limes. Not to mention his cigarette.

I sat down across from him and the waitress appeared almost before I could tell him hello. I ordered a Jack Daniel's and water. When she brought it, Clive raised his glass to me and asked how I was doing.

I took a sip of the drink and let its warmth spread through me.

"You mean personally or on the case?" I said.

"Either one," Clive said. "But I'd be interested to know what you hear from Sarah."

I took another sip, a much bigger one.

"Nothing," I said. "Her lawyer talks to me, but she never does. She wants half of everything I have, including my retirement. That's fine. She's welcome to it. She can have it all. It's not worth much to me if she's gone."

"I know what you mean," Clive said. "But at least you have a chance to get her back. I don't."

Clive's wife had died of colon cancer only a couple of months after being diagnosed. She'd been gone for nearly a year now, but Clive was still as grief-stricken as he'd been in the beginning.

I knew that I shouldn't have been so insensitive, and I regretted what I'd said, but it was too late to take it back.

"How're you sleeping?" Clive asked.

"Not very well. How about you?"

"The same."

I thought he might tear up again, but the waitress came to take our orders, and he smiled at her when he asked for the grilled snapper. I ordered fried shrimp, and Clyde said he wished he could have something fried just once.

I grinned and said he could have a bite of mine if he wanted it, but I knew he'd turn me down rather than run the risk of messing up his stomach.

"And another thing," I said, while he was pretending to think over my offer, "I think you should quit smoking. Your stomach would feel a lot better."

"To hell with that idea. I can't eat what I want, but I'm not giving up smoking and drinking. A man's got to have some pleasure in life."

"Whatever you say."

"And I don't want any of your damned shrimp, either."

"I don't blame you. What about those two lawsuits involving Ralph Parker that you're looking into for me?"

"I know the defense lawyers in both of them," he said, stubbing out his cigarette after lighting a fresh one from it.

One reason that Clive had better sources of information than most cops in town was that he knew more people on both sides of the law than just about anybody in Houston.

"Randall Thomas's client company is being sued in the car accident," Clive said. "Big State Insurance. The people there hate plaintiff's lawyers with a passion. But Randall says they're in a real bind in this case. There's pretty much no way out for them. They've agreed to settle, and they have plenty of money to do it with. So you can mark that case off your list of possibilities. Nobody involved in it would have a reason to kill Ralph Parker."

It always helps to narrow things down. I thanked Clive and asked about the other case. He started to tell me, but our food arrived, so he waited until after he'd said his blessing.

I thought about all the detectives I'd seen on TV and in the movies. I don't think I ever saw a one of those fellas say a prayer. But Clive was the real thing, one of the best and toughest private investigators in the country, and here he was, bowing over his food in a restaurant.

And then there was his relationship with his Anna and their kids. When Clive was working on a case out of town, there had been plenty of times when he'd load up the whole clan and take them along. That was another thing you'd never see on television.

After Clive finished praying, he crossed himself, and we started on our food. As we ate, he told me about the other case. The defense attorney was a man named Will Hall, and his client, Sam Lindley, didn't have any insurance on his workers.

Lindley owned the American Way Machine Shop on Long Point, and his idea of the American way was to let his employees pay for their own insurance if they wanted it and could afford it. One of his employees, Zach Monroe, either wasn't making enough to buy insurance or he'd decided to take a big chance, because a malfunctioning machine had torn four fingers off his right hand.

Lindley, through Hall, had offered ten thousand dollars to Monroe to settle, but Monroe's expenses had been a good bit more than that, and of course Parker had encouraged him not to settle but to sue for a hell of a lot more money to cover "pain and suffering," not to mention loss of future wages. So Monroe was asking for two hundred and fifty thousand dollars. Clive said he would have been likely to get it if Parker could have gotten a sympathetic jury.

According to Hall, Lindley was in bad financial shape, and if Parker had won the suit, Lindley would be likely to lose his business and everything else that he had. He'd told Hall that he hated Parker and would "like to see the son of a bitch dead."

"What did Hall tell him?" I asked.

"He told him that another lawyer would just take over the case and ask for twice as much," Clive said. "But Lindley said there was no way to know that and he'd be willing to take his chances if he could just see Parker wiped off the face of the earth."

I thanked Clive for the information. I figured that Sam Lindley had a solid motive for the murder, or thought he did, so he was someone else I'd have to check out.

We finished our food, and Clive grabbed the check even before he lit a cigarette.

"I thought I was paying," I said.

"Sometimes I like to surprise you," Clive said. "I need to keep in practice."

I surprised him, too. I didn't protest. He paid the bill cheerfully, though.

We walked out of the Fish House together. The rain had started coming down in earnest, washing the sheen off the parking lot and bouncing off the tops of the cars.

When Clive drove away through the downpour I thought about how he'd feel, going back alone to his empty house. For what was probably the first time since Sarah had left me, I felt sorrier for him than I did for myself.

CHAPTER 9

Before going back to my own office, I went by to see Bolce. I told him what I'd found out, and he asked about my source.

"Clive Watson," I said. "And before you tell me to stay away from private eyes, he's doing this for free because he's my friend. And he's already been very helpful."

"I wasn't going to say anything," Bolce told me. "I'm not like Wetsel."

Wetsel hated private eyes. He thought they were a pimple on the ass of society. Maybe my friendship with Clive had something to do with why Wetsel didn't like me.

While I was in Bolce's office, I asked him for all the reports that Wetsel and McGuire had turned in, and he handed them over.

"I have the crime scene reports, too," he said, and he gave those to me as well.

I took all the reports to my office and put them on my desk. I planned to read them carefully, but first I wanted to check out Sam Lindley. It turned out that he didn't have any criminal record, at least not in Houston or the state of Texas.

But I didn't stop there. Like Clive, I know a lot of people, and one of them, Wayne Forster, worked for the FBI.

I gave him a call, and we exchanged a few pleasantries, mostly about how bad the weather was in Houston. Then I asked if Forster could check on Lindley for me.

He said that he could, but I'd owe him a favor somewhere

down the line. I'd expected that and agreed without an argument. I was glad that I did because he came up with something almost immediately.

"Seems like your friend's got a federal rap sheet," Forster said. "He was charged with an assault on a federal marshal."

"He's not my friend," I said. "What's the story?"

"Well, Lindley was a witness in a federal case about ten years ago. I guess he didn't like the way he was questioned while he was on the stand. He got visibly upset and had to be reprimanded by the judge a couple of times. He stormed out of the courtroom after his testimony and took a swing at a U.S. Marshal as he was leaving."

"Does the report say why?"

Forster laughed. "The marshal claims he told Lindley to have a nice day."

"And we all know a United States Marshal wouldn't tell a lie," I said.

"Right. So it's pretty obvious that your client is one hot-tempered son of a gun. You Texans are known for being like that, though."

"Sure we are. So don't ever cross me."

"You don't have to worry about that. At least not as long as you remember you owe me one."

"I doubt that you'll let me forget it."

"You got that right," Forster said.

I made a note of what Forster had told me and started reading the reports I'd picked up from Bolce. One of them had to do with an interview McGuire had conducted with the maid who worked for the Parkers. McGuire was better at that sort of thing than Wetsel, and I usually trusted his reports to be accurate. According to him, the maid had been at the Parker house on the day before the murders, and she'd overheard some interesting things while she was cleaning the den.

Stanford Parker, Ralph Parker, and Stanford's girlfriend, a woman named Emily Jackson, had all been in one of the bedrooms. They were arguing in loud voices that carried all the way to where the maid was dusting.

The loud talk had become shouting, and Ralph Parker had stormed out of the bedroom, red in the face, yelling at his son and telling him to get out of the house and never come back. A few minutes after that Stanford Parker and Jackson had come through the den and left through the front door.

Like most eyewitnesses, the maid couldn't remember anything that was said, at least not exactly. She was sure of one thing, however. The argument between the father and son was about money. Stanford, who must have been on some kind of allowance, or who had been getting money from his father semi-regularly, wanted more of it. And his father had adamantly refused to give him any and had told him never to ask again.

The maid had said some other things, but none of them seemed to point in any particular direction, so I turned to the crime scene reports. The first one I read said that there were no prints on the open window in the bedroom.

I didn't buy McGuire's "fresh air" theory. Nobody runs the A/C and opens a window at the same time, not with all the rain we'd been having. It would have been ridiculous to open a window in the first place.

The investigators hadn't found any footprints outside the window, but the lawn had been disturbed there, so they were reasonably certain that the perp had gotten into the house through that window. The only conclusion I could draw from that was that someone had wiped the window clean or worn gloves.

The front door was the type that locked automatically when it shut, so I supposed that Dot Parker had left it open behind her every morning when she went to get the paper.

The Medical Examiner hadn't been able to fix the time of death exactly, but he said it had happened sometime between midnight and when the bodies were found, probably around four a.m. That fit with what I'd been told by the Reitmans.

I put the report down and leaned back in my chair, which squeaked in protest. I'd learned a lot that day, but I wasn't sure how it all fit together, or even if it did fit. But now it was time to go home, so I put everything away and got ready to leave.

When that was done, I found myself not wanting to move out of the office. The thought of the empty house was a little too much for me. For once, I wished I liked to hang out in cop bars. Even Wetsel would be better company than nobody at all.

On second thought, maybe he wouldn't. I put that idea out of my head, drove home, and watched the early news. It seemed that Teddy Kennedy had driven his car into a lake or river, and a young woman passenger had drowned. I figured that would be the end of his political career right there.

The weather forecaster said that we'd have more rain. No surprise in that. In the summers there's almost always rain in the forecast on the Gulf Coast. I turned off the TV set and popped a frozen pizza in the oven. Gourmet cooking is a little beyond me, but I can heat up a pizza with the best of them. I couldn't eat the whole thing, but I'd save the leftover part and have it cold for breakfast.

Somebody had given me a copy of a new book called *The Godfather,* so I read a few chapters of that after I'd cleaned up in the kitchen. It was a wild story about the Mafia, and as far as I could tell there wasn't a word of truth in it. I thought it might make a good movie, though. I put it down easily enough and went to bed.

I lay there and thought about Sarah and how much I missed her. It was a long time before I got to sleep.

CHAPTER 10

I was about to leave the house the next morning when Clive called. He was beginning to make a habit of it.

"I can't talk on this phone," he said. "Meet me at the donut shop, off Kirkwood on Memorial, and I'll give you some news."

"I'm about to leave for the office," I said.

"Free donuts," Clive said. "What cop can resist that?"

"Not me. I'll call Bolce and tell him that I'm going to be late."

Since Bolce had taken me off all other cases, I had a lot of leeway and didn't really have to call in. But I thought it would be a good idea to keep in touch. When I mentioned that I'd be meeting with Clive and might be getting some more information about the Parker case, Bolce told me to go ahead.

The rain had moved on, and the sun was shining. My leg, which usually ached a little on damp mornings, didn't hurt at all for some reason. The dew on the grass was so heavy that my lawn seemed to be covered with sparkling glass beads. The humidity, of course, was fierce, and I could smell the dampness in the air. My shirt collar was wet before I could get to the car and turn on the air conditioner.

I plowed along in the traffic, and I kept the windows rolled up. I wasn't in the mood to inhale exhaust fumes. As soon as I could, I got off the freeway and drove along Memorial. It's a pretty street, with plenty of trees and nice houses. People sometimes think that Houston, being in Texas, must be a desert, but they couldn't be more wrong. Because of all the rain and the mild temperatures, the whole city is covered with trees, mainly oaks, but with plenty of other kinds as well. There's a lot of shade, which is a good thing in the summer.

The donut shop was in a little strip mall just off Memorial. When I went inside, Clive was smoking a cigarette while drinking coffee and talking to Bruce, who owns the place. They were good friends, and Clive went there just about every day.

Sitting on the table by Clive were a couple of boxes of donuts, a dozen in each one.

"You can take these back with you," Clive said. "Then nobody will care if you come in late."

"Cops and donuts is a real cliche," I said.

"Every cliche has some truth in it," Clive said. His head was wreathed in smoke from his cigarette. "That's how it becomes a cliche. Right, Bruce?"

Bruce nodded his agreement and said, "Did you hear about Teddy Kennedy?"

I told him that I'd heard it on the news last night.

"That girl's family should hire Clive. He'd have Kennedy in the pen within a year. Either that or get a settlement up in the millions."

I said I didn't doubt it and went over to get myself a cup of coffee. Bruce has a couple of big urns, and the coffee is strictly self-service. When I got back to the table, Bruce got up to leave, as if he knew that Clive and I had some private business to discuss.

Clive waited until Bruce was back behind the donut counter, then asked me if I'd heard anything from Sarah.

"No. I thought you called to talk to me about the case."

"You don't have to be snippy," Clive said. He lit a cigarette from the butt of the one he was holding. "I have plenty to say about the case." He opened one of the boxes on the table. "Take yourself a donut and calm down."

I reached in and got a plain glazed donut. It was still warm, and its sugary taste did help soothe me a little, along with the coffee I was drinking.

When he judged that I was calmed down, Clive said, "I got a call from Elmer Gann last night. He wanted to talk about the Parkers. Do you know who Gann is?"

"A lawyer," I said, brushing sugar off my tie. "There seem to be a hell of a lot of lawyers mixed up in this case."

"He's not exactly mixed up in it," Clive said. "He was a good friend of the Parkers, and he's got plenty of money. He wants to hire me to look into the murders."

"He doesn't trust the police?"

"Don't get your dander up. He thinks the police are fine, but he thinks a little private help wouldn't hurt them. You don't mind private help, do you?"

"Not as long as I get free donuts."

"You're really touchy today," Clive said. "You don't have to eat the damn donuts if you don't want to."

"Who's getting snippy now?" I said.

Clive laughed. "Okay, I get the point. The thing is, I'm helping you out already, and I'm glad to do it. I'm not sending you a bill, and I'm even paying for your donuts and coffee. But if Gann's willing to hire me, I can keep on helping you and make a little money at the same time. I don't see anything wrong with that. Do you?"

I told him that I didn't, and took another bite of the donut.

"Gann thinks Stanford Parker's guilty as sin," Clive went on. His cigarette was down to nothing, and he lit another one.

"So does Bob Wetsel," I said around a mouthful of donut.

"Uh-oh," Clive said. He knew Wetsel and Wetsel's feelings about private eyes. "I hope he doesn't know I've been helping you out."

"I haven't said a word."

"Just as well. Let's keep it between us."

I said that was fine with me, and Clive went on with his story.

"Gann told me that Ralph Parker had talked to him about his problems with Stanford. Seems that Stanford has a terrible temper. Ralph was afraid of him, and he'd made some threats when Ralph cut off his money supply."

I told Clive about McGuire's interview with the Parkers' maid.

"Well, it all fits," Clive said. "Maybe for once in his life, Wetsel's right."

"Maybe," I said. "What does Gann want you to do about all this?"

"He wants me to run a surveillance on Stanford Parker. Do you have any problem with that?"

When Clive said you, he meant the department in general and Bolce in particular.

"I don't think there's a problem," I said. "As far as I know, nobody's ordered a surveillance on Stanford Parker."

"Good. I didn't want to get in your way, even for the money. But if you think it'll be all right, I'll let Gann give me a retainer. Then I'll get some surveillance started on Stanford."

"Naturally you're going to keep me posted on what you find out, if anything."

"Sure," Clive said. "You know that."

I finished my coffee and told Clive that I had to get back to work. Before I could stand up, he asked me about Sarah again.

"Remember, Steve," he said, "God works in mysterious ways."

Sometimes those ways are entirely too mysterious for me, but before I could tell Clive that, I saw the glint of tears in the corners of his eyes.

"I'll talk to you later," I said, and got out of there.

I just couldn't stick around, not if Clive was going to start talking about Anna, or about God. If I'd stayed, I'd have become more depressed than I ordinarily was. I don't usually mind Clive's talk about religion, and I even think of myself as a religious man, most of the time. But now wasn't the time for that kind of talk, not as far as I was concerned. I got in my car and drove to the station.

The first thing I did was stop by Bolce's office and tell him about my meeting with Clive.

"I want you to write up a report on what Parker told Gann," Bolce said. "We might want to interview Gann later."

I told him I'd write the report and mentioned that Gann had hired Clive to run a surveillance on Stanford Parker.

Bolce sat there and thought about that for a few seconds. Then he nodded and said, "Okay."

I waited, but he didn't add anything to that. So I went back to my office to start on the report.

Before I wrote it, however, there was something I thought I'd better do. I asked for the records on Elmer Gann. It wasn't that I didn't think he was a fine fellow, hiring Clive to find his friend's killer. And it wasn't that I didn't trust lawyers. It was just that I like to check everything out.

As it turned out, Gann wasn't exactly Mr. Clean. He'd been handled most recently for a couple of DWIs, but earlier he'd been involved in some illegal gambling that involved a poker ring. He'd almost been disbarred but had managed to hang on to his license. Finally, according to one of the informants who'd been questioned, he was also heavily in debt to a couple of the big casinos in Las Vegas, and he'd passed a few hot checks around town.

None of that really made any difference to my case that I could see, but I wrote everything down before I sent the reports back, just in case.

After that was taken care if, I started on the report for Bolce. I'd hardly begun on it when Wetsel showed up. His face was red and so was his neck, all the way down to the long-pointed collar of his blue shirt.

"What did your private eye pal want with you?" he said. "Did he tell you how to run your investigation? Or did he just want to suck up to the cops some more?"

I sat there and looked at him without saying anything, trying to think how he could have known I'd talked to Clive. But the answer was easy. I hadn't told anyone except Bolce where I was going, so Bolce had told Wetsel. There was no way around it. Maybe Bolce wanted Wetsel to know that Clive was helping out. Or maybe he just wanted to piss Wetsel off. It's hard for anybody who knows him to resist doing that, sometimes.

After I'd thought things over, I took a deep breath, let it out slowly, and said, "What makes my meeting with Clive Watson any of your business?"

"The Parker case should be mine, that's what. I don't need any cheap private eye messing it up."

If Wetsel had known anything about Clive's rates, he wouldn't have used the word cheap. It didn't apply.

Wetsel got out a cigarette and lit it, maybe trying to calm himself down. He didn't offer me one.

I guess smoking did have a calming effect, as his face got a little less red by the time he'd taken a puff or two.

"There's no use in getting mad at me," I told him. "Bolce put me on the case, and I'm just doing what he tells me. It's not like I have a choice."

"Your damn private eye buddy has a choice."

I decided I might as well let Wetsel in on what was going on. It might settle him down, and he'd find out sooner or later, anyway.

"Clive has to make a living," I said. "He has a client who's hired him to look into the Parker murders, and he wanted to clear it with me."

Wetsel blew a jet of smoke. "He didn't clear it with me."

I shrugged. "He has Bolce's okay."

"Well, he doesn't have mine. If that son of a bitch gets in my way, if he interferes the least little bit, I'll file on him for obstruction of justice quicker than a cat can lick its ass."

"He likes you, too," I said, hating that I was going to have to tell Clive that Wetsel knew about his involvement.

"The hell he does. I know who his friends in the department are, and there aren't too damn many of them. You'd better keep him out of my way, Steve, or your ass is grass, and I'll be the lawnmower."

Like anybody could control Clive Watson. I laughed at the thought, and my laughter must have made Wetsel angry all over again. He tossed what was left of his cigarette down on my floor and ground it under the toe of his shoe. Then he turned and stomped out of the office and down the hall.

A little bit of Wetsel's company went a long way. He was one of those guys who brightened up the place by leaving, and I was happy to see him go.

I decided to get a hamburger for lunch, and while I was on the way, a call about a shooting came in over the car radio. I was probably the closest car to the scene, which was a bar called the Olde Salt on Navigation, so I headed over.

The Olde Salt wasn't located in one of the best areas of town. Old cars with rust-pitted bodies were parked along the street, and winos lay asleep with their backs against the walls in the shade of the alleys, the empty bottles in the paper bags lying by their sides or still gripped tightly in their closed fists. Seagulls swooped and dived around one of the Dumpsters, calling raucously to claim the garbage for themselves.

No one else had arrived on the scene when I got there, so I went inside with my sidearm drawn.

It was cool and quiet inside. A jukebox over on one side of the room was playing "Mama Told Me Not to Come," which seemed somehow appropriate.

Only seven people were there, and one of them was dead.

CHAPTER 11

The dead man lay on the floor not far from one of the tables. He wore a T-shirt that had once been white but that was now stained red with his blood.

The bartender saw me, and he nodded in the direction of the third man, who sat at the end of the bar. I already had my pistol trained on him. He had his left hand wrapped around a glass of beer and his right hand wrapped around a Saturday Night Special. He wasn't looking at me, but I knew he could see me in the mirror behind the bar.

Four other men sat at a table not too far from where the dead man lay. They all looked at me, but they had nothing to say. Either they were too scared, or they just didn't want to talk about what had happened in the bar. Their eyes were all wide, and one of them was tapping his foot rapidly on the floor, not in time to the music from the jukebox, so I figured that they were more scared than reluctant.

I heard the faint sound of sirens, and I said, "Somebody go out there and tell those cops not to come in here."

Nobody moved. I motioned to one of the men at the table with my pistol.

"You," I said. "What's your name?"

"Leon," he said. His voice was shaky.

I switched the pistol back to the man at the bar. "Okay, Leon. You go on outside and tell those fellas to stay there. Tell them I have things under control in here."

The song on the jukebox ended, which was fine with me. I was tired of it anyway. Leon got up and started outside. The man at the bar didn't seem to care, so I told the other three to go with Leon and help him out.

They got up and headed for the door, not slowly, but not panicking, either. When they opened the door, sunlight flooded in. The door swung closed behind them, and the dimness gathered inside the bar again.

"You want to tell me what happened here?" I said to the bartender.

He looked at the man who was sitting in front of him. The man took a drink of his beer, draining the glass while continuing to watch me in the mirror the whole time.

The bartender said, "This guy came in here with his buddy, and they were both drunk."

" 'S a damn lie," the drinker said, setting his glass on the bar. "Never been drunk in m' lie. Life. Goddammit."

The bartender looked at me and raised his eyebrows. "They looked drunk to me," he said. "And they acted drunk, too. So I refused to serve them, and this guy here pulled a pistol on me. Said he was gonna shoot my ass if I didn't give them a drink."

"Woulda done it, too," the drinker said. "But Sham . . . Sham . . . Chingada! Sammy! Shammy, he got in the way."

The bartender nodded. "That's what happened. He was gonna shoot me, but he got to waving the gun around and shot his buddy instead."

"Didn' mean to. Sham . . . Sham . . . Mierda! Sammy! Shammy shoulda stayed home."

"After he shot his buddy, I gave him a beer," the bartender said. "Then I called you."

Well, he hadn't called me, exactly, but this was no time to argue semantics. He'd been cool under pressure and done the right thing, probably avoiding getting someone else shot. Now all I had to do was get the guy's pistol.

"Will you trade that pistol for another beer?" I said.

The drinker turned his head to look at me. "You mus' think I'm shtu . . . shtu . . . Hijo de puta! Stupid!"

"I don't think that at all. I just thought you might be thirsty."

"You can besh . . . besh . . . Goddammit! Besa! Besha mi culo!"

He turned on the stool and threw the beer glass at me and tried to bring up his pistol at the same time.

But he was too drunk and uncoordinated to do much of anything. The beer glass hit a table ten feet to my right and shattered, and the drinker fell off his stool, firing a shot that hit the wall behind me, well over my head.

He struggled to right himself, pulling himself up on the stool with one hand and aiming the pistol with the other.

Maybe aiming was the wrong word. It was more like he was waving it around in hopes that if he pulled the trigger he might hit something.

And he did. He hit the jukebox, and some of its flashing lights immediately went dark.

"Shoot the son of a bitch before he does any more damage," the bartender yelled at me.

I didn't plan to shoot anybody, much less a hapless drunk, not if I could help it. As it turned out, I didn't have to shoot him. In trying to pull himself up, he instead pulled the stool over and sprawled on the floor, the stool on top of him. While he struggled to get it off, I walked over to him and kicked the pistol out of his hand. It skidded across the floor, and I told the bartender to leave it there. I didn't want him to get any prints on it.

"Don't worry," he said. "I don't want to touch it."

"Good. Now go outside and bring in the patrol officers."

He came around the bar and headed for the door. I looked

down at the drinker. He was passed out cold on the floor.

By the time the patrol officers got the drinker into a car, the Medical Examiner's people had arrived. While they did their thing inside the bar, I went outside to help the patrol officers take statements from the witnesses. They all told pretty much the same story, which agreed in all details with what the bartender had already said, so I was fairly certain there would be only one set of prints on the gun.

One of the patrolmen had taken the drinker's billfold and gotten his name and address, or he thought he had. The name on the license was Felipe Lopez, but the license itself was a poorly made fake, and it was a good bet that the name was a fake as well. The address was probably wrong, too. Another good bet would be that Lopez, or whatever his name might really be, was an illegal. That would complicate things a little, but not too much. He'd be headed for jail sooner or later, no matter where he came from.

We were just about to finish up with the statements when one of the patrolmen came running up.

"That drunk's passed out in my patrol car! He fell off the seat and he's choking!"

We all ran to the car. The man had fallen face up and was choking on his own vomit.

"Flip him over," I said.

Nobody seemed interested in helping, so I turned to the young patrolman. "It's your car," I told him.

"Damn! This makes the fifth time in less than three months that a drunk has barfed in my car."

In spite of his complaint, he turned Lopez over, but it wasn't much help. Lopez still wasn't breathing well, and I thought maybe some of his nasal passages might be clogged by the vomit. The bartender was standing not far away, so I told him to go inside and call for an ambulance.

When the ambulance came, one of the patrolmen rode in it with Lopez to make sure he got to the hospital all right. And of course to make sure that he got to the jail after he'd been taken care of.

I felt sorry for the poor kid who had to drive that patrol car, but I didn't worry about him long. He might have to sit in the stink for a while, but he could get the car cleaned out. I had to deal with Bob Wetsel, and he was a lot harder to get rid of than a bad smell.

I got back to police headquarters and wrote up a report on the bar killing. When I finished, I realized that I hadn't had any lunch, but by then it was time for me to leave for the day. On the way home I stopped off at a WhopperBurger and got a Number One, which is a plain old hamburger with all the trimmings. I had some fries and a root beer to go with it. I ate at a little Formica-topped table. I wasn't in any hurry to get home.

I got there eventually, after driving around a little and thinking about Sarah. She and I had always liked to drive downtown and see the crowds going home in the afternoons, gathering at the bus stops near the office buildings and department stores, guessing about what kinds of lives they had, wondering if any of them could be as happy as we were, and telling each other that nothing would ever come between us.

Now something had, and I didn't have any idea what it was. For the first time I considered asking Clive to see if he could find out something for me, specifically who might have given her the idea that I was having an affair. It was a crazy idea, and not even Wetsel would tell her something like that.

Then my thoughts turned another way. It was the word *crazy* that had done it. What if Sarah had some kind of mental problem and was imagining everything? It was about the only explanation that made any sense, but I didn't like anything about it.

Still, I couldn't get it out of my head. I drove home and watched the news. It was mostly about the men on the way to the moon, and I knew the people at NASA must be feeling a pride in their accomplishment that would be hard to beat.

I read a few more chapters in *The Godfather,* and they were no more believable than the earlier ones. I had to admit that the author could tell a good story, though, no matter how fanciful it was. But it didn't get my mind off Sarah. I called her number, but she didn't answer.

I watched Johnny Carson and went to bed, but sleep was a long time coming.

CHAPTER 12

The next morning I was sitting at the kitchen table in my underwear, reading the newspaper, when the telephone rang. I picked it up and said, "Hello, Clive."

"How did you know it was me?"

"It's always you. Nobody else calls me, especially not at this hour of the morning. And you've been doing it every day lately."

"You're a regular Sherlock Holmes."

"Elementary, my dear Watson. And what does my faithful assistant have for me this morning?"

Clive didn't like the idea of being anybody's assistant, faithful or not, but he didn't let on that I'd slipped him the needle. He said, "I've got something that's going to surprise you. I put a man on Stanford Parker starting at noon yesterday. Parker left his house around three o'clock and walked about twelve blocks to a gay bar."

That was a surprise, all right. Parker had a girlfriend, after all. I wondered if he was bisexual or if the girlfriend was just a beard. And why walk?

"Maybe he just wanted a drink," I said.

"Could be," Clive said. "But when he came out of the bar about forty-five minutes later, he was with an older man. They got in the man's car and drove to an apartment. They were inside for over two hours, and when they left, the man drove Parker home."

"Maybe they were playing Scrabble."

"And maybe I'm the king of France."

"France doesn't have a king anymore."

"You know what I meant."

I tried to fit this new information into what I already had and came up with an idea.

"It could be that Parker's prostituting himself to get money," I said. "His father had cut him off, remember."

"I remember, but that theory won't fly. When they got to Parker's house, Parker walked around to the driver's window and handed him a bunch of bills."

"He paid the driver?"

"Don't go jumping to conclusions. I didn't say he paid him. I said he handed him some money. I don't know why he did that, and neither does my investigator. Do you want the license number of the car?"

"You know I do," I said, and I wrote it down when Clive read it off to me.

"I'll let you know if I find out anything interesting," I said. "And now I have a little news for you."

I told him about Wetsel.

"I can't believe Bolce would do that," Clive said. "Wetsel is just crazy enough to file on me. He can't make anything stick, but he could really mess up our investigation."

Wetsel wouldn't care about that, of course. In fact, he'd probably enjoy doing it.

"You'd better talk to Bolce," Clive said. "Tell him to call Wetsel off."

"I'll talk to him," I said. "I can't make any promises, though."

"I'm going to keep on feeding you information," Clive said. "Because we're friends. But if Wetsel gets in my way, I'll have to take care of him myself."

I didn't ask what he might do along those lines. I figured it was better not to know.

As soon as I got to my office I ran the license number and got the information on the man who had picked up Parker. He was Dave Persons, forty-six years old, five feet, ten inches tall, brown hair, blue eyes. Clive had most of that already, and he had the address of the apartment house, which also came up. I had Persons' name and date of birth run through the computer, but Persons had no record at all, not even a parking ticket or a speeding citation.

I wrote everything down and went in to see Bolce. I gave him an update, and then I braced him about Wetsel.

"You shouldn't have told him I was meeting Clive Watson," I said. "You know how he hates private investigators."

Bolce actually apologized, which surprised me. I'd never known that to happen before.

"I made a mistake," he said. "Wetsel came by to make a report, and I mentioned that you'd had a call about the case. When he asked who'd called, I told him. It just slipped right out. I knew I'd screwed up as soon as I said it."

"He's not happy," I said. "He's threatening to file on Clive for obstruction of justice."

"He won't, though. I'll have a little talk with him before things get out of hand. You let me know if he causes any trouble. We've got to handle this case right because it's becoming political. Ralph Parker had a lot of friends, and he was a fairly prominent attorney. The papers are starting to call and ask what's happening. I haven't told them much. But then there's not much to tell."

Which meant that he was putting them off. I remembered the reporters I'd seen outside the house the day of the murders. They weren't going to give up, no matter how Bolce tried to stall them.

"I'll trust you to handle the papers and Wetsel," I said. "Just keep them off my back. All of them."

"I'll do what I can," Bolce said.

I'd been so busy checking out other leads that I'd neglected Sam Lindley, the man who hated Ralph Parker and had told his lawyer he wouldn't mind seeing Parker dead. So I drove out Long Point to the American Way Machine Shop.

It was sandwiched between a tool warehouse and a used-car lot. The outside was sheet metal with rust bleeding from the nail heads, and there were potholes in the asphalt parking lot. There was water from the rain in the potholes, and a scruffy looking dog was lapping water from one of them. He looked up and ran away when I got out of my car, limping just a little.

Lindley's office was just inside the front door of the building, sort of a roofed cubicle that set it apart from the rest of the building. I could hear grinding and see sparks flying in the dim interior.

I didn't bother to knock on Lindley's door. I just opened it and went inside. A small air conditioner hummed from its hole in the wall, and a man sat at an old wooden rolltop desk talking on the telephone. There was a big ashtray on the desk, and it overflowed with stubbed out butts. The smell of stale smoke hung in the air.

The man talking on the phone had a big, hard-looking stomach that pushed his double-knit shirt out over his belt, short black hair, and a jowly face. He looked up, saw me, and said, "I'll call you back" into the phone. Then he hung it up and said, "What can I do for you?"

I showed him my badge and asked if he was Sam Lindley. He said that he was.

"I'd like to ask you a few questions about Ralph Parker," I said.

"That son of a bitch. If you want me to say I'm glad he's dead, I will, but I didn't kill him."

"I guess you can prove that."

"You're damned right. I was at a party in Galveston until after midnight when he was killed, and my wife was with me. She'll be glad to testify to that."

Wives had been known to lie to protect their husbands, but I didn't bother telling Lindley that.

"And it's not just my wife," he went on, as if he'd known what I was thinking. "We spent the night with the couple who gave the party and didn't leave Galveston until after breakfast the next morning."

"I'll need the name and phone number of the people who gave the party," I said. "And if you have the names of some of the other guests, that might help."

"I have all that," Lindley said. "I'll write it down for you."

He pulled a pack of Chesterfields from his shirt pocket and extended them to me. "Smoke?"

"I've quit."

"Not me. I love these damned things." He lit a Chesterfield, sucked in smoke, and exhaled with deep satisfaction. "Fills my lungs with tiny little vitamins."

I didn't comment.

"Let me write that stuff down for you," Lindley said after another deep drag on the cigarette.

He put the cigarette on the edge of the already overfilled ashtray and pawed through the papers on his desk until he found something to write on. Then he located a pencil and scrawled the information I'd asked for. He handed the paper to me and I could see the nicotine stains on his fingers.

"Thanks. I'll give them a call."

"You go right ahead." He picked up his cigarette again and

took a puff. "But I didn't kill Parker, even though the bastard deserved it. Just like every other plaintiff's lawyer in the state. He was trying to drive me into bankruptcy, and he was going to do it, too."

"But you didn't kill him."

"That's right. That'd be stupid, since there's always another plaintiff's lawyer where he came from. They're just like rattlesnakes. When you find a hole with one of 'em in it, you know there's a hundred more just like that down there in the dark."

"But Parker's death did buy you some time," I pointed out. "You might be able to get your ducks in a row before your case ever comes to court."

He puffed his Chesterfield. "Maybe. Maybe not. No way I could know that. Wouldn't be worth taking a chance on killing him to find out."

That wasn't exactly what he'd said to his lawyer, but it didn't matter. If he was solidly alibied, then he was out of the running as Parker's killer. However, it wasn't just wives who'd been known to give false alibis. Good friends had done it all too often. Lindley certainly had enough rage in him to kill, or so it seemed to me.

"You'll see," he said. "I'll check out. You'll have to look somewhere else for your killer."

"I guess so," I told him. "Thanks for your time."

"Hey, you got a job to do, just like everybody else." He stubbed out the cigarette in the ashtray, knocking a couple of butts out on the desk. He ignored them and picked up the telephone. "You through with me?"

"For now," I said, and he started dialing the phone as if he'd already forgotten I'd ever been there.

I put the piece of paper he'd given me in my shirt pocket and left.

★ ★ ★ ★ ★

A man can say he has an alibi, and he can even be free to give you the information about the alibi. But that doesn't prove anything. So I went back to my office and started making calls.

The first people on the list Lindley had given me were Robert and Susan Eversole. Beside their names, Lindley had written "Party at their house" and a Galveston phone number.

I got the operator and made the long-distance call. A woman answered. When I asked, she said that she was Mrs. Eversole, and told me that Lindley had indeed been at the party, just as he'd said.

"But he's not really a friend of ours," she added. "We like his wife, and he sort of comes along as part of the deal."

"But he was there all night?"

"That's right. He was so drunk that Bob and I had to put him to bed. I heard him get up several times and go to the bathroom. He was awfully sick."

"You don't sound too sorry for him."

"Well, he's pretty obnoxious. He hates just about everybody, and doesn't mind telling you. Mexicans, Indians, Orientals, Blacks, and plaintiff's lawyers. You name it. He's just a pure-dee hating man, and he lets everybody know it. His wife is welcome here anytime, but we won't be asking him to come back."

So much for my idea that Lindley might be getting an alibi from his good friends. I thanked Mrs. Eversole for her time and looked at the second name on the list.

Marianna Gaston. She had a Houston number, so I dialed it, and she answered on the first ring.

"Oh," she said when I told her I was calling about Sam Lindley and the Eversoles' party. "What a horrible man."

"You know him, then."

"Not very well, but I was at that party at the Eversoles' house down in Galveston. I wish I could say I hadn't noticed him, but he was hard to miss. He was drunk and offensive and couldn't keep his hands off the single women. Or off the married ones, either. And the things he would say! He's a very prejudiced person. It was embarrassing to everybody, I'm sure, especially his poor wife." She paused. "Why are you asking about him?"

I told her about the murders I was investigating.

"Well, I'm sure he's capable of murder, if anybody is. And worse. He's a stupid, horrible man."

"You said he was drunk that night."

"Oh, my, yes. By the time I left, he could hardly stand. I believe he and his wife were spending the night there. I'm sure they had to pour him into the bed."

We talked a little longer, and she continued to let me know how much she disliked Lindley. By then I didn't much like him, myself, but I had to admit that he had a pretty good alibi for the night of the murders.

I was writing everything down when Bolce came into the office.

"I have to pull you off the Parker case," he said.

CHAPTER 13

"What the hell?" I said, giving Bolce a glare. "I thought you were getting heat over this one. I thought you wanted me to devote all my time to it."

"What you want and what you get aren't always the same thing. This is an emergency."

"Send Wetsel and McGuire."

"They're out of the office, working another case. If I had anybody else to send, believe me, I'd do it. It's probably open-and-shut, anyway."

"And if it's not?"

"If it's not, we'll shuffle it off on somebody else later. But I need somebody on it now."

There was no use in any more argument. I knew that Bolce wouldn't have asked me to take the call if he'd had anybody else to send, and in fact this sort of thing happened all the time. One guy, or even a team, would be assigned to some high-profile homicide case full-time. That was the theory, at any rate. More often than not, however, there'd be some "emergency," and Bolce would have to change his mind about the "full-time" deal.

"Where's the stiff?" I said.

"In a hot-sheet motel out on South Main." He gave me the address. "You know the way."

I did. Main was the longest street in Houston, and after it passed through downtown, it got seedier. The farther south it went, the seedier it got. I checked out a car and went to see what I could find.

The Lone Star Motel was so old that at one time it had been what people called a tourist court. Its rooms were all in separate units, and some of them didn't even have air-conditioning. The parking lot was just a coating of gravel over the black gumbo soil, and all the low places were full of water. Seagulls were swirling and diving around a paper sack near one of the units, and one of the smaller birds came away with a french fry. He soared upward, pursued by eight or ten others, all of them after that fry. I didn't watch to see if they got it.

A patrol car was parked by the motel office. I went inside and asked the desk clerk where the officers were. He was a fat, red-faced young man with long, greasy hair, and he had a red and white bandana tied around his head to keep his hair out of his eyes. He was reading a ragged paperback copy of *Rosemary's Baby.*

When I came in, he looked at me over the top of the book and said, "The cops are at Unit Six." His voice edged with contempt to let me know how he felt about the police. "You must be with them."

It's not just cops who can identify other cops. Lowlifes are pretty good at it, too. I thanked him politely and went back outside.

The patrol officers were standing outside the door, smoking. I knew one of them, Mike Atkins, and I asked him where the body was.

"In the bathroom." He shook his head. "It's pretty weird."

The door to the unit wasn't locked, and I went inside. The room smelled like years of smoking and hurried sex, drenched in Pine-Sol. The bed didn't look like anything I'd want to sleep on, and I didn't even like to think about the last time the linens might have been washed. There was no carpet on the concrete floor.

I stepped back outside and asked about the Medical Examiner.

"He's been called," Atkins said. "Should be on the way. We haven't touched anything."

"Who called in about this?"

"The desk clerk. He said the maid told him."

I must have looked surprised because Atkins laughed.

"Yeah," he said, "they have one. I don't think she works every day, though."

I went back inside. The bathroom door was ajar and I looked in. There was a tub with a plastic shower curtain. The curtain was open, and the body of a small man hung from the shower nozzle, a white nylon rope around his neck.

A short-legged stool lay on its side on the floor by the tub, with a grayish towel beside it. The towel had been white once upon a time, probably during the Truman administration. A magazine, some cheap *Playboy* imitation but much cruder, lay beside the towel.

The dead man was fully dressed. Flared jeans, washed nearly white, a cheap shirt with a jagged brown lightning pattern, and black shoes.

What must have seemed weird to Atkins was that the zipper of the jeans was pulled down, and the dead man's penis was hanging out. It wasn't so weird to me. I'd seen that kind of thing before.

The Medical Examiner's team and the crime scene analysts came in about then, and I got out of the way while they lowered the body to the floor. The M.E. was Bradley Pulkrabek, a short, balding man with mild blue eyes.

"What killed him?" I asked when he'd finished his preliminary examination of the body.

"I'd say asphyxiation, from all appearances. He choked to death."

That's what I'd figured. There were no signs of a struggle, no bullet holes, no sign that anyone else had been in the room. So my guess was that it was a case of auto-erotic asphyxiation. A guy tries to reach a super-intense climax by masturbating and choking himself at the same time. Except that he's supposed to release the rope when he climaxes. The dead man hadn't. Maybe he'd been too excited.

I've always been a little surprised at what people will do for sexual gratification, especially when they try something danger-ous. I'd worked at least seven other cases of auto-erotic asphyxi-ation, so I knew how hazardous it could be.

Pulkrabek agreed with my assessment. But of course they'd have to be thorough. They'd check the fingerprints on the shower, the telephone in the room, the commode, and every-thing else to compare them with the dead man's. And then there would be an autopsy. Pulkrabek wasn't going to make a ruling just based on what we could see with our naked eyes.

While the fingerprinting was going on, I went back to the motel office to talk to the desk clerk. He was eating a po-boy sandwich, and he didn't appear to be too happy that I was interrupting him.

I asked about the man in Unit Six, and the clerk, without bothering to stop chewing his sandwich, told me that the man had checked in alone and that his name was James Delgado. He lost a piece of lettuce and picked it off the desk to stuff into his mouth.

"Anybody join him?"

"Not as far as I know," the clerk said around a mouthful of sandwich. Or at least it sounded something like that. It was hard to tell for sure.

"Where's the maid?"

"Should be cleaning the units. Must be on Unit Twelve by now. It's the last one."

I went back outside and found Unit Twelve. The door was open, and someone was moving around inside. I knocked on the door facing, and the maid came to see what I wanted. She was Hispanic, around fifty, with bright eyes and a big smile.

When I told her why I was there, she stopped smiling. She said, "What a nasty man he must have been. I'm sorry I had to see that."

I told her I was sorry, too. "Did anybody else use that unit?"

"I don't think so. I didn't stay around long enough to see. I banged on the door and called out, but nobody answered. So I went in to clean." She gave me a look. "They don't pay me much, but I do a pretty good job."

"I'm sure you do. What happened next?"

"I went to the bathroom, which is where I always start, and I saw that nasty man, hanging from the shower with his thing sticking out. I screamed. Didn't anybody come, though, so I went and told Freddie."

"He's the desk clerk?"

"That's right. Freddie's okay. He told me to skip that unit and he'd call the cops. You're a cop, right?"

I admitted that I was and thanked her for her time. When I got back to Unit Six, the crime scene investigators were going over the car that was parked by the unit, fingerprinting the steering wheel and door handles. Atkins was watching, and I asked him if he'd called in the license number.

"Yeah," he said. "Car belongs to James Delgado, and that's him in there if the ID in his wallet means anything."

One of the investigators opened the trunk of the car, and I saw a plastic bag with some nylon rope hanging out. I looked in the bag, and there was a sales slip with the words Janzen Hardware printed in blue at the top.

No doubt about it, this was a throw-down case that wasn't going to take up much more of my time. I was glad, because that meant that I wouldn't have to do anything more than write up the report. As soon as I finished, I could get back on the Parker murders.

But of course it wasn't as simple as that. Someone had to find out if there was a Mrs. Delgado. I asked one of the investigators for the address from the driver's license and drove to a little neighborhood on Quitman Street, not that far from the motel. Delgado had lived in a small frame house on a lot barely big enough to hold it. I parked at the curb and went to the door.

A small woman about forty-five wearing a blue house dress answered my knock. She had dark hair with streaks of gray in it and a sad, tentative smile. I showed her my badge and asked if she was Mrs. James Delgado.

"Yes," she said. "Ellen Delgado."

"Is there anyone here with you?"

"No. No one. Why do you ask?"

"It's about your husband. Can we go inside?"

She invited me in, and we sat in the tiny living room, me in a rocker, and her on the couch.

"He's dead, isn't he?" she said.

"Yes. I'm sorry. It looks like he might have committed suicide." I knew that wasn't true, but sometimes the truth isn't what people need.

"He hung himself, didn't he?" she said.

I was surprised at that, but I said that it was correct.

"I thought so," she said. She bowed her head and started to pray.

At least she didn't seem distraught, and I was grateful for that. When she'd finished her prayers, she looked up and told me a little about her life with her husband. They hadn't been close for years and in fact lived as if they were two strangers sharing a house rather than a married couple.

"James goes to work every morning," she said. "Without speaking. But he pays the rent, so I do all the housework, and I don't complain."

They had separate bedrooms, she explained, and James kept his locked at all times, whether he was inside it or not. He brought his dirty clothes and bed linens out of the room and left them on the kitchen floor once a week. Ellen would wash and fold them and put them on the kitchen table for him.

After this had gone on for several years, she got curious about his room.

"I know it was wrong," she said, "but I called a locksmith and had him make me a key. I had to know what was inside. Do you understand?"

I nodded, though I wasn't sure I did. I didn't understand the whole arrangement.

"Would you like to see the room?"

I said that might be a good idea if it would help me with my investigation.

"I believe it will," she said. "Excuse me."

She went to another room and came back with a key that she used to open a bedroom door. The first thing I saw when I looked inside was a rope hanging over the partially opened closet door. It was tied to the knob on the other side. Then I saw the skin magazines lying on the floor and on the dresser.

"What he was doing was wrong," Ellen said. She was standing in the narrow hallway behind me and to one side, not looking into the room. "And now he has paid for it."

She dropped down on her knees in the hall and started praying again. I waited until she was finished and asked if there was anyone I could call for her.

She looked up at me. There were tears on her face.

"Connie Taylor next door is a good friend. If you could ask her to come over, I'd appreciate it."

I left her kneeling there and went next door. Connie Taylor was a large, smiling woman, who stopped smiling as soon as I'd told her that Mrs. Delgado needed her, and why.

"I'll go right over," she said, and went past me, leaving me standing on her porch.

I knew that Mrs. Delgado was in good hands, and I'd done all I could do. I'd also confirmed what I already knew about Delgado and knew it would be all right to close the case.

When I got home that afternoon, I poured myself a bourbon on the rocks. I thought about the strange marriage of James and Ellen Delgado and wondered if my own marriage had somehow gone wrong, not like theirs but in some other way I didn't comprehend. Could it be that Sarah and I had somehow become strangers to each other?

It didn't seem possible, and I was convinced that on my part it hadn't happened. I wondered again if Sarah might not need professional help, but I didn't know how to get her to agree to it. If she wouldn't answer my calls or see me, how could I do anything?

I read until midnight and then went to bed, thinking that if I stayed awake long enough, I might be able to sleep more soundly.

It was a fine idea.

But it didn't work.

CHAPTER 14

Clive didn't call the next morning, so I knew he didn't have any fresh information for me. I ate a bowl of shredded wheat and went to the office, where I spent most of the morning going over everything related to the Parker case one more time.

It was beginning to look as if Stanford Parker was our best suspect, but of course there was that one little problem: he had an alibi.

I read Wetsel's report on Emily Jackson again. She'd been interviewed in Wetsel's office, and Parker had been nowhere around. She hadn't asked for a lawyer, either. Her story was that she and Parker had been together the entire night of the murders, from around seven-thirty that evening until the next morning.

Parker had told substantially the same story, and I wondered again about Parker's sexuality, not that it seemed to be relevant to the case. More to the point was whether Jackson was telling the truth.

If she was, I was going to have to develop some new leads. I'd eliminated all the other suspects. They all had alibis just as good as Stanford Parker's. Better, in fact. I decided it was time for me to pay a visit to Stanford Parker.

Parker's house wasn't in the same neighborhood where his parents had lived. It was only a mile or so away in distance, but it could have been a thousand miles away in other ways. The houses were small, and old cars were parked along the curb. There were tricycles in driveways, and many of the yards could have used a trim. The worst yard of all was in the middle of the block. Grass grew over the edge of the curbing and sidewalk. Four or five newspapers lay in the grass. In the yard was a sign that said For Sale, and below that was the name of the listing agency. It was obvious that the house was deserted.

I went to the door, anyway, and rang the bell. I got no response, so I knocked. Nobody came to greet me. None of the neighbors came out to see what was going on. I got back in my car and left.

Since I couldn't think of anything better to do, I drove over to Clive's office, which didn't really look like an office at all. Anyone driving by would think it was just another house. It was at the end of the block in a sparsely populated area off the Katy Freeway, shaded by tall pine trees that had dropped cones here and there on the grass. There were no other houses nearby because Clive had bought several of the surrounding lots. I parked on the extra-wide driveway and went to the door, which had a discreet sign on it. The sign said, Clive Watson and Associates, Confidential Investigations. Enter without Knocking.

I was about to do as instructed when the door opened and a man started out. He was putting a piece of folded paper that looked like a check into his pocket.

He was one of the most handsome men I'd ever seen, well over six feet tall with long, wavy brown hair and wide brown eyes. He was dressed like one of the Beatles, but he looked as if he spent a lot of time in a gym, working out. His shoulders were so wide that he almost had to turn sideways to get out the door.

"Excuse me," he said, as I stepped aside.

"Hold on, Gene," Clive said from inside the doorway. "I want you to meet Steve."

Gene had already gone a few steps down the walk, but he

turned back and stuck out his hand.

"Gene Moore," he said as we shook.

"Ted Stephens," I said. "Steve."

For a man with such a strong build, he had a gentle handshake. He hardly gripped my hand at all.

"Gene's one of my investigators," Clive said. "Steve's a cop."

"Always happy to meet one of Houston's finest," Gene said, but he didn't look all that pleased to me. He told Clive he'd see him later and left.

We went inside and each got a cup of coffee. Clive's secretary, Jane, has a pot going at all times.

"Who was that guy?" I asked when Clive and I had gone inside to his office.

It was much bigger and more comfortable than mine, and the furniture was much newer. There was a big window that looked out into the yard, and I could see the pine trees and the street beyond. But the place reeked of smoke, and Clive lit up even as I thought about it.

"I told you who he was," Clive said letting out a cloud of smoke. "Gene Moore."

"Is he really one of your investigators?"

Clive grinned. "That's right. He's been with me for a long time. He started back about ten years ago, in Dallas. He infiltrated the Communist party for me."

"You're kidding."

Clive shook his head.

"Like that old TV show? *I Was a Communist for the FBI*?"

"I'm not the FBI. Never liked the Feds all that much."

"You know what I mean."

"Yeah, then, it was like that. A little. There was a homosexual major in the Air Force who was feeding information to the commies."

"Wait a minute. Gene's a homosexual?"

"Sure enough. I interceded for him with the Dallas Police Department and got his case dismissed. There was nothing to it. There was a guy who had trumped up the charges against him because of some trouble they had at work. Anyway, Gene owed me a favor, and he turned out to be pretty good at investigation. He got into the party and got the evidence on the major. I couldn't have made the case without him."

"And now he's living in Houston."

"Moved here five or six years ago. He was working at a furniture store where I bought this desk." He put his hand on the mahogany desk he was sitting behind. "Anna was with me. She helped me pick it out."

As soon as he thought of Anna, he started to get sentimental again, but he caught himself, brushed his hand at his eyes, and went on with his story.

"We heard someone back in the office going bananas after the order was turned in, and Gene came out. He said that as soon as he saw the name and address, he had to talk to me. It was like old home week. He's been doing little jobs for me ever since, and that check you saw was an advance."

"He's going to check out Stanford Parker," I said.

"You got it in one guess."

"You have it pretty good," I said, thinking it over. "Your informants are a little higher-class guys than the ones we cops have."

"And you probably don't even have any homosexual informants at all."

He was right. It was next to impossible for us to get anybody from that community even to talk to us, much less give us any worthwhile information. I blamed some of the archaic laws that were still on the books, but this being Texas, the laws weren't likely to change anytime soon. If ever.

"You don't have to waste any time reading people their

Miranda rights, either," I said, referring to the new rules that had been in effect for the last couple of years.

"Well," Clive said. He lit another cigarette. "I have some disadvantages, too. I'm not a sworn officer, and I don't have the power of arrest. But then because of that, I don't have to warn anybody about his civil rights under the law. I guess that does make things easier for me."

"So what's Gene's approach going to be?" I said. "How's he going to get next to Parker? So to speak."

"Have you checked out Parker's house?"

"I drove by there on the way here. It's for sale."

"That's right, and before the day's over, Parker's going to get a call from a prospective buyer."

"Named Gene Moore."

"That may not be the name he uses, but, yes. That's how we're going to work it. Gene will approach Parker that way at first and take it from there. Maybe it won't lead anywhere, maybe it will. If it doesn't, we'll try something else."

"I had our guys find out about Parker's financial situation," I said. "And it's not good. He owes a lot of money all over town. He has the house, but his father made the down payment. I can see why he needs to sell it, because he's been effectively cut out of his parents' wills and his grandmother's, too. He'll want to talk to your boy Gene, all right."

"Yeah. I know. I did a little checking of my own."

"You didn't tell me."

"I haven't had a chance. You want to hear it, or just complain?"

I said of course I wanted to hear, and Clive told me about having called the real estate agency that had the house listed. He'd pretended to be interested in buying it.

"I found out that Parker's father didn't pay cash for the place," Clive said. "He made the down payment, all right, but

Stanford's been responsible for the monthly payments, and he hasn't kept them up. That means that the mortgage can't be assumed, so whoever buys the house will need a new loan. I gathered that Stanford's borrowed all the money he can against the mortgage."

"As far as I know, he doesn't have a job," I said.

"I've had him under twenty-four hour surveillance, and he hasn't been going to work anywhere. And here's something else that's funny."

He paused and thought about whatever it was. After a few seconds, he went on.

"It's the girlfriend," Clive said. "His alibi. You told me that she'd spent the night with him when his parents and grandmother were killed, but she's living at her own place and she didn't spend the night with him last night. My investigator talked to a neighbor who says she doesn't remember seeing the girl there much at all."

I'd been worried about the girlfriend all along.

"Goodbye, alibi," I said.

Clive nodded. "It's a possibility," he said.

CHAPTER 15

Emily Jackson lived on Trinity Street, so I drove to her place when I left Clive's office. I knew that Wetsel would be pissed off if he found out I'd been following up with people he'd already interviewed, but to hell with him. He hadn't gotten anywhere with Jackson, and I was hoping to break Stanford's alibi.

The neighborhood I found myself in wasn't any better than the one where Parker lived. There was a big oak tree in front of the Jackson house, and there were acorns in the sparse grass and dirt that it shaded. There wasn't much grass because the tree had never been trimmed. The sun couldn't get through all the limbs and leaves, so the grass didn't grow very well. An old Chevrolet sat in the driveway. It sagged down on one side, as if the shocks or springs were bad. As I approached the house, a cat with a patch of hair missing from its flank slunk off into some hedge bushes planted along the property line.

My knock on the door was answered by a woman around twenty years old. She was thin as a broom handle and quite short, no more than five-three. She had dirty blonde hair that hung straight down nearly to her waist.

I identified myself and showed her my badge. Her eyes widened, and I thought she might cry.

"I want you to come down to the station for an interview," I said. "There are a few things about your boyfriend that have to be cleared up."

"I . . . . I'll have to tell my mother," she said.

She turned abruptly and left me standing there in the door. I waited for about a minute, and a woman came to meet me. She was short, like her daughter, but the resemblance ended there. She was built like a fullback, but she had the crazy black eyes of a linebacker.

She didn't wait for me to introduce myself. She said, "My daughter's already been down to your damn station once, and she told that other cop all she knew. I've talked to my lawyer, and Emily doesn't have to go anywhere with you unless you got a warrant for her arrest."

She stopped and glared at me. "Well?" she said.

"Well, what?"

"You got one?"

"One what?"

"One warrant, dumb-ass. You got one or not?"

"I don't have one."

"Then fuck off, pig," she said, and she slammed the door in my face.

It wasn't the first time I'd been called a dumb-ass or a pig, and it wasn't the first time I'd been told to fuck off. And it certainly wasn't the first time I've had a door slammed in my face. So I wasn't too upset.

I went back to my car. Before I left, I wrote down the license plate number of the Chevy in the driveway.

When I got back to my office, I had the license number of the Chevy run. The record showed that the car was registered to Ruby Jackson at the address where she'd slammed the door on me. Ruby was fifty-six.

The age I could have guessed. Nothing helpful there.

I recalled from Wetsel's report that Emily Jackson had no prior criminal record, but now I wondered about her mother. I decided to check, and I discovered that Ruby was a paperhanger.

She'd served two six-month sentences in the Harris County Jail for writing hot checks and had been arrested a couple of other times but not charged. She'd probably made good on the checks.

The record also showed that she was single but had a daughter, which I knew already, and that she'd worked as a nurse's aide at a couple of local hospitals, which I hadn't known. But I didn't see that it helped me any.

I called Stanford Parker's house but got no answer. I decided I'd go there again and sit and wait for him to show up. He had to come home sooner or later.

When I got there, two cars were parked in the driveway, and Gene Moore was knocking on the door. I parked down the block and waited to see how long Moore would be inside.

I hoped it would be a short time because the sun was bearing down on top of the car, and the humidity inside turned it into a sauna even with the windows down. I'd taken off my jacket, but I was sweating heavily nevertheless.

I'd been there sweltering for about ten minutes when a car pulled up beside me. It was a Ford Crown Victoria Police Interceptor, but the driver wasn't a cop. It was Clive.

Clive had always liked to drive fast. I'd been with him a couple of times when I thought he was going to crack the sound barrier, though he never quite made it. He'd slowed down some as he'd gotten older, but if you wanted to get somewhere fast, he was still able to take you there, and take you even faster than you wanted.

Clive's window was rolled down a little way to let the smoke from his cigarettes out of the car. He rolled it down the rest of the way and said, "What's the matter, Steve? Didn't you trust me?"

I knew it wasn't a serious question. I said, "How much do you pay somebody like Moore to run a surveillance? It had better be plenty if they have to sit in hot cars for very long in this kind of weather."

"I pay a hell of a lot. More than enough to make it worth his while to sit in the sun for a few hours. But that's all I'm going to say. If you'd retire and come to work for me, you'd find out about the pay."

Clive had been after me for a couple of years to retire from the force and become one of his investigators. One of these days I might take him up on the offer, but for the time being I was satisfied to be a cop. I liked the work and I was good at it. Clive knows that, which is why he wanted to hire me, and he didn't give up easily, on me or anything else.

"I'll think about it," I said. It was mid-afternoon, but I'd skipped lunch, so I asked Clive if he'd eaten.

"No. As a matter of fact, I was on my way to Dino Vallone's place. How does that sound?"

Vallone was a young man who was just getting started in the restaurant business. He provided great food, great atmosphere, and great service. Clive and I didn't see how he could miss becoming a star.

"I'll meet you there," I said.

The restaurant wasn't crowded at that hour of the day, and we asked for a back table in the smoking section. Clive was laughing and joking and didn't seem as depressed as usual. Maybe he was coming out of his grief. I hoped so. There had been a time or two after Anna's death when I'd been afraid that he might try to kill himself.

We'd even talked about it once. He said that he'd heard there were two sides to the arguments about suicide. One, and this was the one that mattered to Clive, was that if you killed yourself, you'd never go to heaven.

"And that's where Anna is," he'd told me. "If anybody's there, she is."

I'd stopped worrying about him after that. Clive wasn't about to kill himself and miss the chance of seeing Anna again, no matter how slim he thought the chance might be and no matter how much grief he felt.

But I'd heard a slightly different version of the suicide answer.

"I thought you went to Purgatory if you killed yourself," I'd told Clive. "And after you've served your time there, you moved on up."

"I don't think so," he said. "And you ought not to tell me that. It might encourage me to do something I shouldn't."

He was right. I said, "Well, we're not exactly theologians, and I'm not even Catholic. Maybe we should ask a priest and a minister about it, see what they have to say."

"So you've thought about it, too."

"Not seriously," I said. "Lots of cops eat their guns, but I'm not going to be one of them, not because of Sarah and not because of anything else. I'm too vain to deprive the world of my presence."

Clive had smiled at that, but I didn't think he'd believed me. He should have. It was the truth. When Sarah had packed up and left, I'd thought for about ten minutes about how easy it would be to end everything right then, but then I wondered who would profit. Not me, for sure. And besides, I knew that Sarah's leaving hadn't been my fault, no matter what she believed. Sooner or later, I hoped, she'd change her mind about me.

It was beginning to look like it would be later rather than sooner. A lot later.

After the waitress seated us in the restaurant and took our drink orders, Clive lit a cigarette and said, "You know one of the things I miss most now that Anna's gone?"

I thought he might be about to get maudlin on me, but he was smiling. So I said I had no idea.

"I miss bragging on myself."

I laughed. "Not that you mind doing that to just about anybody."

"Now you know that's not true," he said. "But I did like to brag to Anna about breaking a big case or about how much money I'd been paid. I told one man that I was so busy I couldn't take his case for less than a hundred and fifty thousand dollars, and he wrote out the check right there in the office without blinking an eye. Handed it to me and asked me how soon I could start. That was good, but the best part was taking the check home to Anna, handing it to her, and telling her to go spend it."

"I'll bet she didn't, though," I said.

"No. She just put it in the bank the next day. That's what she always did. She'd say, 'We might need this money for the kids.' "

The waitress brought our drinks, and we ordered. I had steak, and Clive got the trout. Anna had once said that he ate so much fish that he was going to grow scales. He took a sip of his gin and tonic with plenty of limes.

"The work's not the same anymore," he said. "It doesn't mean shit to me when I break a big case or get a big fee. I don't even know why I keep on doing this job. I have more money than I can spend, and the kids don't need it. They're all on their own now. The only fun I ever really had was bragging to Anna. I never cared all that much about the money or the personal glory, getting my picture in the papers and all that. Just seeing her smile when I told her what I'd done was my best reward, and now she's not here to listen to me." He paused and looked across the table at me. "I just want you to know that I'm still praying for Sarah to realize she made a mistake by leaving you. Have you heard from her?"

"I haven't heard a damned thing, and I don't want to talk about her right now."

116

Clive put his cigarette in the ashtray, then put up his hands, palms out. "Hey, don't take it out on me. I'm just trying to help."

"Well, you're not helping."

We might have gotten into an argument at that point, but the waitress brought our food, and we both shut up. By the time we'd been served, I'd cooled down. Clive said his blessing, and we started to eat.

After he'd had a couple of bites of his trout, Clive said, "From what I gather, it's beginning to look like Wetsel might be right about your case. Stanford Parker might have killed them all."

"How in the hell do you know what Wetsel's thinking? I didn't tell you that."

"I seem to remember that you did. But even if you didn't, I know Wetsel. Give him the obvious answer, and he'll run with it. And if he's right, well, even a blind hog turns up an acorn now and then."

He had a point. And since all my other suspects seemed to be solidly alibied, I had to agree with him.

We finished eating, and Clive said that he needed to go by Elmer Gann's office and pick up a check for ten thousand dollars as a retainer on the Stanford Parker case.

"I thought you didn't brag to anybody but Anna," I said.

Clive grinned. "Maybe I've changed my ways."

"Does he know that he's already going to have expenses on top of that?" I said. "Like that informant of yours?"

"I haven't mentioned Gene to him yet. There's really no reason to tell him or not to tell him, but some people are a little paranoid about the use of informants. I'll wait until I see what Gene comes up with before I give up that little piece of information."

"Makes sense to me."

"See, you're already thinking like a private investigator. Are

117

you sure you don't want to come to work for me?"

I told him again that I'd think it over, and when the check came he grabbed it.

"I thought it was my turn," I said.

"If you were working for me, you could afford it. Since you're not, I'll pay."

"Next time it's on me, for sure."

"Right. If we can find a hotdog stand." He thought about it for a second and added, "You know, that wouldn't be a bad idea. We can go to James Coney Island."

"Not with your stomach," I said.

Clive laughed and agreed. When he'd paid and we were leaving, he said, "Don't forget that I'm praying for you and Sarah. You never know when something good might happen."

"Yeah," I said. "Right."

About an hour after I got home that evening, Sarah called.

CHAPTER 16

I'd just finished watching the news, which was entirely taken up with the Apollo 11 moon landing. For the first time, men were going to walk on the surface of another world. It wasn't a miracle, just good science and a lot of dedicated people working together to make something happen, but it was an unprecedented occurrence. It made me feel good, not just for the people down at NASA but for the whole country.

When the phone rang, I was still smiling from the news. I said, "Hello."

There was a slight pause, and then Sarah said, "Steve? It's me. Sarah."

Just hearing her voice was a shock. What she had to say next was an even bigger shock. I was in the kitchen, and I had to sit down in a chair by the table.

"I want us to try to get back together," she told me.

"So do I. I never wanted us to be apart. But if you still think I was having an affair, I don't know how we'll be able to work it out."

"What I think about that affair doesn't matter. Maybe I was wrong about you. I'm all mixed up, Steve, but I know one thing for sure. I know that I still love you. I'm not mixed up about that."

"I love you, too," I said. "I never stopped."

"I know. I know. I can't live with you, but it seems I can't live without you, either. What are we going to do?"

119

"We're going to meet and talk about it. Where are you?"

But she wasn't ready to tell me that. She said, "I'll come to the house."

"When?"

"In the morning."

"What time?"

"I'll be there before you leave for work."

"I won't be going in tomorrow," I told her. "We have too much to talk about."

"I'm not sure we can talk for long."

"We can try," I said.

"All right, Steve. We can try."

I hung up the phone and sat back down. I was in a state of shock. I hadn't ever expected to hear Sarah's voice again, and now she was telling me that she wanted us to patch things up. I started to think about what I'd tell her when she arrived.

And about whether I should call Clive and tell him that his prayers had been answered.

The next morning I was too nervous to eat. I sat at the table, reading the *Post* articles about the moon landing, hardly taking in anything at all, and waiting for Sarah to come home.

The doorbell rang. I tossed the paper on the table and went to the door. Sarah stood there, tears in her eyes.

I'd hardly slept at all the previous night, thinking about what I'd do when I saw her. Now that she was right in front of me, I still didn't know.

"Steve," she said.

I opened my arms, and she came into them.

For a long time we just stood there and she cried against my shoulder. After a while I said, "We should go inside. The neighbors might start to talk about us."

"If they haven't already," Sarah said. She dug a tissue from her purse and wiped her eyes. "I must look terrible."

"No," I said, "you don't."

In fact, I thought she'd never looked so beautiful. Whoever coined that phrase about absence and the heart growing fonder was right on the money.

We went into the kitchen and sat at the table. Sarah looked around as if she might be checking on my housekeeping.

"You don't have any dirty dishes," she said. "And the counters are clean."

I couldn't tell if she was disappointed or pleased. I said, "I didn't have anything else to do."

"I'm sorry, Steve. I know I was wrong to leave you. But I didn't think I could stay, not when I believed you were cheating on me."

"I never cheated," I said, looking at her. "I never will."

She didn't meet my eyes. "Why can't I believe that?"

"You should. It's the truth."

"Maybe. I hope so." She started to cry again. "What are we going to do?"

"We're going to get help," I said.

She got out another tissue and wiped her eyes again. "Help?"

"A psychologist. Dr. Milton Coffee. We have a ten o'clock appointment."

I had called Clive last night and asked him what he thought. He'd been elated to know that Sarah had called and that she was coming to talk.

"I told you that God works in mysterious ways," he said.

"Too mysterious for me. I need somebody who can get this mess straightened out in a practical way here in Houston, not in heaven. Do you know anybody?"

Clive had worked on a case for Coffee, whose secretary had been stealing from him.

"He's exactly what you're looking for," Clive said. "Everybody

I talked to said he was topnotch, and I liked him a lot."

Clive was as good a judge of character as anybody I'd ever known. If he liked Coffee, that was good enough for me. Clive had volunteered to call him.

"Right now? At home?"

"Damned right. This is an emergency, and he owes me a favor."

"Go ahead," I said, and about an hour later Dr. Coffee had called me to set up an appointment.

"It will be a real pleasure to help out a friend of Clive's," he said, and we'd set a time for me to bring Sarah in, assuming that she'd go along with the idea.

Sarah was reluctant at first, but I told her that we'd tried to work things out ourselves and hadn't had much luck.

"And the lawyers we hired certainly aren't doing us any good," I added.

"I fired my lawyer yesterday," Sarah said. "I didn't want a divorce. I didn't want to take your money."

"It's our money," I said.

"I don't care. I didn't want to take it. I wanted us to be together again. But I don't know how to do that."

"Dr. Coffee will help."

"I hope so," she said. "I really hope so."

Dr. Coffee had offices on the tenth floor of a building near the medical center. We entered it at five minutes until ten, gave the receptionist our names, and sat in stiff, uncomfortable chairs to wait.

We didn't have to wait long. Dr. Coffee was punctual, something I approved of. He said that he'd like to talk to Sarah first, without me.

I nodded. This was something we'd discussed last night. Sarah looked at me over her shoulder as she started to follow Dr. Coffee into his office. I tried to give her an encouraging smile, but it might have come off as just sickly.

I knew what Dr. Coffee was going to recommend, but I hadn't had the guts to tell Sarah.

She was in his office with him for around forty-five minutes before he called me in. Her eyes were red, and it was obvious that she'd been crying, though she seemed in control of herself now.

Dr. Coffee asked me to have a seat. I sat down beside Sarah and took her hand.

"Sarah and I have had a productive talk," he said.

He was a round little man, with round shoulders and a round head. He wore glasses with thick black plastic rims, and the lenses magnified his eyes, which might have been a little frightening if he hadn't had such a kind voice.

"I've recommended that Sarah admit herself to a hospital for a couple of days so that some tests can be run," Coffee said. "She's agreed that it's a good idea."

Sarah's hand tightened on mine.

"After that," Coffee continued, "she'll be coming to visit me once a week. We'll work out a convenient time later. I've already called the hospital, and Sarah can check in this afternoon. You might want to go by and do the paperwork this morning, however."

I looked at Sarah. "Are you sure about this?"

"Whatever it takes," she said.

We got the paperwork done, and Sarah checked into the hospital around three o'clock. I stayed with her for the rest of the afternoon, and we talked about inconsequential things, avoiding any mention of what the next few days or weeks would bring. There would be plenty of time for that later. For now it was enough to recall some of the happy times we'd had together, the vacations we'd taken, the people we knew.

When I left that evening, I was feeling better than I had in months. I called Clive when I got home to let him know how things had gone, and he was happy to hear from me.

"I feel almost as good as I would if I had Anna back," he said, and while it was a nice thing for him to say, I knew it couldn't be true.

"Are you going to take any more time off?" he asked. "To be with Sarah, I mean?"

I told him that I couldn't just drop the case or even let it sit idle for any longer than a day. If I did, Wetsel would be after Bolce to let him take it back, and Bolce would have to let him because of the pressure from the newspapers and the politicians.

"I guess you know best," Clive said, but I could tell he didn't really think so.

"Listen," I said. "You know how Wetsel is. You know I'm right."

"I know how the son of a bitch is, and I know what your case is like. But some things are more important."

"I've talked to Sarah about this, and she understands. Things are going to be fine."

"I hope so," Clive said.

CHAPTER 17

I went by the hospital the next morning to check on Sarah. She smiled and said that everything was fine.

"They'll be starting the tests later this morning," she said.

She looked good even without makeup, and I told her so. That made her smile some more.

"I'm sure this was the right thing to do, Steve," she said. "We're going to make it. You'll see."

"That's what I've wanted all along," I said.

There was a message from Dr. Coffee on my desk when I got to work. I gave him a call, and he said that he needed to talk to me.

"When?"

"This morning, if possible. I can fit you in at nine-thirty."

That would only give me half an hour, but I knew it must be important.

"I'll be there," I said, and then I went to tell Bolce that I'd need another day off.

I'd thought that Coffee had something to tell me about Sarah, but I was wrong.

"This is about you," he told me.

"What about me?"

"You have a problem."

I didn't need a psychologist to tell me that. My wife thought

I was cheating on her, which wasn't true, and she'd left me because of it. That was a big problem, all right. Anybody could see that.

"That's not it," Coffee said when I told him.

"Is this about Sarah?"

"It is, and it isn't. It's possible that she has a medical problem, something that can be helped by medication. But part of her problem, and yours, is that affair she believes you had."

"There is no affair," I said. "There never was. I told Sarah that over and over."

"And she didn't believe you, is that right?"

"That's right."

"And she had no basis for believing that you were seeing someone else?"

"None. I swear to you, I've never even looked at another woman. Not in all the years I've been married. I know some men do, but I'm not one of them. Sarah's the only woman I've ever cared about, at least since the first time I saw her."

Coffee settled back in his chair. "Fine. I believe you."

I relaxed a little. He was on my side. Or that's what I thought until he said, "I want you to take a week off from your job."

I was so surprised that I couldn't answer for a second. When I'd recovered, I swallowed hard and said, "I can't do that. I'm working on an important case. There's a lot of pressure to get it solved."

"You said you loved your wife. If it was important to her that you take a week off, could you do it?"

Why did he have to put it that way, make it a choice between Sarah and the job? It wasn't fair.

"Look," I said, "I don't see how my taking any time off would help Sarah. If I thought it would help, I'd do it, but she's in the hospital. I'll go by to see her every day. I'll spend some time with her there. But I have to keep working on the case."

Coffee leaned back at his desk and folded his hands on his ample stomach.

"Now," he said, "let's imagine how what you've said would sound to your wife."

I started to react angrily, but I caught myself before I said anything. I saw where he was going, and it didn't make me feel very good about myself.

Coffee smiled. "I see that you get my point. Let me elaborate. You weren't having an affair, but your wife seems to have gotten it into her head that you were. What is there in your life that might have made her feel that way? What is it that you might have been putting ahead of her or neglecting her for?"

"I've never put anything ahead of Sarah," I said, but even as the words passed my lips, I knew they were a lie.

More than once, more than a hundred times, probably, I had put the job first.

There's something seductive about working a case. Ask Clive, or ask any cop. Even Wetsel. The case draws you in, and you want to gather up all the pieces and put them together so that they make a perfect whole.

When I'm working on something I'm always thinking about it. Day or night, awake or asleep, it's always on my mind. Even after Sarah had left me, when getting her back should have been uppermost in my mind, I was still thinking about my caseload, still worrying about how to put the pieces together, still looking for the one answer that would bring everything into focus.

If I'd concentrated that hard on Sarah, would she ever have left me?

I looked at Coffee. "You're telling me that I've been having an affair with my job?"

"You're the one who's saying it. I'm just asking you to think about it. And I'm asking you to take a week off to spend some time with your wife. Just with her. Not with the job, not with anything else. Can you do it?"

I wanted to say hell, no. I wanted to get up and walk out of Coffee's office, slamming the door behind me.

What I did was say, "I don't know."

"When is the last time you took a vacation?"

I had to think about it. "Five years. Maybe six."

Coffee didn't say anything.

"All right," I said. "I give up."

"There's nothing to give up. We weren't having a contest. But does this mean that you'll take a week off?"

"Will it help Sarah if I do?"

"I can't promise anything. But I believe it will."

"Then I can do it," I said.

Bolce didn't like it, not even a little bit.

"The chief called me just this morning," he said. "He wants us to get this wrapped up."

"So do I," I told him, and that was an understatement. Just thinking about leaving for a week was making me sweat like I had a fever. "But I have to take this time to be with my wife. I don't have a choice."

I'd already explained to him about me and Sarah. He was sympathetic, but only a little.

"Clive Watson has some men working on things," I said. "Wetsel and McGuire are interviewing the relatives. You can tell the chief all that."

"Not about Watson."

He was right. The chief wouldn't like the idea that we were taking help from a P.I.

"You can tell him that I have some informants getting information," I said. "That's close enough to the truth."

"I don't want to get my ass in a crack over this."

"Neither do I, but my marriage is more important than any murder case."

"I never thought I'd hear you say that."

"I never thought I'd say it."

And maybe I wouldn't have said it then if Clive hadn't been offering me a job just yesterday. If I had to walk away from the cops, I could go right to work for Clive, and I wouldn't even have to leave the case, thanks to Clive's client. The best part was that Clive wouldn't mind giving me a week off.

"All right," Bolce said after a while. He must have figured out that I was going to take the week off no matter what he said, one way or the other. "You can take the time. I'll cover for you with the chief."

One other thing worried me. "Wetsel will try to get control of the case back."

"That's fine. Let him try. He won't get it. But I want you back on the job in one week. I can't promise you anything after that."

I got out of there before he could change his mind.

I'm not sure if the following days were harder on me or on Sarah. I know that I didn't sleep well, and this time it wasn't because I was worrying about Sarah. It was because I couldn't stop thinking about the Parker case.

And every time I thought about it, I felt the job tugging at me, trying to pull me back.

I didn't let it. I didn't call Bolce, and I didn't talk to Clive, except to tell him not to call me unless he wanted to talk about Sarah.

"But not about the case," he said.

"Not about the case. Don't even say 'the case.' "

"This is all going to work out, Steve. I know it is."

"It had better," I said, and when I put down the phone the

receiver was damp from the sweat of my palms.

I don't want to overemphasize my problems. It's not like I was a junkie going cold turkey. Or maybe it was. Maybe I was addicted to the adrenaline high of a case the way a junkie was to his drugs. But at least I wasn't seeing pink tarantulas crawling on the walls.

Somehow I got through the week. I visited Sarah in the hospital and stayed all day. I went back in the evenings and stayed until they chased me home.

She was released from the hospital and came home after a couple of days. Dr. Coffee prescribed something for her.

"It won't solve anything," he said to me. "Not by itself."

I took that to mean I'd better hold up my part of the bargain, and I intended to. Sarah and I drove to Galveston and checked into the Galvez, the oldest and fanciest hotel on the island. We walked on the beach in the mornings and swam in the late afternoons. In between we went to a movie or talked. And in the night, for the first time in what seemed like years, we had sex. It was wildly passionate at first, almost ferocious, and then it was calm but even better. By the time we started back to Houston, I was sure we'd never be apart again.

"I don't know how I could have believed there was another woman," Sarah said as we drove across the bridge that separated Galveston Island from the mainland. "I don't know what put the idea in my head."

I told her what Coffee had said, and I told her that I was ashamed to think that my devotion to the job might have come before my devotion to her. I promised it would never happen again.

"I'll hold you to that," she said, kissing me on the cheek. "But don't think I'm going to let you retire."

"I'm not ready for that, either," I said.

"Good. I don't want to have to support you."

I hadn't asked her about her own job. Unlike mine, it had regular hours and a generous vacation plan, although the stress level was just about equivalent. She was an elementary school teacher. Third grade.

"I was able to finish the semester," she said, in answer to my unasked question. "I wasn't sure if I'd be able to go back in the fall, but now I know I can. I think everything is going to be just fine."

"I guarantee it," I said.

On Monday morning as we lay in bed, Sarah told me that I could go back to work if I wanted to. I told her that it had been only six days, and that I wasn't going back until the full week had passed.

"It's like I've been given a test," I said, "and I want to pass it."

"Are you sure you'll have enough to do if you stay home?"

"What are you suggesting?"

"I have a feeling that if we stay in bed a little longer, something will come up."

And sure enough, something did.

Chapter 18

On Tuesday Bolce called me to his office as soon as I got to the station.

"How are things going?" he asked, and I knew he wasn't talking about the case. Sometimes, though not all that often, I think he's almost human.

"Fine, so far," I said. "We're just getting started."

"What about the Parker case?"

Well, that didn't take long. "Nothing new for my part. I haven't even thought about it for a week." That was a lie, but Bolce wouldn't know it. "What's Wetsel come up with?"

"I've kept him away from Stanford Parker. He's still interviewing the Parker relatives. That should keep him busy for a while yet, and he won't be interfering with what you're doing. You won't have to worry about him getting in your way anymore."

That was good news. I'd have to let Clive know. I told Bolce I'd get to work on the case immediately and left his office. When I got back to my own office, I had three messages from Clive, so I gave him a call.

"How's Sarah?" he asked.

"Fine. And so am I. I think this is going to work out."

"That's what I told you," Clive said. "You may have to work at it, though."

"I plan to. Do you have anything for me on the Parker case?"

"Quite a bit. We need to talk, but not on the phone."

"You think the phones at the police station are tapped?"

"There's a switchboard. And I don't trust Wetsel."

I told him what Bolce had said.

"Great. I hope it's the truth."

"We'll find out. I'll be at your office in an hour."

I've worked a couple of arson homicides in my day, and the burned-out houses didn't smell one bit smokier than Clive's office.

"You really do need to quit those things," I said, looking at the Chesterfield he held between his fingers.

"That's what Anna always said, but they haven't killed me yet. Anna never smoked a cigarette in her life. . . ."

His voice trailed off, and to get his mind off the irony, I said, "What was it that you couldn't talk to me about on the phone?"

Clive shook himself as if coming awake from a deep sleep. "I've had a report from Gene Moore."

"What's he found out?"

"I'll let him tell you himself. He's on his way here right now."

We talked a little more about Sarah while we waited for Moore. In about fifteen minutes, Clive's secretary buzzed him and said that Moore had arrived.

"Send him on in," Clive told her, and Moore breezed through the door.

He was wearing a paisley shirt, tight bell-bottomed jeans, and square-toed Beatle boots. As soon as he saw that Clive was smoking, he pulled out a package of Camels and lit up.

Clive must have noticed the look on my face because he got up and opened a door that led to the outside. The muggy air invaded the air-conditioned room.

"Might as well let some of this smoke out," he said.

Through the open door I could see a couple of bushy-tailed squirrels running around under the pine trees.

"I hope you don't asphyxiate the local wildlife," I said.

"Don't worry about them. There's plenty of space out there for them to move around in. They can get away from the smoke."

"But not from the smell of Houston," Gene said.

"That's the smell of money," Clive said, and Gene laughed.

We made small talk for a while, discussing the return of the astronauts, the Teddy Kennedy affair, and the war in Vietnam, until Clive thought that Gene was comfortable enough with me to make his report.

"Okay, Gene," Clive said. "Tell us about Stanford Parker. From the beginning."

Gene lit another cigarette and blew out a stream of smoke. He said, "I called Parker and told him that I'd been driving by and seen the sign in his front yard. Then I asked if the house was still for sale. He said it was and that he'd sell it to me himself. We could avoid the Realtor's fee that way. So I said I'd like to have a look."

"We saw you there," Clive said. "Here comes the good part, Steve."

Gene looked at me. I wasn't sure if he trusted me. I was a cop, after all.

Clive said, "It's okay, Gene. Steve and I have been friends for a long time. Everything that's said in this office stays in this office."

Gene shrugged. "All right. I went to the house and looked it over. It was pretty obvious that Stan liked me, if you know what I mean."

I nodded to show that I knew.

"Yeah. So I told him I thought the house was just what I'd been looking for but that I'd have to let my friend Walt look at it before I made a decision. He asked me who Walt was, and I told him that Walt was a very close friend.

"Stan had been interested in me from the start, but now his

eyes lit up. We had a cigarette, and I let him light mine. Our hands touched, and he looked into my eyes. He was making a play."

I wasn't sure I wanted to hear the rest, but I didn't interrupt.

"Stan wanted to know when Walt could come by, and I said that Walt was out of town."

" 'Aren't you lonely when he's gone?' Stan said.

"I told him that I was, and he suggested that he keep me company. When I explained that Walt might come back unannounced, Stan said, 'Why don't you stay here and keep me company, then?' "

Gene crushed out his cigarette and leaned back in his chair. "So I did," he said.

Gene had been with Parker most nights after that. After a few days he told Parker that he'd sent the imaginary Walt on his way, and Parker had begged Gene to move in with him.

"He claimed it was love at first sight on his part," Gene said, "but I'm not sure. Maybe he just wanted me to pick up the payments on the house. He said that if I did that, we could live there forever."

I said, "So I guess we can pretty much take it as a given that Parker is . . ."

"Queer?" Gene said with a wry grin. "You can say it. The word doesn't bother me. But that doesn't mean what you think it does about Stan's alibi."

I'd been thinking that Parker's alibi was down the tubes, but Gene's comment brought me up short. "Why not?" I said.

"Tell him about the girl," Clive said.

"Sure. There's this girl . . ."

"Emily Jackson," Clive said for my benefit.

"That's her. She's a pill head. Stan says he met her at a coffee shop. She needed money for pills and was willing to clean house or do anything else, so Stan took her home and put her to work. After she cleaned the house, she gave him a blow-job that he didn't enjoy all that much. And it's no wonder, since Stan doesn't like women. I think he let her do it in hopes that he might like it. Anyway he got all that for twenty bucks. So he let her spend the night, and she hung around after that, for the drugs he was supplying her. He needed a maid, I guess. He even took her to meet his father, who gave her some money to help her out of a jam. But the second time they asked for money from him, he blew up and threw them out of his house."

"So Emily's his girlfriend, after all," I said.

"No, she's not," Gene said. "She's just a poor girl Stan's trying to help."

Uh-huh, I thought.

"I don't see why you're checking up on Stan like this, Clive," Gene said. "I don't think he killed anybody."

"We're just trying to find out about him," Clive said. "It's just something we have to do. To tell you the truth, we're trying to clear him."

I've found that whenever Clive says, "To tell you the truth," you might hear just the opposite. Gene, however, didn't know Clive as well as I did. He seemed to relax a little, and he said, "I'm sure Stan's in the clear. I don't think he'd ever hurt anyone. I can tell you who you should be investigating, though."

Clive raised his eyebrows. I had a feeling we were about to get some information that he hadn't heard yet.

"You mean Stan gave you the name of somebody that you think is involved in the murders?" Clive said.

"That's right. Stan was telling me about him last night."

"Good," Clive said. "Stan told you, and now you can tell us."

"It was some lawyer his father knew," Gene said. "In fact, the whole family knew him."

"What's his name?" I said.

"Elmer," Gene said. "Isn't that a funny name. Just like Elmer Fudd."

"But his last name's not Fudd," I said.

"No," Gene said. "It's Gann. Elmer Gann."

According to what "Stan" had told Gene, Elmer Gann had hated Ralph Parker and Ralph's mother.

"Stan said that Gann had robbed them," Gene told us. "He was a friend of the family, so Dorothy, that's the elderly one— not that she looked elderly, according to Stan—hired him to collect some money that was owed to her late husband, a gambler named Aaron Winetroub."

"We know who he is," Clive said.

"Yes. Well, the deal was that Gann could keep a percentage of what he collected. He did a good job and collected about twenty thousand dollars, but he never turned any of it over to Dorothy. So Ralph told Gann that he'd give him thirty days to turn over the money. If he hadn't done it within that time, Ralph would file suit against him and also file a complaint with the state bar."

Gann had been in trouble with the bar association before. Another suit wouldn't be good news. In fact, it might mean the end of his career as a lawyer and the loss of his livelihood. And of course a civil suit over the money wouldn't work in his favor, either.

"Steve," Clive said, "you need to run a check on Gann."

"I did that already."

"And you didn't tell me?"

"I didn't think of it. I had a lot on my mind."

Clive nodded his understanding and said, "There's something I neglected to tell you, too."

"What?"

"The check that Gann gave me to pay for the surveillance bounced."

We both laughed at that one. Gene must have thought that we were crazy.

"I don't think that's very funny," he said. "And I think Gann's the man you should be investigating, not Stan. I like Stan a lot, and I plan to continue seeing him."

I wasn't surprised, not considering the way Gene had been talking. Clive wasn't surprised, either. He said, "What you do with your private life is your own business. You know how I feel about that. Now let me give you a check for the rest of the time you've spent on surveillance."

Gene stood up. "No thanks. This one's on me."

Clive didn't argue with him.

"I hope you can find out who killed Stan's family," Gene said. "But I know it wasn't Stan."

He left, and Clive and I sat there for a minute or two, not saying anything. Clive smoked, and I watched the squirrels through the window. A mockingbird in one of the pine trees was dive-bombing one as it raced across the grass.

Finally Clive said, "Whenever you think your life is screwed up, just think about the Parker family."

"My life's not screwed up anymore," I said.

"Thank God for that," Clive said, and I assured him that I did.

CHAPTER 19

That afternoon I started to work on verifying the information that Gene had given us. I wondered who might be able to tell me about Gann's owing money to Dorothy Parker, and the only name I could come up with was Dr. Reitman. I called his home, and Mrs. Reitman told me that he was in the office that day.

"Seeing patients," she said. "There are so many people who need his help."

I explained to her that I needed to talk to him about the Parker case, and she gave me the office address and telephone number.

"But you don't have to call," she said. "You just go on over there. I'll let him know you're on the way."

Reitman's office was on Bissonnet, not far from Main, and it was very crowded. I gave the receptionist my name and looked around the waiting room full of coughing, sneezing people. There was a small lighted aquarium on a table, and the fish swimming around in it were supposed to have a calming effect on the patients. They didn't have that effect on me, and I hoped Reitman would see me quickly.

And in fact, he did. I didn't have to wait at all, at least not with the patients. The receptionist took me right to Reitman's office and said, "He'll be right with you."

It was about ten minutes, but that wasn't bad, especially as I knew he'd been with a patient. He asked what I wanted to know, and I told him about Gann.

"Yes," he said. "She once mentioned that a man by that name had stolen some money that was owed to her, but she didn't go into any details. Is this Gann a suspect?"

"He could be."

"Do you have any others?"

"More than we need, but they all seem to have alibis," I said.

"What about Stanford Parker?"

"He's still on the list. Did Dorothy Parker say who owed her the money that Gann took?"

"It was a bookie. Her husband was a gambler, you know."

I said that I knew. "Do you remember the bookie's name?"

He thought it over and said that he didn't. "But it was an Italian name. Something like Anthony."

"Could it have been Antonelli?"

"Why yes, that could have been it. I believe it was."

I asked him if he remembered any more details, but he couldn't come up with anything, and I knew he needed to get back to his patients. I thanked him for his time and left his office.

Outside, the day was partly cloudy, and the sun was occasionally obscured by those big, flat-bottomed clouds that come floating up our way from the Gulf of Mexico and look as if they're threatening rain, even though they're not. I thought I could even smell the salty, seaweed smell of the beach, but that was probably my imagination.

Sergeant Harvey Beck was a sad-looking man with a face that seemed to indicate that it had seen about every form of human depravity imaginable. Which it probably had. Beck had been on the Vice Squad for more than fifteen years, and I figured he knew all about bookies, among other things. I asked him if Tony Antonelli was still in business or if he'd retired.

"He's retired five or six times. But right now he's back at the same old game. Has one of the biggest books around. Just not in Houston."

"Where is he?"

"He's set up in Sealy."

Sealy was a small town just across the county line, best known for its high school football teams. It didn't seem a likely spot for a bookie joint.

"The Texas Rangers know he's there," Beck said. "They've been investigating him for a good while. I expect they're going to raid him one of these days. Why are you so interested in him?"

I told Beck that Antonelli's name had come up in a homicide case.

"Well, whatever else he is, and that takes in a lot of territory, Tony's not a killer. You can check his records and find that out."

"I'll check, all right," I said, and I did. I should have done it sooner, but I excused myself by saying that his name had come into the investigation only tangentially.

I discovered that Antonelli had been arrested for gambling-related offenses on ten different occasions. He was either making so much money at it that it was worth the risk, or he was addicted to gambling. Well, there was always another possibility. Maybe gambling was the only way he knew to make a living.

I called Clive and said that Tony's name had come into the investigation again. Then I explained his connection to Gann.

"Damn," Clive said. "I hope Tony didn't have anything to do with the murders. I like Tony. And I'm sure he's not a killer. He doesn't even like crime."

"What about gambling?" I said.

"He doesn't think of that as a crime. I remember once when Buster Kerns was sheriff and Tony got the word that Bugsy Siegel was sending Al Smiley to open a book in Houston. Tony didn't like the idea of anybody connected with the Mafia setting up here, so he called Buster. Buster and a Texas Ranger met the plane and welcomed Al to Houston in a little room in the airport. Al could still walk when they finished with him, so they put him on a plane back to Los Angeles and told him never to come back. As far as I know, he didn't."

That sounded to me as if Tony disliked competition more than he disliked the Mob.

"He sounds like a strange friend for you to have," I said.

"He's a strange one, all right," Clive agreed. "We both go to the same church, and . . ."

"Hold on," I said. "You never mentioned that."

"No reason to. Anyway, one Sunday we were both asked to take up the collection. Tony was on the other side of the church from me. He handed the collection basket to a well-dressed man, and when he got it back, he shoved it at the man again. That happened two or three times, and the man finally took out his wallet and put some bills in the basket. When we got to the back of the church, I asked Tony what was going on. He said, 'That cheap bastard just put a little change in the basket. He bets with me, and he hit it big last week. I wasn't gonna let him off so easy.' "

I laughed at the story, but it didn't change anything. I said, "He might not like cheapskates, but that doesn't mean he wouldn't kill for money."

"Tony wouldn't kill anybody. I know him better than that."

"Maybe not personally. But would he hire it done?"

There was a pause on the other end of the line while Clive thought that over. Finally he said, "I couldn't swear that he wouldn't. He has the connections, for sure, in Las Vegas and New York both."

Tony was beginning to sound like a character right out of *The Godfather*.

"I don't think Tony would ever pull the trigger," Clive went

on, "but his father damn sure would have. He was a contract killer for the mob. He screwed up somehow, and they put out a contract on him. He owned a fancy restaurant and club here, and the shooter flew in from New York, got a ride in from the airport to the club, shot him, and went right back to New York. Or so the story goes. I wasn't in town at the time, and I've never asked Tony about it."

Tony might not have been a killer, but he did have an interesting history. I said as much to Clive.

"A history like that might make him less likely to kill. But if you want to talk to him, here's his phone number."

Clive not only knows everybody in Houston; he has everybody's phone number. He read it off to me.

"I'll give him a call," I said.

"You do that," Clive said.

Tony Antonelli answered his own phone. As soon as I identified myself as a homicide detective, he said, "Do you have a warrant for my arrest?"

Before I could even answer, he said, "Never mind. I don't talk on the phone."

I could see why, considering his occupation. Maybe he even knew that the Rangers were onto him.

"I need to talk to you," I said. "I don't have a warrant, but I do have some questions."

"I don't mind answering them. I'll come to your office, and I'll have my lawyer with me."

"By all means bring your lawyer," I said. "And the sooner, the better."

"Damned right, I'll bring the lawyer. I'll call you back and let you know when I'm on the way."

"Fine," I said. "Make it soon."

He didn't hear the last part because he'd already hung up.

That didn't bother me. I figured he'd be in as soon as he got in touch with his lawyer.

People like Tony, who've had a lot of experience with the law, always like to get lawyered up before they talk to the police. Not that I blamed them. They usually had plenty to hide.

While I was waiting for Tony's call, I went over his arrest records to see who his lawyer was, and I got a surprise. He never had one until he went to court, and after they got there, the lawyer did next to nothing. Tony always pled guilty, got a fine, paid it, and walked away.

The phone rang, and Tony Antonelli said, "We're on the way."

He hung up before I could ask him who we included, but I knew I'd find out soon enough. In about thirty minutes the desk sergeant called me to say I had a couple of visitors.

"I'll be right down," I told him, as I had to sign them in. I was interested to see who Tony's lawyer would be.

But when I got there, Tony didn't have a lawyer with him at all.

He had Clive Watson.

CHAPTER 20

Clive grinned at me and said, "Hey, Steve. I'm here to see that Tony doesn't get pistol-whipped."

I didn't say anything. I just signed them in and pointed in the direction of the interview room, not that I needed to. They both knew the way.

Antonelli didn't head for the room. He headed straight for me. He was about six feet tall, and hefty. Over two hundred pounds, easily. His brown hair was thinning on top, and he had the round face of a rascally angel. His suit was wrinkled, his shoes hadn't been shined in months, if ever, and his tie was loose around his neck.

When he reached me, he stuck out his hand, grabbed mine, and shook it.

"I'm Tony Antonelli," he said. "And you're Steve, right? Clive's told me all about you. What can I do for you? Anything at all, you just name it."

I was still too surprised to say anything. I led him and Clive to the interview room and indicated that they could have a seat.

As soon as they sat down, Clive lit up a Chesterfield. The room already smelled like smoke. Everybody who came in there smoked. The top of the wooden table by which Clive and Tony sat was covered with burn marks.

I gathered my wits and said to Tony, "What did Clive tell you about me?"

Tony glanced at Clive then back at me. "He said that you

were a square shooter and that I should just answer your questions and tell you the truth."

I looked at Clive. "I've known Clive for over twenty years, and I never knew he had a law degree."

Clive just grinned, and Tony said, "He ain't a lawyer. I don't need one. I called Clive, and he was willing to come with me. What the hell, he's not even charging me. So I told him to come along."

"You're not charging him?" I said to Clive. That would be a first.

"Nope. Just came along for the ride."

"I can't think of any reason you called me in," Tony said. "I've never been involved in a homicide." He paused. He must have thought about his father's murder. "Well, not in a long time. Anyway, I guess you know I'm a bookie. Not in your county, though," he added.

"I've heard about your occupation," I said.

"I figured. If one of my players has been murdered, one that owes me money, believe me, I had nothing to do with it. You say you know Clive. Fine. He knows me, too, and he knows I'd never kill anybody."

"So what do you do if somebody owes you?" I asked.

"I give them as much time as they need to get the dough to pay me. Hey, they can't pay me if they're dead, right?"

He looked at Clive as if for confirmation, and Clive nodded.

"It wouldn't make sense," Tony went on. "Dead men don't pay off. If somebody owes me, I don't take any more bets from them till I'm paid off, but that's it. No kneecapping, no broken thumbs, no murders. I'm a gambler, not an enforcer, and I don't hire enforcers, either."

Maybe he was telling truth. "Do you know a man named Aaron Winetroub?" I asked.

"Hell, yes. I knew him, anyway. He's dead now. Aaron and I

146

were in business together for a while. He never owed me any money. He was my banker. I'm the one that owed him, but he died, so I figured my debt was canceled. That's the way it should work, right?"

I said that I didn't know.

"Well, it is. His wife, though, Dorothy, she didn't feel that way. I thought we were friends. We used to have some good times when she was married to Aaron. But she was a hard woman. She sent a lawyer after me to collect the money she said I owed Aaron." He paused, then said, "Is this about Dorothy?"

I didn't answer his question. I said, "What was the lawyer's name?"

"Elmer Gann," Tony said. "He's a smart, no-good son of a bitch. I don't like him even a little bit."

"How much did he get from you?"

"Twenty thousand. He claimed I owed forty thousand, but I don't know if that was true. Aaron and I were friends, and we didn't write anything down." He gave me a straight look. "You can understand."

I understood, all right. In their line of work, they probably kept as few records as possible.

"The way we'd do it," Tony continued, "is that he'd say, 'Tony, you own me X amount of dollars,' and I'd pay him. If there were any records at all, I never saw them." He folded his hands and tried to look innocent. "I'm asking you again. Is this about Dorothy?"

He could ask all he wanted to, but that didn't mean I had to give him a direct answer. I said, "Where were you on the night she was murdered?"

"How should I know? What day was it? I've forgotten."

I told him the date.

"Hell, I don't remember where I was. I don't have any idea.

But I damn sure didn't kill anybody over twenty thousand dollars. I'll take a lie detector test if you want me to."

I believed him. I figured that if he'd had anything to do with the murder, he'd have had a solid alibi ready to lay out for me.

Like everybody else who was involved.

"Do you own a gun?" I asked.

"I have a thirty-thirty rifle."

"But not a pistol?"

"Well, I have one, but it's not mine. It belongs to my wife. I can't get a permit for it because of my record."

"I'd like to have a look at it," I said.

"Sure, if that's what you want. It's under the front seat of my car."

"Where's your car?"

"It's parked at Clive's office. We can go there right now if you want to."

I was tired of the interview room, and I was tired of hearing Tony's denials. "Let's go, then," I said.

Tony's car was a long black Cadillac. Tony unlocked it and got the pistol out from under the seat. It was a Walther P38 with a black matte finish and black plastic grips. It looks a lot like the Luger, but it's not quite the same.

Tony popped the clip out and handed the gun and the clip to me. I could smell gun oil, so I knew that the pistol had been cleaned recently. Tony took good care of it. I wondered if he had a reason.

I unloaded the clip and put it and the eight bullets in my pocket.

"I'd like to borrow this for a few days," I said, holding up the pistol.

"If you're going to try to make a weapons charge against me, it won't stick. This is my wife's car."

"I'm not interested in charging you with anything," I told him. "I just want to have the pistol test-fired and check the ballistics."

"Was Dorothy killed with a nine millimeter?" he asked.

She was. The Medical Examiner's guess at the scene had turned out to be right. But that was none of Tony's business, so I didn't answer. By this time Tony probably didn't expect that I would.

"You really think I'm so small-time that I'd kill somebody over twenty thousand?" he said.

"I've known plenty of times when people were killed for a lot less," I said.

"Not by me," Tony said. "And not by anybody I know. Hell, I heard Dorothy's grandson killed her, and his parents, too."

"We have to look at every angle," I said. "I'm going to take this pistol back to the station now."

"Sure, sure. Go ahead. You can give it to Clive when you're finished. He'll see that I get it back. I mean, that my wife gets it back. Right, Clive?"

"Right," Clive said.

When I left, he and Tony were talking about Anna, and by the time I got to the car both of them were crying. Maybe Tony hadn't killed anybody. Like Clive, he was too sentimental.

I logged in the pistol as soon as I got back and took it to Marv Sherman in Ballistics. When I explained what I wanted, he said he'd get right on it.

"What kind of shape are the bullets from the scene in?" I asked.

"Not too bad," Marv said. He always had a toothpick in his mouth, and it moved from one side to the other when he talked. "They went through the bodies into the mattresses, and then lodged in the wood floor. They're in good enough shape for us to get a decent comparison."

"Call me when you get something," I said, and Marv said he'd be glad to.

After I dropped off the pistol, I stopped by to see Bolce. I asked him what Wetsel was up to.

"He's in New Mexico," Bolce said.

"That's a good place for him. Any chance he'll be staying there for a while?"

Bolce almost smiled. But not quite. "He won't be there long. He's supposed to interview the Parkers' daughter."

I remembered that the daughter's name was Amy and that she was coming into a lot of money. She hadn't been at the funeral, so I hadn't given her much thought. It was about time someone interviewed her.

"She lives in Roswell, and she couldn't come here for the interview," Bolce said. "She had a heart attack right when she got the news about her parents and grandmother, and she had to be hospitalized. She's at home now, but she hasn't been able to travel since then. I thought sending Wetsel out there to talk to her would keep him out of your hair for a while."

"I wish you could get him to bring his reports up to date. I haven't seen anything on the sister at all."

"I'm on his ass all the time about the reports," Bolce said. "It never does any good. That's just the way Wetsel is. You know?"

I knew.

Thinking over the Parker case as I walked back to my own office, I couldn't help but wonder if there wasn't something I'd missed.

I took a detour and got all the reports again. When I got back to my office, I started through everything as if I hadn't read any of it before, right from the beginning. I read the autopsy report, the crime scene analysis, the interviews, everything.

I was trying to figure out who had a motive to kill all three victims. So far, I couldn't see that anybody did, or at least not for any reason I could see.

Stanford Parker was angry at his father, but why kill his mother and grandmother? It didn't make sense, considering the size of his inheritance.

The daughter, Amy, stood to inherit a million, which was certainly a motive, but she was supposedly wealthy herself and was married to a respected doctor in Roswell named Jellicoe. With her heart condition, she was a highly unlikely killer, though of course she could have hired someone for the job. But why?

Hal Grubble might have had a motive for killing the grandmother, but why would he kill Ralph and his wife?

Tony Antonelli also had a motive for killing the grandmother, but no reason at all to murder the others.

Someone, somewhere had to have a decent motive for killing all three.

What about Elmer Gann? I asked myself. He'd taken money from Tony that belonged to the grandmother and refused to give it to her. He'd been threatened with a lawsuit by Ralph Parker, and Parker had also promised to expose him to the State Bar Association. As far as I knew, Gann was the only one with a motive to kill more than one of the victims.

But not all three of them.

I was thinking that over when the phone rang. It was Clive.

"I wanted to let you know," he said. "Tony Antonelli's just had a heart attack."

CHAPTER 21

"You mean I scared him that bad?" I said.

"I don't think it was you," Clive said, "but he started having chest pains right after you left. I took him to the emergency room, and he's doing okay. He's going to have to rest and lose weight. They even mentioned doing that bypass surgery, but Tony's not ready for that kind of thing yet."

"Where are you?" I asked.

"I'm still at the hospital, but I called his family, and they're all here now. Meet me at the donut shop in the morning, and we'll talk about things."

"No," I said. I didn't feel like meeting him there. "I'll just meet you at your office."

"That's fine," Clive said. "What time?"

"I have to go by the office first," I said. "Let's make it around eleven."

Clive said that was fine, and I hung up.

Before I left the office for the day, I looked at Elmer Gann's record one more time. The hot checks he'd given had all been filed with the county constable in Precinct One. I knew the chief deputy in that precinct, J. C. Monroe, who had worked in homicide with me before going to work for the county, so I gave him a call.

J.C. said he was glad to hear from me, but that he knew it was business. "You never call for anything else."

"You sound like somebody's mother."

"Yeah. People call me a mother all the time."

"But what kind?"

"Never mind. What did you want to know?"

I told him about Elmer Gann and the hot checks.

"I can look into that for you," J.C. said. "But I can tell you right now that Gann's sorrier than owl shit. Hell, he almost lost his license once for showing up in court drunk. Hang on while I pull his records."

Gann was getting more interesting all the time. I waited for a couple of minutes and J.C. came back on the line.

"We have two warrants out on Gann," he said. "Both for hot checks."

I wondered if Clive would file on Gann. Maybe not. Clive was more forgiving than most people think. I asked J.C. how much the hot checks came to.

"One's for five thousand," he said, "and the other's for two thousand, five hundred. Sergeant Foley's out looking for him even as we speak."

"Let me know if he brings him in," I said, and J.C. promised that he would.

When I got home that afternoon, Sarah was already there.

"Long day?" she said when she got a look at me.

"Long enough. The case I'm on is getting more and more complicated. But I'm up to speed now. At least I think so. How about you?"

"I've been reading that book of yours, *The Godfather*. You should give it to Clive. He likes to read, and he knows people like the ones in the story."

I thought of Tony Antonelli. "You got that right. I'll give it to him when you're finished."

We had smothered pork chops for dinner, one of my favorites, and chocolate pie for dessert.

"You're going to spoil me," I said when we were cleaning up the kitchen.

"I hope so. Why don't we go to a movie tonight?"

"Which one?" I asked. I didn't even know what was showing.

"You like John Wayne, don't you? We could see *True Grit*."

The truth was that I'd have preferred to stay at home and think some more about the Parker case, but if Sarah wanted to go to a movie, I was game. I didn't want her to think that the case was more important than she was.

"Sounds like a good idea," I said. "Who else is in it?"

"Glen Campbell."

"I like his singing," I said. "I hope he can act."

He couldn't, as it turned out, but we didn't mind. We both had a good time, and I didn't think about the Parker case again until the next morning as I drove to the station, fighting the early-morning traffic all the way.

On my desk there was message saying that I should call Ballistics, which I did, and Marv said that the slugs from the Parker murders didn't match up with those fired by Tony's Walther. Or, to be completely accurate, his wife's Walther.

"I'll come by and pick up the pistol later this morning," I said, and Marv said he'd have it ready for me.

After that, I went through the reports again, but I didn't come up with anything useful. By then it was time to leave for Clive's.

Clive was outside under the pine trees, breaking off tiny pieces of bread and feeding the birds. Dozens of them were gathered around him, mockingbirds, blue jays, sparrows, and even a cardinal or two, all of them chirping and fluttering, snatching up each piece of bread that he dropped. The blue jays were the most aggressive, but even the sparrows were getting their share.

"Anna used to feed them," he said when I joined him. "So

the birds know where to come when they get hungry. I figured I'd better keep doing it, or they'd all starve."

I told him that I was glad to see him outside doing something and that it was good that he could continue Anna's kindness to the birds.

"I guess I could put up a bird feeder, but then the squirrels would just steal all the food. Anna thought this was the best way."

"Probably makes the squirrels jealous, though."

"I don't care. Those rascals get plenty to eat, one way or the other. Besides, I always put out some pecans for them in the fall. They're fatter than town dogs."

"I always knew you were a softie," I said.

"Well, don't tell anybody. You think being able to feed the birds without crying means I'm getting better?"

"Yeah," I said. "I do."

"So do I," he said, tossing out the last handful of little pieces of bread. "At least I hope so. Come on. Let's go inside."

We went in, and the birds started to scatter, flying off to sit in the trees and wait until Clive showed up with more bread.

Once inside, we got coffee and went to Clive's office, where, of course, he lit a cigarette.

"How's Sarah?" he asked, exhaling smoke.

"She's doing fine. Still seeing the shrink and taking the medication, but we're getting along. We went to a movie last night."

I told him about *True Grit.*

"I might like that one. John Wayne's my kind of guy."

In a way Clive reminded me of the characters Wayne played. Big, with a little bit of a swagger, and not afraid of anything.

"How about Tony?" I said.

"He's going to be okay, but like I said, he'll be on a diet for a good long time. He's gonna hate that. He loves to eat. And he'll be staying in the house for a while."

"Then maybe he won't be needing this," I said. I pulled the Walther from my waistband and laid it on the desk. "Give it to him when he's feeling better."

Clive said that he would and put the pistol in a desk drawer. Then he told me about a case he'd had while I was off work.

"It was for C.M.E. Tool Works," he said. "Somebody had been stealing tools from them for about two months, and when they called HPD, they were told 'engrave the tools with the company name.' And that was it."

He looked at me.

"Hey," I said. "I'm not responsible for burglaries."

"You'd have done better than that, I'll hope. The owners gave me a call, and I told them to get me the names of any employees they'd hired within the last three months and I'd come check the place out. When I got there, I met with them. They had the list of names for me. I took it and asked if there were any signs of forced entry. They said there weren't, so I asked to see where the tools were kept. They were all in big chain-link cages about seven feet tall. Pretty good protection, you might think. But the cages were open at the top."

"So anybody could climb right in them," I said.

"See? I keep telling you that you should come to work for me. Hell, a man could climb over the fencing, fill his pockets with tools, and climb right back out again."

"If he was about half monkey."

"It wouldn't be that hard. Even you could do it. I took that list of names to the nearest pawnshop and introduced myself to the owner. He recognized my name."

Clive got his name in the papers quite a bit, and it always tickled him when somebody recognized him.

"I showed him the list," Clive continued, "and I asked if anybody on it had pawned any tools there lately. Guess what?"

"You hit it on the first try," I said.

Clive had never been shy about telling me what a good investigator he was, and when I'd said I thought that luck played a part, he told me that good investigators made their own luck. But the truth was that Clive did get lucky now and then. And this was one of those times.

"That's right," he said. "The pawnshop owner pointed to one of the names and said, 'That guy brings in a bag of tools every week or so.' I drove back to the tool works, talked to the man, and got his confession. One of the easiest fees I ever earned. Nothing like this Parker business that's dragging on and on."

"I'd like to close it," I said. "But I still don't have a handle on it."

"You'll find one. Are you hungry?"

I said that I was, so Clive buzzed Jane and asked her to go out and get us some sandwiches. In a little while she came back with some soft drinks and two sandwiches, one for Clive and one for me.

She was a cheerful brunette, a little overweight, but not minding it much. I said, "Where's your sandwich?"

"Don't you worry about me, honey," she said. "It's out on my desk. When it comes to food, I never slight myself."

Clive got a cheese sandwich. Mine was barbecue. I suppose that his stomach problems made it tough for him to eat barbecue. After he gave me a couple of envious looks, I made a big show of how much I was enjoying the barbecue. It was soaking in sauce, so it was a good thing that there were plenty of extra napkins.

When we finished the sandwiches and drinks, I told Clive about Gann's current hot-check troubles and asked if I could use his phone to call J.C.

"Go ahead," Clive said. "I'd be interested to hear if they've caught up with the son of a bitch."

When I got J.C. on the line, he told me that Sergeant Foley had caught up with Gann at his house.

"He was about to get in his car and leave," J.C. said. "Foley didn't have any trouble with him, but he said there was a nine-millimeter pistol on the front seat of his car."

"I'd like to come out there and have a talk with him," I said, "before you put him in jail."

"Come ahead," J.C. said.

I filled Clive in and told him I'd see him later.

"And thanks for that sandwich," I said. "Best barbecue I've had in years."

"Get out of here," Clive said, so I did.

CHAPTER 22

I arrived at the constable's office just as Foley was walking in with Elmer Gann. I'd met Foley once before, so I gave him a nod and checked out Gann.

He was short and stocky, with brown hair that hung down over his ears, a popular look these days, but not one that suited Gann. His flesh was soft and puffy-looking, and his belly hung over his belt. He had no more chin than Andy Gump. He was around forty-five and not much more than five and a half feet tall. He looked as if he'd spent his life with a sullen look. Or maybe he was just sullen because he'd been arrested. I couldn't really blame him too much for that.

He wasn't dressed like a lawyer. His shirt was some kind of psychedelic blue and orange combination, and his bell-bottom Levi's had frayed cuffs. His Hush Puppies were a sort of bilious yellow.

J.C. came up and handed me a paper bag. It was heavy, and I nearly dropped it.

"That's the pistol that was in Gann's car," he said.

Gann overheard us. He said, "Damn right, it's my gun. I've had it for ten years. And I have a perfect right to carry it. I have a permit for it."

"That's wonderful news," J.C. said. "Now stand right there while I read you your rights."

"I know 'em already."

"I'm sure you do, a smart attorney like you, but because of

159

the Supreme Court decision in that Miranda case, I have to tell you what they are, whether you know them or not."

J.C. took a little card from his pocket.

"I should memorize this stuff, but I might forget something," he said, and then he read off Gann's rights, hardly stumbling a single time.

When he was finished, Gann said, "What the hell have I done that you're treating me like this?"

"You've been writing hot checks," J.C. said. "Didn't Sergeant Foley tell you that?"

"Sure." Gann looked at me. "But who's your friend there? I haven't seen him around this part of town, but he looks like a cop to me."

"This is Ted Stephens," J.C. told him. "He's a detective lieutenant with HPD, homicide division."

"Homicide?" Gann said, looking even more sullen. "What does that have to do with me?"

"Probably nothing," I said. "But it's always nice to be sure. If you don't have any objections, I'd like to talk to you for a few minutes."

"I'll talk to you," Gann said after a short pause. "But first tell me who's dead."

"Ralph Parker, his wife, and his mother," I said.

"Okay, yeah, I heard about that."

"So will you talk to me?"

"Sure. Why not? Those people don't have anything to do with me."

"We'll have to sit in," J.C. said, indicating Foley with a nod. "Let's go to my office."

He went first, followed by Gann, who was gently prodded along by Foley. I trailed along behind them. There were plenty of chairs in J.C.'s office, and there was plenty of room for all of us to sit. I looked the place over. I figured it was about three times the size of my little cubbyhole at HPD. It even had a window. Of course all he could see was the parking lot and the sky. No squirrels and pine trees. But his view, as unexciting as it was, was better than the one from my office, since my office had no window at all. Maybe there were more advantages to working for the county constable's office than I'd have thought.

When we were all seated, Gann asked if he could smoke, and J.C. told him to go ahead. Gann got out his Winstons and lit up. When he'd taken a puff or two he asked what I wanted to know.

"Tell me about you and Ralph Parker," I said.

"He's a lawyer. We've run into each other a time or two, but we never had anything to say to each other. I've never had any business dealings with him."

"What about his wife and his mother? Did you ever meet either one of them?"

"I know who they are," Gann said, "but I never had any dealings with them either. I damn sure didn't shoot them or have anyone do it!"

He looked angry and arrogant now instead of sullen. I couldn't figure out the reason for his arrogance, especially since I knew that at least half of what he said wasn't true.

I decided to see if I could shake him up a little. "Nobody suggested that you killed the Parkers, Gann, much less that you had it done. Why are you in such a hurry to deny it? Guilty conscience, maybe?"

He stubbed out his cigarette in a clean ashtray on J.C.'s desk and said, "I want a lawyer."

Sergeant Foley spoke up. "What lawyer do you want? We got half a dozen in the lobby right now, making bond for their rat-bastard clients."

"I don't want any of those damn shysters. I want my own lawyer." He paused. "What the hell. Forget the lawyer. Just book me on whatever trumped-up charges you have on me and take me to my cell. I'll call a guy I know."

"Just give us his name," J.C. said. "We'll call him for you."

"To hell with that. I'll call him myself, later."

"Do you want him to advise you on the hot-check charges or on the murders?" I said.

"Goddammit, you people are pushing me. I need time to think about all this shit."

"Take your time," I said. "I'm not in any hurry."

I looked at J.C.

"Fine by me," he said. "I'm not going anywhere until five o'clock." He turned to Gann. "You can sit right there and think it over for as long as you want to. Or until five o'clock, anyway. After that, you'll have to do your thinking in a cell."

Gann lit another Winston and smoked it right down to the filter without saying a word. When he'd finished smoking it, he stubbed it in the ashtray and said, "Okay, forget the lawyer for now. I'll talk to you. What do you want to know?"

"For starters," I said, "I want to know where you were when the Parkers were murdered."

"Hell, how should I know where I was that night? You think I keep a record of where I am every Tuesday night?"

"How did you know when they were murdered?"

"I read that in the papers."

"Sure you did," I said, knowing that was another lie. "What about your connection to Tony Antonelli?"

Gann didn't answer. He rose from his chair and said, "I want a lawyer!"

"What lawyer you want?" Foley said. "We got . . ."

"Screw that shit," Gann said. He folded his arms across his chest. "I'm not saying another goddamn word."

And then, like most people who lie too much, he went right on to say another word. Or several.

"You sons of bitches are trying to railroad me. I don't know any of those people, Parker, his wife, or his damn mother. Just let me bond out of here for those hot checks, or charge me with something else. I'm tired of you and all the crap you're giving me."

"Before they charge you," I said, "why don't you give me a statement about how you didn't know any of the Parkers."

"He won't have to do that," J.C. said. "I have everything he said on tape. I turned the recorder on when we came in the office."

Gann started screaming about how his civil rights had been violated and how he wanted his lawyer. "And I want out of here right goddamned now!"

"He's all yours," I told Foley. "Lock his ass up."

As they started out the door, I said to Gann, "You don't mind if I borrow your pistol for a while, do you? I'd like to have some tests run on it."

He stopped and turned his head to look at me. "As far as I'm concerned," he said, "you can take that pistol and jam it up your ass."

"I think I'll take a pass on that, if you don't mind."

He didn't respond to that, and Foley led him off down the hallway, with Gann muttering all the way. I couldn't make out what he was saying, but I had a feeling it wasn't flattering to me or J.C.

They'd gone about halfway down the hall when Gann turned around and looked back at me.

"You sorry son of a bitch," he said.

He jerked his arm from Foley's grip and started running down the hall, straight for me.

I grabbed the ledge at the top of the door to J.C.'s office, swung up both feet, and kicked him squarely in the chest. His breath whooshed out and his eyes bugged wildly. Then he went over backward, and before he knew what was happening, Foley had flipped him onto his stomach and cuffed his hands behind his back.

I let myself down to the floor and rubbed my right leg. Whenever I jarred it like that, I always remembered my war wound.

All the commotion in the hall brought the constable out of his office. His name was Jack Allen, but everyone called him Constable Jack. He was an imposing but kindly looking man, given to wearing western-cut shirts and cowboy boots.

"What the hell's this ruckus about?" he said.

J.C. gave him the short version. When he'd finished, Constable Jack turned to me and said, "You better put a hold on him for attempted assault on a police officer in case he bonds out of here on those hot-check charges."

"I'll clear it with my lieutenant," I said.

We all watched as Foley jerked Gann to his feet and frog-marched him down the hallway. Gann didn't mutter this time. He started cursing every one of us in a loud voice. Son of a bitch was the mildest of the names he used, and he didn't let up until he was helped through the door at the end of the hall. He may not have let up even then, but at least we couldn't hear him anymore.

I thought about what he'd told me in J.C.'s office. He'd been lying about not knowing the Parkers, but even more interesting than that was his comment that he hadn't killed them and that he hadn't had them killed.

His denial that he'd killed them wasn't surprising. Anybody might have said that, whether it was true or not. The second comment was the one that bothered me. Why had he added the bit about not having hired anybody to kill them? Why had he even thought of it?

And how had he known when the murders occurred? That

information had never been printed in the newspapers. The stories merely said that the bodies had been found, not when. Sure, Gann could have guessed that the murders had happened at night, and he might have guessed the day from when the articles appeared. But why would he have remembered it so well?

Gann had the motive to kill Parker and his mother, if not Parker's wife. And I was sure he'd had the opportunity as well. I thought it would be a good idea to follow Constable Jack's suggestion.

Constable Jack went back to his office, and J.C. and I shot the breeze for a few minutes. He told me how much he liked working for the constable's office, and he said I should consider retiring from HPD and getting a job with the county.

It was beginning to look as if everyone wanted me to quit my job and take another one. I had to admit that it was tempting, but I still liked what I was doing, and I told J.C. that I intended to stick with it for a while.

"If you change your mind," he said, "let me know. I can put in a good word for you."

"Thanks," I said.

I took the bag containing Gann's pistol with me when I left and told J.C. to give my regards to Gann.

When I got back to HPD, I had to log in the pistol, and for the first time I took it out of the bag and had a look at it. It was an old Beretta in miserable condition, and it looked as if it hadn't been cleaned since the day I'd been shot in France. Flecks of rust marred the barrel and the trigger guard, and there was no smell of gun oil at all.

Marv looked the Beretta over when I took it to Ballistics and said, "I'd say this thing hasn't been fired in years. In fact, it might be dangerous to fire it. There could be dirt in the barrel.

Probably is."

"You can test it, though, can't you?" I said.

"Sure. We can test it, but we'll have to clean it up first."

"That's okay," I said. "I know it's not likely to be the murder weapon, I'd like to be sure about it."

"You don't have to worry about that," Marv said. "We'll make sure."

CHAPTER 23

I looked around my crowded little office. The one without a view of anything except the hallway. The view was thanks to the fact that the cubicle had no door. I was accustomed to the place, and it served my needs just fine, I suppose, but I couldn't help comparing it to J.C.'s spacious office with its window. I sat down in my squeaky chair. I was willing to bet that J.C.'s chair didn't squeak. But I couldn't sit there and envy somebody else's situation. I had more immediate problems to worry about.

I didn't know any of Elmer Gann's friends or business associates, and they probably wouldn't have talked to me if I'd known them. But I thought I could get some information about him from a source I'd already cultivated, so I called Dr. Isaac Reitman's office. The receptionist told me that he was with a patient but that he'd call me back as soon as he could. I started to work on my reports while I waited.

Dr. Reitman called back in about fifteen minutes. He said that he really didn't have time to talk, but that Dorothy Winetroub Parker had confided in his wife as much as she had in him.

"I was just her doctor," he said. "Ruth was more like her friend. I'm sure she'd be glad to help you if she can."

I thanked him and called Mrs. Reitman, who seemed happy to have someone to talk to, especially if anything she knew might help to find the Parkers' killer. So I asked her if she'd ever heard of a lawyer named Elmer Gann.

"Oh, yes. Dorothy mentioned him several times. He was going to help her get some money that was owed to her, I believe. I thought it was strange that she'd hire a lawyer when her own son was one."

"Did she say who recommended him?" I asked.

"No, and I'd never heard of him before, either. Dorothy told me that she'd gotten his name from a woman at the Hair Hut. That's where she went every week for her wash and set. She was very particular about her hair. Anyway, one of the women who was a customer there mentioned him to Dorothy. She said that Gann had collected some money for her son. That's all he did, according to her. Collection work. And that's what Dorothy wanted to have done."

"Not the best way to pick out a lawyer," I said.

Mrs. Reitman agreed. "I told her that she should have Ralph check him out, but she said it was too late for that, that she'd already hired him. Dorothy was a very strong-willed person, you know. She didn't want her relatives involved in any of her personal affairs, not even her son."

I thought about the fact that Dorothy had hired Clive's son-in-law to do the real estate deal for her rather than have her son do it. He might not even have known about her selling the house in Las Vegas.

"Did she ever mention if Gann got the money for her?" I said.

"Yes. She told me about that. She was very upset with Gann. She said that he got the money but didn't give it to her. She was considering legal action."

Her son had known about that, I thought, and in fact he was the one who'd threatened to sue Gann. Maybe his mother had decided that a little family help wasn't so bad, after all, not when it came to dealing with a lowlife like Gann.

I asked Mrs. Reitman a few more questions and let her go.

I'd hoped she could tell me if Gann had ever been to the Parker house, but she didn't know the answer to that one.

I took a few minutes to think about the phone call, and then I looked up the number for the Hair Hut. The owner, whose name was Susanne Scott, answered my call, and after I told her who I was and why I was calling, I asked her if she could give me a list of the customers who had regular appointments on the same day that Dorothy Parker did.

"It's crucial to our investigation of her murder for me to find out which of those women had contacts with a lawyer named Elmer Gann."

"I can check my appointment book and find the names," Susanne said. "I know all of them, and I can find out if they knew Gann. Give me your number, and I'll call you back."

"That would be a big help," I said, and I gave her my number.

My next call was to Clive Watson. I wanted to find out how Tony Antonelli was doing.

"He's in St. Luke's, and he's doing about as well as can be expected," Clive said. "They have him in the VIP section that they call the Terrace. That's the one with the big rooms and the special meals."

"And the one where they bring around coffee and finger sandwiches in the middle of the afternoon," I said.

"That's it, all right. I can meet you there around three-thirty if you want to talk to Tony. That's the best time because that's when they bring those goodie trays around."

I looked at my watch. It was a little after three. I told Clive that I could make it and that I'd see him there.

"Meet me at the valet parking area," Clive said, and I told him I would.

Clive got to the hospital ahead of me, which was no surprise, considering the way he drove. His car had already been driven away by the valet, and he was talking to a young woman in a nurse's uniform. I handed over my keys and went to where Clive was talking to the nurse.

"This is M. C. Deboult," Clive said, introducing me. "She took care of Anna."

I'd thought Clive was getting better, and maybe he was, but the chance meeting with M.C. outside the hospital was too much for him. He turned his head to the side so we couldn't see his tears.

I shook hands with M.C. and asked her about her job. We talked about this and that while Clive recovered himself. It didn't take as long as it would have only a week or so earlier. He turned back to us and told M.C. that we were on our way to see Tony Antonelli.

She smiled and said, "He's in room six forty-three. He's quite a character."

"It seems like everybody knows Tony," I said.

"He's a very outgoing sort," M.C. said. "I don't know if he's told you, but he's scheduled for a heart catheterization in the morning. He has a blocked artery."

"So they didn't recommend a bypass?" I said.

"No. This procedure's not as serious. And not as dangerous."

"Will it be okay if we talk to him?"

"If Clive's with you, it will be. He and Clive are very good friends."

We left her there and went on inside. We waved at the receptionist as we crossed the lobby and took the elevator up to the sixth floor. I'd been there before, so I wasn't surprised at how elaborate the set-up was. Tony had a regular suite: a big bedroom for himself, a smaller one for his wife, and a private bath.

When we came through the door, Tony was on the bed, which was cranked up to put him in a sitting position.

"Hey, Clive," he said. "Come on in. Hey, Steve. What's up?"

"I've been talking to Elmer Gann," I said. "He told me that he didn't know you or the Parkers."

"The little bastard," Tony said.

His face reddened, and he pushed the call button for the nurse. She came into the room, and he said, "Bring me my clothes. I'm getting out of here."

The nurse was a sturdy woman about forty years old, and I'm sure she was accustomed to dealing with unruly patients. She said, "No you're not. You're not going anywhere. You're staying right there in that bed."

Tony threw back the covers, showing his hairy white legs.

"That's what you think," he said, and he started to slide off the bed.

The nurse told him to stay where he was, but he didn't listen. She put her hand on his chest to push him back down on the bed, but he brushed it aside. However, Clive and I had moved to the bed by that time, and each of us took hold of one of his large arms. With the help of the nurse, we forced him back onto the bed.

"You're going to have a heart attack right here if you don't calm down," the nurse told him. "And then your wife will sue us. You wouldn't want that to happen, would you?"

"I guess not," Tony said, but he was still angry.

"Then behave yourself." The nurse looked at me and Clive. "And you two had better not get him excited again, or I'll throw you out of here."

We believed her and told her that we'd behave, too. I wasn't sure that she believed us, and when she left the room she looked back and gave us both a glare that was supposed to be intimidating. It didn't bother me, and it bothered Clive even less.

Tony didn't even notice. He said, "That Gann is a lying son of a bitch. I have six people who saw me hand him the money

171

for Dorothy. And I know he was representing her because he had a letter she'd signed that authorized him to collect from me."

"Are you sure the letter was genuine?" I said.

"Damn right it was. I didn't just fall off the potato truck."

Just then, the nurse came back into the room. She hadn't believed us after all. She had two men with her, and she introduced them as Dr. Leachman and Dr. Lufchanoski, Tony's cardiologists.

Leachman was tall and thin. He had black eyes and black hair with just a little gray in it.

"We can't having you get excited," he told Tony. He walked to the bed and started taking Tony's pulse. "It's not healthy. Not in your condition."

Lufchanoski was about six inches shorter than Leachman and a good bit older. He shook his head and said that Tony shouldn't even think about leaving the hospital. And he told us that we would have to cut our visit short.

We said that we would, and Leachman said that Tony's pulse was elevated. Not dangerously, but it was higher than it should be. Leachman looked at me and Clive as if to imply that we'd be responsible if Tony kicked off right there in the room.

"We'll go quietly, doctor," Clive said. "Just let us tell Tony goodbye."

"Fine. But don't say anything more."

Clive nodded, and the doctors left the room, followed by the nurse. I had a feeling that she was lurking somewhere right outside, just to be sure we left promptly.

I told Tony that I'd follow up with him later, and we turned to go. But the door was blocked by a candy-striper teacart loaded down with pastries, finger sandwiches, and fruit.

"Hey, you can't leave now," Tony said. "Stay and have a bite."

The candy striper pushed the cart on into the room, and

while she was telling Clive and Tony what was available, I took a look outside. The nurse was nowhere in sight.

"We can risk it," I told Clive.

"Good," he said, sitting down in one of the chairs and lifting a sandwich off the cart.

I had one or two myself, and they were delicious. Even the coffee was good. Clive cheered up considerably and started telling the story of another time when Tony had been in the hospital and Clive had posed as his doctor. He'd told a floor nurse to give Tony an ice-water enema.

Anna had been with Clive, but she hadn't overheard what he was telling the nurse. She was horrified when she found out what he'd done and insisted that he stop the nurse before she got to Tony's room.

"But it was too late," Tony said. He had a reflective look. "That enema was worse than this heart attack, I think. You're a real bastard, Clive."

"It was the right procedure for somebody who's full of shit," Clive said. "And you know it."

They were both laughing about it when Tony's wife came into the room. She was short and solidly built, with graying hair and a big smile. She went right to Clive and gave him a hug, then told him how much she missed Anna.

"I miss her, too," Clive said, but he was in too good a mood to get teary-eyed this time.

We left Tony with his wife and headed down to the valet parking area. Clive ran into three or four other nurses that he knew by name before we got there, and they all wanted to hug him and tell him how sorry they were about Anna. I was beginning to think there wasn't anybody in Houston that Clive didn't know.

"There must be somebody," Clive said when I mentioned it to him. "But I can't remember who it is. Nobody important, that's for sure. Aren't you glad I'm on your side?"

"Damn right," I told him.

CHAPTER 24

It was time for me to go home, but I kept thinking about the letter that Tony had mentioned, the one authorizing Gann to make collections for Mrs. Parker. So when I left the hospital, I went back by the office and checked the inventory on all the paperwork the crime scene team had gathered at the Parker house. There was no mention of a copy of the letter Mrs. Parker had given Gann when she'd hired him to collect her money.

I thought about that. Surely someone whose son was a lawyer would have kept a copy of the letter as a precaution. I wondered what could have happened to it, but I couldn't figure it out. So I called Bolce to ask if Wetsel had gotten back from New Mexico.

"He's back, but there's no report, if that's what you want to know."

I could have guessed about the report. Wetsel was lazy and never turned in his paperwork until forced to. I asked Bolce if it would be okay if I got in touch with Amy Parker Jellicoe and talked to her myself.

"Go ahead," he said. "Nobody's going to tell Wetsel, and it could be a week before he gets that report done."

I found the number for the Jellicoe residence in the reports and got the long distance operator to call the number.

A woman answered and said that she was Amy Jellicoe. I explained why I was calling, and she said, "You sound much nicer than that officer they sent out here to talk to me. Detective Wetsel."

The way she said his name told me plainly how she felt about Wetsel. Which was pretty much the same way everybody else felt about him.

I said that I was sorry she was having medical problems and apologized for bothering her, but she didn't seem to mind talking to me. Unfortunately, she couldn't help me much.

"I never talked about money with my parents or my grandmother," she said. "I didn't need their money, and I certainly didn't feel it was my place to tell them how to spend it. They had their lives to live, and I had mine."

"What about your brother?" I said.

There was a long pause, and I thought maybe the connection had been broken. Finally she said, "Stanford and I were never close, and we haven't kept in touch. He was a constant source of sorrow to the whole family. I think it's the whole hippy generation that's to blame. All that 'turn on, tune in, drop out' philosophy they talk about. Stanford's done all those things, I'm afraid."

"Drugs?"

"I'm sure he's used them. And he didn't have any kind of job. If my parents hadn't given him money, he couldn't have survived. He'd be living under a bridge somewhere. The detective who came here, Wetsel, said that in his opinion Stanford was the killer." There was another long pause. "I'm afraid he could be right."

"Any specific reason you feel that way?" I asked, but she couldn't give me one. It was just a feeling that she had, and I couldn't get any more out of her than that.

When I finished up the conversation, it was after six o'clock, and by the time I got home, it was close to seven. Sarah wasn't happy.

"You're late," she said.

I couldn't deny it. I'd let myself get caught up in the investigation, and I'd put it ahead of my obligation to her.

"Look," I said, "I don't blame you for being upset. You know that sometimes in my job, I have to work overtime and at odd hours."

"I know that. I also know that you do it because you want to do it."

That was true, this time, but it wasn't always true. I started to tell that to Sarah, but I realized I was just rationalizing. I'd promised her that I'd be home on time, and I hadn't been.

"I won't do it again," I said. "Not unless I call you and let you know. I love you, Sarah, don't think I don't. I hated every minute that you were gone, and I don't ever want you to leave again."

She smiled. It wasn't much of a smile, but at least it was a start.

"We could go out to dinner," I said. "Have a good meal, come home and watch a little TV, then see what develops."

Her smile got marginally wider.

"Italian food?" she said.

"I know just the place," I said, thinking of Dino Vallone's restaurant.

"You're trying to bribe me, you know."

"I know. Is it working?"

"I think it might. It'll take me a few minutes to get ready."

"I'd wait for you, no matter how long it took."

"You're really trying, aren't you?"

"I really am."

"I'll be ready in ten minutes," she said, and she was.

The next morning I called J. C. Monroe and asked if Gann had bonded out.

"Nope," J.C. said. "His bondsman wouldn't put up the money. Seems that Gann's not doing too well financially, and all the bondsmen know it. They think he might run."

"I'd like to have another talk with him," I said.

"And I'm sure he'd love to see you again since the two of you got along so well."

He made a kissing sound into the phone.

"Just let them know at the jail that I'm coming," I said.

The jailer brought Gann down to an interview room, and he and I faced each other across a gray metal table that was scarred and scraped from years of hard use. I told the jailer it would be all right to take the cuffs off, but Gann didn't thank me. As soon as his hands were free, he lit up a Winston.

"What do you want?" he said when he'd had a puff or two.

"Why don't we try starting with the truth this time. You lied to me yesterday, and I know it. You know Tony Antonelli, and you knew Ralph Parker and Dorothy Winetroub Parker. She hired you to collect money from Tony, and she even gave you a letter that said you were acting on her behalf."

He smoked about half the Winston without talking. Then he said, "So I lied. So what?"

Gann hadn't looked good the day before, and he looked even worse now. His hair was matted, and his eyes were bloodshot as he peered at me through the smoke of his cigarette.

I didn't bother to answer his question. I said, "You also knew when the Parkers were killed. You said you read it in the paper, but the day and time were never published. Somebody's going to get the needle for this one, Gann, and I think it might be you."

I'd always thought the hint of a seat on Old Sparky was a better threat than a lethal injection, but the state had phased out the electric chair about five years previously.

Gann gave me a sullen grin. "Could be I heard about the murders from somebody."

Now we were getting somewhere. Maybe.

"Who told you about them?" I said.

"You know him. It was a homicide cop."

I got a bad feeling.

"His name's Wetsel," Gann said. "He and I are drinking buddies."

It was bad enough that Wetsel was pig-headed and wouldn't keep his reports up to date. Now it turned out that he couldn't keep his mouth shut, besides. And that he had really bad taste in drinking buddies. I wondered if he'd met Gann in a cop bar, but it didn't seem likely. Gann would avoid places like that if he could.

"Does Wetsel know you're talking to me?" Gann said. "Because he might not like it."

"I don't give much of a damn what Wetsel likes or doesn't like," I said. "And he doesn't tell me who to talk to."

"Kind of touchy, aren't you?" Gann said. "When Wetsel told me you were on the case, he also mentioned what a sorry asshole you are."

I thought about squashing Gann like a bug against the metal table, but that's probably what he wanted me to do, and I wasn't going to give him the satisfaction. So I smiled instead. "Wetsel's a good judge of character, all right. Did he know you were collecting money from Tony Antonelli for Dorothy Winetroub Parker?"

"Sure he did. We talk all the time."

"And did he know you got the money and kept it for yourself?"

Gann snuffed the Winston, lit another one, and breathed out smoke. "Hell, yes. He's the one who gave me the idea. He told me that it was all illegal money, so she wasn't entitled to it anyway."

"That Wetsel's a really smart guy, all right," I said. "Did he tell you to lie to me about knowing Mrs. Parker and Tony Antonelli?"

"Why would he tell me that? He didn't know you were going to talk to me. He just said for me to keep quiet about the money, and everything would be okay. He said nobody would ever know because you sure as hell weren't smart enough to find out about it."

"I guess he's not quite as good a judge of character as I thought," I said.

Gann didn't respond to that. He said, "How did you find out, anyway?"

"It wasn't anything smart," I said. "I just happened to see a copy of the letter that Mrs. Parker signed for you, the one that authorized you to act for her in making the collection."

"Oh, yeah, that." He paused for a few puffs. "How the hell did you see it? I thought . . ."

"What did you think?"

"Nothing. I just . . ."

I reached across the table and snatched the lighted cigarette out of Gann's fingers, threw it on the floor, and stepped on it.

"Don't smoke in front of me again without asking permission," I said. "Now tell me what you started to say, or I'll break your fucking nose and tell the jailer you fell off your goddamned chair."

"Hold on," Gann said, sliding his chair backward. "Hold on."

"Fuck you," I said. "I'm tired of you and your lies. I'm gonna break your fucking nose and a couple of your fingers, too."

I kicked over my chair and started around the table.

Gann cringed away from me. He said, "All right. All right. Calm down. I didn't think you could've seen the letter because I had the original, and Wetsel gave me the copy that he found in the Parker house. He was going through some papers and saw my name on the letter. He didn't know what it was, but he stuck it in his pocket so he could give it to me and keep my name out of the investigation."

I walked back around the table, picked up my chair, and set it upright. Then I sat back down. I'd always known that Wetsel was a bad cop. I just hadn't known how bad until now. Of course there could be even worse things about him. Maybe I'd find out someday.

"That Wetsel's a stand-up guy," I said.

"Damn right he is. He sticks by his friends. Can I smoke now?"

"No. Let's talk about your alibi for the night of the murders. I'm assuming you have one."

After all, I thought, everyone else did.

"I think I have one," Gann said. "But I'll have to check and make sure."

"What the hell is that supposed to mean?"

"It means that I was with a married woman whose husband was out of town at the time. I have to ask her if she'll vouch for me."

The women of the world were harder up for male companionship than I would have guessed. Or at least one of them was.

"I'll take your word for it," I said. "For now. And while we're being frank with each other, maybe you want to go ahead and tell me everything you know about the murders."

"I don't have anything to say about that. I'm through talking to you. I want to go back to my cell."

"I'm disappointed, Gann. And here I thought we were starting to trust each other. But since we're not, you're going to have to give me the woman's name."

"Fuck that. You're not getting it."

"I'll be discreet," I said. "Nobody else has to know."

"Yeah, right. Wetsel's told me about you. You'll blab it all over town. I'll tell you one thing, though, and it's the straight poop. Stanford Parker killed them. And that's all I'm going to say."

CHAPTER 25

I called the jailer to let me out. He led Gann away, and I went down to the sheriff's office to put a "hold for homicide" on Gann in case he found a bondsman who'd bail him out. As I was signing the papers, the sheriff walked in.

Ray Thompson is big, tall, and good-looking. He looks like a cop, but a pleasant one, and he's a down-to-earth type. He still lives in the same little house in Katy, Texas, that he bought twenty years ago, long before he became the high sheriff of the county.

"Hey, Steve," he said in a rumbling bass. "What've you got going?"

"I've been talking to one of your customers about the Parker case," I said.

"I've heard about that one. The papers are getting a lot of mileage from it."

"So I've noticed."

I'd been reading the articles in case they might have something to help me, but they hadn't. They never did. But I kept hoping.

"Who's the customer you're interested in?" Ray asked.

"Elmer Gann. You've got him for hot checks, and I just put a hold on him for homicide."

"You want some help with him?"

"I can always use some help. What did you have in mind?"

"I can put a trusty in the cell with him, one who'll cooperate with us. If Gann lets anything slip, we'll know."

"Sounds good to me. Can you keep a list of Gann's visitors for me?"

"Sure. Anything else?"

"I wouldn't mind having a list of the people he calls. If he calls anybody besides bail bondsmen."

"I'll see what I can do," Ray said.

It's always a good feeling to leave a jail. It was especially good this time because it was a beautiful day. If there was a single cloud in the blue sky, I couldn't see it. A front had come through during the night and taken most of the humidity out of the air, and though it was hot, it didn't feel nearly as hot as it ordinarily did in Houston in the summer. People who live in dry climates don't know how to appreciate a day like that, when your skin doesn't feel slimed over the minute you walk out the door, but we Houstonians do. Even the drivers on the freeway were in a good mood.

It was such a nice day that I hated to spoil it by giving Bolce the bad news about Wetsel, but he had to know. I stopped by his office and said, "I have something to say that I don't want anybody to hear. You want to go outside, or is this a good place?"

"We can talk here," he said. "Close the door."

I did as he said and sat down in the chair near his desk.

"What's on your mind?" he said.

I went through what Gann had told me about Wetsel. Bolce hadn't looked happy to begin with, and by the time I'd finished, his face was droopy as a beagle's.

"I'm not quite willing to take Gann's word for what he told you," Bolce said. "Wetsel might be a turd, but he's a cop with a lot of years on the force, and he knows better than to do anything like Gann claims he did. Will Gann give you a sworn statement to back up what he told you?"

"Judging from what I've seen of him, he just might. He thinks he's smart, but he's really pretty shallow. I don't know how somebody like that ever gets a law degree."

"It doesn't matter how he got his law degree. Will he swear to what he told you?"

"Maybe if I give him something in exchange."

"Like what?"

"With Gann it won't take much. A candy bar, maybe. He has the backbone of a caterpillar."

Bolce brightened.

"My only concern," I said, "is that Wetsel might get to him before I do. If that happens, Gann most likely won't talk to me again. Wetsel will tell him not to."

"I'll see to it that nothing like that happens."

"Good. I'll visit Gann tomorrow and see if he'll sign an affidavit."

Bolce nodded. "If it turns out that Wetsel really was doing favors for Gann and removing evidence from the scene of a crime, I'll have to turn things over to Internal Affairs and let them deal with it."

"That's what I figured. And in that case, even if Gann gives me a sworn statement, we'll need some corroboration. I.A.'s not likely to take Gann's word for anything."

"Can you blame them?"

"No," I said.

"Then you'd better get corroboration," Bolce said. "Or forget the whole thing."

I worked on my reports and wondered where I was going to get corroboration for Gann's story about Wetsel. And I wondered if I could convince Gann to give me a sworn statement. I might be out of luck on both things, though I thought I had a pretty good chance with Gann.

In the middle of the afternoon Sarah called to ask what I wanted for dinner.

"We'll go out," I said. "Or I'll bring something home. Whatever you want to do."

"I want to cook. I haven't been doing that enough. It makes me feel at home."

"Well, you know I like to eat your cooking. Whatever you come up with will be fine with me."

"I'll surprise you, then."

"Great," I said. "I'll leave here at five on the dot."

And I did. But when I got home, Sarah hadn't cooked anything. She was dressed and ready to go out.

"Let's get barbecue," she said.

I could have said that I thought she was going to cook. I wasn't her psychologist, but even with my limited education, I somehow didn't think a comment like that would go over well. For the same reason, I didn't ask her why she'd changed her mind.

I just told her I loved her and said, "Let's go."

The next morning I stopped off at a Seven-Eleven and bought an apple, a few packages of snack crackers wrapped in cellophane, and a couple of Hershey bars for Gann. I would have taken him some beer or bourbon. Gann probably would have loved it, but it wouldn't have gone over well at the Graybar Hotel.

When I got to the jail, I stopped outside the open door of Ray Thompson's office.

He looked up, saw me, and said, "Come on in, Steve. I have something for you."

I stepped inside, and Thompson said, "Close the door."

"This must be good," I said. "I hope it's going to help my case."

"I don't know about that, but at least it's a piece of information. Gann had a visitor."

"Okay, don't keep me in suspense. Who was it?"

"Stanford Parker."

That was interesting news, all right.

"I wonder what the hell that was all about," I said.

"I can't tell you. But we did put a trusty in the cell with Gann."

"Have you talked to him?"

"Sure. He said he asked Gann who his visitor was, but Gann wouldn't tell him. Gann just said that he asked the guy for bond money and not only did he say he wouldn't do it, but he tried to get money from Gann."

That at least confirmed everybody's comments about Stanford's lack of funds. But it didn't explain why he would have visited Gann.

"Maybe Gann will tell me more," I said.

Except that I wasn't going to mention Parker to Gann. I didn't want to upset him, not when I was going to ask him to sign an affidavit for me.

"Do you have a notary on the premises?" I asked Thompson.

"Sure. Why do you need one?"

"Bolce wants me to get a sworn statement from Gann. I'll need to get the notary to swear him and notarize the statement to make it official."

"I'll take care of it for you. Just tell the jailer when you're ready, and he'll bring her in."

"Thanks, Ray. I need all the help I can get on this one."

We shook hands, and I left the office. I checked my gun at the gate, and told the guard that I had two candy bars, some crackers, and an apple for the prisoner in the sack I was carrying. He looked inside to make sure I hadn't slipped in a file.

The jailer who turned up to escort me to the interview room

was Major Henslowe, a serious-looking man whom I'd met before. Everybody liked the Major, even the prisoners, because he did his job right and treated people fairly, as long as they followed the rules.

"I've already brought Gann down," Henslowe said. "He's waiting for you."

I thanked him and told him about the notary.

"The sheriff called me," he said. "I'll have her standing by. Just knock on the door when you want her to come in."

The room was the same one we'd used the day before. Gann was smoking when I came in. I stopped just inside the door and looked at him.

He took the cigarette out of his mouth and held it up.

"Is it okay if I smoke?" he said.

"It's okay."

"Good. What the hell do you want this time?"

"I just came by for a friendly visit." I put the sack down on the table. "There's a little snack in there for you. In case you get hungry."

"I can't eat the shit they serve here. I'm hungry all the time."

I sat down and pushed the sack across to him. "This should help a little. It's not much, I'm afraid, but it's a start."

Gann didn't touch the sack. He took a puff on his Winston and then said, "I tried to call Wetsel last night. The bastard wouldn't take the call."

To protect the public, prisoners can make only collect calls from the jail. I figured that Bolce had talked to Wetsel and warned him about accepting calls from prisoners, without mentioning any names.

"You can call me," I said. "I'll be glad to accept the charges and talk to you."

Gann blew out smoke and said, "What the hell are we going to talk about if I do call you?"

I replied, "Anything you want to talk about. If you feel you need to talk to somebody and Wetsel won't listen, you can call me."

"If you mean that, then release the homicide hold you put on me so I can make bond."

"The hold is already released," I told him. "If you can make bond on the checks, you can get out of here as soon as I leave. That's if the paperwork has been processed. That might take a while."

What I didn't tell him was that the hold was good only for twenty-four hours, after which it was automatically dismissed. He might as well think I had something to do with it.

"And since you're likely to be a free man pretty soon," I said, "there's a little favor you could do for me."

"I knew there was a reason you brought me something to eat. Well, fuck you. You can't buy me that cheap. I'm not doing you any favors."

"I'm sorry you feel that way," I said, reaching across the table and dragging the little sack of goodies back to my side. "I was hoping you wouldn't mind trading favors. But since you do, I'll just take this stuff and get out of your hair."

I stood up, holding the sack.

"Hold on, goddammit," Gann said, eyeing the sack. "What's the favor?"

"Nothing much. I told my lieutenant that you and Wetsel were buddies. I told him what you said about Wetsel picking up the copy of the letter of agreement between you and Dorothy Winetroub Parker when he was in the Parker house and giving it to you." I smiled ruefully. "The lieutenant listened, but he didn't believe it."

"Well, it's the truth," Gann said.

"Hey, don't get upset with me. I believe you. It's the lieutenant who doesn't. He's always showing favoritism to Wetsel.

Everybody in the department notices."

"Yeah, he told me that he was the fair-haired boy."

Bolce would love to know that, but I didn't think I'd pass it along.

"I'd love to change that attitude of Wetsel's," I said. "I just don't know how."

"I'd like to change it, too. The bastard. Wouldn't even take my call, as many drinks as I've bought him."

I pushed the sack over to Gann.

"Go ahead," I said. "Eat one of those Hershey bars while I think about this."

Gann opened the sack and looked inside. Then he looked at me. "I think I'll have the apple first."

"Whatever you want," I said.

He took the apple out of the sack and crunched down on it. He chewed noisily.

I sat there, not saying anything, pretending to think the situation over.

"There might be one thing we could do," I said after a while.

"What's that?" Gann said, his mouth full of apple.

"If you'd write down what you said and put in a little about you and Wetsel being friends, maybe Bolce would believe it. Of course I'd have to get it notarized to satisfy him."

Gann put the core of the apple in the ashtray on the metal table and said, "If I do that, would Wetsel get in any trouble?"

"I can't make any promises about that. But he might."

"I'll do it, then."

Before he could change his mind, I reached into my jacket and brought out my notebook and pen. I flipped open the notebook to a clean page and set it and the pen on the table.

"Go to it," I said.

Gann pulled his chair up closer to the table, picked up the pen, and started writing.

CHAPTER 26

When Gann had finished, I read over what he'd written.

His handwriting was terrible, and his spelling wasn't much better. I wondered again how he'd gotten through law school. But the content was what mattered, and Gann made it clear that he and Wetsel were good friends, that he'd done a few favors for Wetsel from time to time and never charged him anything, and that Wetsel had taken the copy of the letter of agreement from the Parker house when he was searching the crime scene and had given it to Gann. He'd signed his name at the bottom. Or I supposed he had. The signature wasn't legible.

I knocked on the door, and the Major sent in the notary public, a woman of about fifty with short gray hair and a severe look. She had Gann hold up his right hand while she administered the oath, and she made him sign his name again in her presence. When all that was taken care of, she applied her seal, and the deal was done.

After she left the room, Gann said, "You had that all planned, didn't you? The notary was waiting out there all the time."

I admitted it.

"I don't give a damn. Not as long as Wetsel gets what's coming to him."

"Let's hope he does," I said. "Have a Hershey bar."

Gann took a Hershey out of the sack. "This has almonds in it," he said.

"The best kind."

"Yeah."

He peeled off the paper and broke a bite off the Hershey with his front teeth.

"What kind of favors did you do for Wetsel?" I asked.

"They didn't amount to much. I know a guy who's the lawyer for the county. Part of his job is to sell property that's been foreclosed because of delinquent taxes. I'd find out about what was coming up for auction and make sure that Wetsel got first shot at some of the good stuff. He fixes the places up and sells them again for a nice profit."

"And you did that for nothing?" I said, trying not to sound skeptical.

Gann crammed the last of the Hershey in his mouth. "Now and then I'd get a little money," he said, chewing. "As a commission."

"How about your pal, the county lawyer?"

"He gets a lot more than I do out of the deal. Wetsel gives him a third of the profit."

So Wetsel had been paying off a county employee. He was going to be in deep shit, I thought.

I must have smiled because Gann said, "If you think Wetsel's gonna get caught with his hand in the cookie jar on this deal, you're wrong. He put everything in his wife's name. He'll claim he didn't know a thing about any of it."

The hell of it was that Gann might be right. Nobody would believe Wetsel if he denied knowledge of the deals, but proof was what mattered, not what people believed. Maybe Wetsel would be a man about it and not let his wife take the fall for him. Or maybe she'd rat him out.

"Have the other Hershey," I told Gann.

"I'd rather have some of the cheese crackers."

"Knock yourself out."

While Gann ate the crackers, putting a whole one in his

mouth each time and getting little orange crumbs all over everything, I thought about the case against Wetsel. It wasn't great, but it would cause him some aggravation at the very least. That was better than nothing.

"Am I still a suspect in the Parker murders?" Gann said, spewing crumbs before wiping his mouth with the back of his hand.

"Yeah. You have a motive, and I'm not convinced that your alibi's any good. It'll have to be checked out when you get ready to name a name for me. And you had a visitor after I left yesterday."

"A visitor? I don't remember anybody."

"The hell you don't, Gann. Why do you want to fuck with me? They keep records here, and I can read."

"Okay, okay. So somebody came by. That fucking Stanford Parker. The son of a bitch has a lot of nerve. He said he wanted the money I owed his grandmother."

"What did you tell him?"

"I said that in the first place, it was illegal money, and in the second place nobody could prove I had it."

Gann was a real credit to his profession, no doubt about it.

"The money was the only reason he came by," Gann said. "And that's the truth."

"Kind of hard to prove, though," I said, even though it tallied with what the trusty had told Ray Thompson.

"There must be some way I could convince you."

I told him that I couldn't think of one.

"Hey, would I have hired Clive Watson to investigate the murders if I'd been guilty?"

"Maybe. You could have thought you could use hiring him as an alibi. Just like you're trying to do right now. So that doesn't mean a thing to me."

He thought about that for a minute, then said, "Maybe I

could take a lie detector test."

"It wouldn't be admissible in court," I said.

"Hell, I know that. I'm a lawyer, remember?"

"I remember," I said, though I kept thinking that the state of Texas had some pretty lax standards if Gann could pass the bar exam.

"Anyway, I don't care about the court. Would it convince you?"

"It might. If I can pick the person who administers the test."

Some people don't put much faith in polygraph tests, but I happen to believe in them as an assist in interrogations. If they're done right, that is.

"I don't have anything to hide," Gann said. "I'll take the test if it'll convince you I'm innocent."

"No test in the world would convince me of that," I said.

Gann didn't laugh. He didn't even smile.

"I meant about the murders," he said.

"Okay. If you pass the test, I'll assume you had nothing to do with the killings. But if you don't, I'm gonna be all over you like white on rice."

"You already think I'm a suspect, so what do I have to lose by taking the test?"

"Not a thing."

"Then I'll do it," Gann said.

I went back to HPD and showed the notarized statement to Bolce. He read it quickly, and his eyes widened. Then he read it again, more slowly.

"Goddamn," he said finally, laying the paper on his desk. "What was Wetsel thinking about? Has the son of a bitch lost his mind? I had no idea he was buying and selling real estate. If he's really been paying off a county attorney to get first shot at good deals, the way you tell me, that constitutes commercial bribery. I.A.'s gonna nail his ass to the wall."

Couldn't happen to a nicer guy, I thought.

"It's all in his wife's name," I said. "He'll claim he didn't know squat about it."

"We'll see," Bolce said. He picked up the statement and waved it at me. "What else do you have?"

"Gann's willing to take a polygraph test on the Parker murders. I think we should let him."

"Good idea. I'll set it up. Who do you want to administer it?"

"How about Mary Barclay? She's the best in town."

She was also Clive Watson's daughter. She had her own office, but she did contract work for the city as well as the county. She was married to a Houston cop, and she knew what she was doing when it came to giving a lie detector test.

There are two kinds of polygraph examiners. One kind is just a paper roller. He'll tell you whether a suspect is lying or not, but that's it. The other kind of examiner will do the interrogation and will try to get to the bottom of the case for you. Mary was the second kind.

"Why don't you give Clive a call," Bolce said. "See if Mary can run a polygraph exam for us in a real hurry, without an appointment."

I said I would and went to my own office to use the telephone.

Clive was feeling cranky.

When I asked how he was doing, he said, "How do you think I'm doing? Hell, I'm eighty years old. I've got all kinds of aches and pains, I have heart problems, and I have bad stomachaches."

"Hang on," I said. "Back up. What's this about heart problems? I thought your friend Tony was the one with heart problems."

"Tony's better off than I am. They did that heart cath on

him, and he's going to be fine. Probably go home in a day or two. He'll miss that good hospital food, though."

I said I was glad to hear that Tony was okay. "But what about you?"

"It's Anna. I miss her, and it hurts my heart."

I felt sorry for him, but I didn't want him to get started on that. "She's in a better place now," I said. "You just have to believe that."

"I do believe it."

"Good. Now listen, Clive, I need a favor."

That perked him right up. He likes for people to ask him for help, because he knows he can usually do something for them. And he enjoys that.

"You name it," he said.

"Okay. I need to get a polygraph run on a suspect in the Parker case. It's a rush job, and if you could persuade Mary to do it, it would be a big help. It has to be her. I don't trust anybody else."

"Consider it a done deal," Clive said. "I'll get in touch with her and call you back. Who's the suspect?"

"Elmer Gann."

"That hot-check–writing son of a bitch."

"And worse," I said. "Did you ever file on him?"

"No. But I think I will. I'm not going to let him get away with giving me a hot check."

"I don't blame you. Why don't you call the constable as soon as we get off the phone and file charges. That way he won't be bonding out before I get to him."

"You got it."

"Good. I want to be sure he's not lying about the murders, and I think the polygraph will help a lot."

"Speaking of those murders," Clive said. "I got a call from

Gene today. He's completely changed his opinion of Stanford Parker. He says Parker's crazier than a shit-house rat."

"Well, well, well," I said.

CHAPTER 27

What had changed Gene Moore's opinion of Stanford Parker was a ride they'd taken a couple of nights previously. Gene had thought it sounded like a romantic idea. They'd gone in Stanford's car, but Stanford had asked Gene to drive. They'd gone only a few blocks when Stanford pulled a 9mm automatic from under the front seat. He'd then proceeded to screw a silencer into the barrel.

When Gene asked what the hell was going on, Stanford had said, "Just keep driving. We'll have us a little fun."

"And you'll never guess what he did then," Clive said.

"No," I said. "I won't. I don't like guessing. Why don't you just tell me."

"You take a lot of the fun out of it."

"It's not supposed to be fun."

"I'm an old man," Clive said. "I take my fun where I can find it."

"I'm still not guessing."

"All right, then, dammit. What happened was that Parker started shooting at everything that moved. I don't mean people. We're talking animals. He shot at a squirrel and a cat, but he missed. He shot at a little black and white dog that was sleeping by the front door of a house. He hit that one. Killed it dead as a doornail, and laughed about it. Gene said it freaked him out, and he's never going to see Parker again."

"I can't say that I blame him, if he's telling the truth. Parker's got to be crazy."

"Gene's never given me bad information before. And I could tell he was scared. He was thinking about moving in with Parker, but now he says he doesn't feel comfortable even living in the same town with him."

I wondered if Wetsel had been right about Parker all along. It would be galling if he had, but even if he was right, we still had to prove it, and so far the evidence wasn't there. Neither was the motive. As far as I was concerned, the one with the best motive was still Elmer Gann, and so far he hadn't provided me with the name of the woman who was supposed to be his alibi. I was hoping the polygraph test would help me decide about him.

"Gann's seen Parker, too," I said, and I went on to tell Clive about Stanford's asking Gann for the money that Gann had collected for Dorothy Winetroub Parker.

"You're making some progress," Clive said. "Even if you don't know what it all means, you're collecting some good information. It's bound to add up sooner or later."

"I'm hoping for sooner," I said.

"Me too," Clive said, and then he got started again on how much he missed Anna.

"There's one thing that's really bothering me lately," he said. "You know how bad off I've been?"

I said that it was pretty obvious.

"Well, I'm afraid I'm not really grieving for her. What if I'm not feeling grief for her after all? What if I'm just feeling sorry for myself because I don't have her?"

I told him that he was getting too philosophical for me, though of course I knew exactly what he meant. When Sarah had left me, I didn't feel sorry for her at all. I felt sorry for me, because I didn't think I could get along without her. As it turned out, I could, but it wasn't a good way to live, and I didn't want it to continue. Now I was feeling guilty because I had Sarah back, even if she was slightly impaired, while Clive was never going to see Anna again.

"I do know that you should try not to feel sorry for yourself," I said, thinking that I was a fine one to be giving that advice. "Self-pity's not exactly healthy."

"I'm trying to do better. Do you think I'm succeeding?"

I wasn't so sure, but I told him that he was doing much better. Then I changed the subject.

"Don't forget to call Mary and set things up for me," I said.

"I might be feeling sorry for myself," Clive said, "and I might have a lot of aches and pains, but I can still remember stuff."

"I'm sorry if I insulted you."

"Like hell you are. But don't worry. I'll call Mary and let you know what she says."

I sat in my squeaky chair, thinking about Clive and what he'd said. If Parker was crazy enough to go around shooting animals on the street, he was certainly crazy enough to kill his parents.

While I was mulling that over, Bolce called me and told me to come to his office.

As soon as I walked in, he said, "Internal Affairs wants to talk to Gann."

"Not now," I said. "I want him to take the polygraph test before they get to him. He has enough on his mind."

Bolce nodded. "You're right. I'll put them off. But you need to get that test run as soon as possible."

I told him that Clive was getting it set up for us and went back to my office. The office set-up is like this: there's a corner office for the Captain, and on each side of him there are offices for the Lieutenants. Each detective has a little cubbyhole with a telephone, typewriter, and built-in desk. The cubbyhole has floor to ceiling partitions on three sides, but one side is open.

There's a bullpen office out in the middle of all that, with telephones, directories, key maps, and such. In other words, privacy isn't much of a consideration, not that I mind, as long as Wetsel isn't around.

But it was hard not to compare my space to the set-up that J.C. had at the constable's office or that Clive had at his place. I was sure that if I'd take Clive up on his offer to work for him, he'd give me a whole room of that house, with big windows and a view of the yard, the pine trees, the birds, and the squirrels.

I put all that out of my mind. I was going to stay where I was for the time being. I liked the work, and I thought I might even be helping the city of Houston. So I started working on my latest report. I spend at least as much time writing reports as I do investigating, which is too bad, but there's nothing I can do about it. It would probably be the same, no matter who I was working for.

While I was plugging along, the phone rang. It was J.C., who was calling to tell me that I didn't need to worry about Gann going anywhere for a while.

"Your friend Clive Watson filed hot-check charges on him this morning," J.C. said.

I didn't bother to pretend that I was surprised. "I had a feeling he might do that," I said. "And I'm glad he did. I'm setting up a polygraph test for Gann, and I need him where I can find him."

"I don't think that'll be a problem," J.C. said.

I hung up and turned to the typewriter, but before I could even get my fingers on the keys, the Captain called me to his office.

"Have you written your report on Wetsel's real estate activities?" he asked.

He'd been with the department a long time, but he looked younger than a lot of the short-timers. He had dark hair, clear brown eyes, and the kind of smooth pink skin that never seemed to age, no matter how much he drank and smoked, not that I knew anything about the drinking part. The smoking, however, was obvious. He had a Marlboro between his fingers while he talked to me.

"I haven't gotten to the part of the report about Wetsel," I said. "To tell the truth, I wasn't sure how much of that stuff to put in. We don't know yet that it's true."

"I want you to put in every bit of it," he said. "I've looked at that statement you got from Elmer Gann, and it's damning. I've already put Wetsel on suspension. He's tainted as far as I'm concerned, and he's staying away from here until we see where all this leads."

"Yes, sir," I said.

"Make the report as complete as possible," he said. And then, just to be sure I got the point, he added, "Everything that's in Gann's statement should be in your report."

"You can count on it," I told him.

And he could. I put everything in. Just the straight facts, no opinions. But even that was bad enough, if you were Wetsel.

I tried to feel sorry for him, but it didn't work. He'd known what he was doing, and he'd been a cop for far too long to have any doubt of what the consequences would be if he got caught. He'd tried to cover himself, but not very hard. He probably thought nobody would ever find out about his little deals with the county attorney. Too bad for him that things hadn't worked out.

I finished the report about four forty-five. I could have called Clive to see if he'd set up anything with Mary, but I decided I'd go home instead. I thought that Sarah would probably be glad to see me.

And she was. She wanted to go out to dinner again, but who was I to argue. As long as she was home, I didn't care if we ate

out every night.

"Chinese?" she said.

"There's a new place called Shanghai River," I said. "Want to try it?"

"Let's go," she said, so we did.

CHAPTER 28

It was threatening rain again the next day. The sky was dark and a fine mist hung in the air. Before I left the house, I turned on all the lights and set the radio on KNUZ, which I figured was the most cheerful station on the dial. I wanted Sarah to have as much light and happiness as I could provide even though I wouldn't be there to share them.

At the office I brushed moisture off my clothes and checked to see if I had any messages. Sure enough, Clive had called.

I dialed his number and asked what was going on.

"I talked to Mary," he said. "She can run the test on Gann at one-thirty today at her office. Is that time all right with you?"

I told him that it was and said that I was eager to see the results.

"I'll have to go to the county jail and get him," I said. "And I'll have to check him back in when we're finished. That's going to take the whole afternoon."

"Are you complaining?"

"Nope. Just making a comment."

"Well, you're right about it, anyway. You need to get there a few minutes early to brief Mary on what you want from her."

"What I'm hoping is that she'll get a confession from Gann," I said.

"If anybody can do it, Mary can. That's assuming he's guilty, of course."

"Right. And I'm not sure that he is."

"Mary can help you make up your mind."

"I know. That's why I want her doing the test."

"If he's guilty, it'll make my job easier, too," Clive said.

"Your job? What the hell job is that? Have I missed something somewhere along the line?"

"You haven't missed anything. I haven't told you yet."

"Maybe you'd better."

"I was just waiting for the chance. I got a call from Amy Parker late yesterday afternoon. She asked about retaining me to look into the murders. I gave her a price and this morning she's transferring the fee from her bank to my bank. So I'm hired on the case."

Sometimes I think Clive gets so many clients because he's lucky. But I know that's not really the reason. It's because he gets so much publicity, and he gets the publicity because he's good. Not that I'd ever tell him that.

"What's the matter?" I said. "Doesn't she think the police can handle things?"

"Well, now that you mention it, she's not so sure. You want to know why?"

"I already know why."

"Then do you want to tell me?"

"Because the cop we sent out to New Mexico to interview her was an asshole."

"You really are good, Steve. She didn't use quite those words, but you're close enough. Are you sure you don't want to come to work for me? You could start today."

"You know the answer to that. I'll call you after we run the polygraph and let you know the result."

I knew Mary would never call him about it unless I told her she could. They kept their businesses separate, and she believes in confidentiality, which is another reason I like to use her to do any polygraph that I need.

"Thanks," Clive said. "You know I wouldn't ask her. I wouldn't want to put her on that kind of a spot."

"That's what I figured," I said.

When I got to the jail, Gann had changed his mind.

"I don't think I want to do it," he said. "I've heard bad things about lie detector tests. I'm sure I'd never let one of my clients take one."

If you had any clients, I thought. But I said, "You don't have to worry. I've lined up the best operator in the state, probably in the country."

"Who's that?"

"Her name's Mary Barclay," I said, hoping he wouldn't know that she was Clive's daughter. He wouldn't take kindly to being tested by a relative of the man who'd just filed hot-check charges on him.

Evidently he didn't know. He said, "I've never heard of her."

"No reason you should have. But there's nobody better. You can take my word for it. And remember, you don't have anything to lose. I'm already about halfway sure you're guilty, and if you turn the test down, I'll be a hundred percent convinced. Even if you fail, you won't be any worse off than you already are."

"You've got me between a rock and a hard place."

I didn't say anything.

Gann looked at me. "Did you bring any more of that candy?"

"As a matter of fact, I did. But it's in the car. I figured you could eat it on the way."

"Damn," Gann said.

I shrugged.

After what seemed like a long time, Gann said, "What the hell. I'll do it."

Mary Barclay's business was located in a strip mall where she

rented five office spaces. One of the rooms appeared to have nothing in it other than a desk, a polygraph machine, and two chairs. The walls were bare, so that there was nothing to distract the person who was being tested. However, hidden in the light fixture were a camera and a tiny microphone.

The office next door had been converted into an observation room outfitted with a TV screen, a tape recorder, and three stools.

The rest of the offices consisted of a waiting room, a coffee bar, and two private offices. In the waiting room were a couch, two chairs, and a desk for the short blonde secretary, who greeted us when we came in about fifteen minutes after one o'clock.

I told her who we were, and she buzzed Mary, who had us sent right to her office. I introduced Gann and told her that he was a little reluctant to take the test.

"So maybe you could put him at his ease," I said.

"Certainly. Here's the way it works, Mr. Gann. First I'll run a chart to see if you have good responses. We call it a stim test. That's short for stimulation. I'll ask you to write the number two or three on a piece of paper with your left hand, and then I'll have you lie to me about it."

"Why would I lie?" Gann asked.

"To see if the machine's functioning properly and to see how you're stimulated. I'll show you the chart, and you'll see how the reaction to the test shows on it. That will let you know that the test works and that you can just relax and go with it."

"What if it doesn't work?"

"Then I'll turn you back over to Sergeant Stephens, and you can go."

Gann still didn't look too happy, but he said he supposed he might as well go through with it. Mary took him to the testing room, and while she was gone, I looked around her office. The walls were as bare as the ones in the room where Gann would be, except for a single crucifix.

I pointed to it when she came back in and said, "You and Clive are a lot alike."

"We're both believers, if that's what you mean," she said. "He's gotten a lot more interested in theology since my mother died."

"I noticed that when I was talking to him yesterday. He sounded like he'd been reading philosophy."

"He reads a lot, but not philosophy. He's been talking to Ben Hall, who's a black minister, and to a couple of priests. Father Frank Rossi's one of them. I think the other one's name is Father Don Schoel."

I didn't know either of them. I said, "Have they helped?"

"I think so. For a while there, I was afraid my father was going to die, too, just out of grief. But he's better now, I think."

I told her I thought so too. Then I asked about Gann. "Is it safe to leave him alone in the testing room?"

"The door locks from the outside when it closes, and I have the only key. So he's not going anywhere. Why don't you tell me what you're trying to find out from him."

I outlined the bare bones of the case for her and said, "I just want to find out if he had anything to do with the murders, and I'd like to know if he's telling the truth about Wetsel's real estate deals."

"I can probably help with those two things. If you want to watch the test and listen in, you can sit in the observation room. You know where the coffee is, so help yourself."

I didn't feel any need to watch the test. I'd seen Mary give more than one of them, and there was nothing I could learn by watching that she wouldn't be able to tell me herself.

I went to the coffee bar and poured myself a cup from the

big pot that was always on. Then I found a fairly recent *Time* magazine that I hadn't read and sat down to wait.

I plowed through several articles on the war in Vietnam, which wasn't going well at all and was beginning to look endless. I thought about my own war, which in some ways seemed like a century or so ago, and about how different it had been. My leg started hurting, so I got up and walked around for a minute. When I sat back down, I turned to the movie reviews and read them instead of the news.

I drank far too much coffee, read three other issues of *Time*, two *Newsweek*s, and every page in that day's *Houston Chronicle* before Mary came in and said, "Would you like to know what I found out?"

"You know I would," I said.

Mary nodded. "I thought you might. Come on to my office, and I'll tell you."

We moved out of the coffee bar and into her office. She closed the door and handed me a piece of paper. "Have a seat and look that over," she said.

The paper had three questions written on it:

1. Did you kill Ralph Parker, his wife, or Mrs. Dorothy Winetroub Parker?
2. Do you know who did kill them?
3. Have you told the truth about everything to the sergeant of Homicide?

"Those are the three pertinent questions that Gann and I agreed to," Mary said. "He answered No to the first question, and the chart showed that he was being truthful. He answered No to the second question, too, but the chart showed that he was lying. And the same's true of the third question. He said Yes, but the chart showed that he was lying again."

"Damn," I said. "That could mean he was lying about any

number of things. Including those real estate deals Wetsel's supposed to have made."

"I'd like to have a talk with him and run some more charts,"
Mary said. "I might be able to find out something for you."

"You're welcome to him. I'll just sit here until you get
through."

"Better go have some more coffee. It could take a while."

"Do you have anything to read besides those magazines?"

"You'll have to ask Linda."

Linda was the secretary. I said I'd check with her, and Mary
went back to work on Gann.

Linda had a copy of a paperback novel called *Airport* in her bottom desk drawer.

"Not that I read on the job," she said when she handed it to
me. "But sometimes there's really nothing to do, and I get tired
of magazines."

"I don't blame you. Is the book any good?"

"It's okay. I finished it the other day. You can take it home
with you if you get interested."

I thanked her and went back to the coffee bar. I shook the
coffee pot. It still had a cup or two left, but I decided against
drinking any. I sat down and started reading the book. Pretty
soon I was more worried about a Chicago airport locked in by a
blizzard, a mad bomber on an airplane, and lots of other things
than about Elmer Gann. When Mary came to get me, I sort of
wished I could just keep on reading rather than stop and deal
with real life.

I closed the book reluctantly and went into Mary's office.

"Here's what we have," she said. "Gann was telling you the
truth about Wetsel. So that part of your case is solid. The bad
news is he claims that he thinks he may know who killed the
Parkers but isn't sure."

"But it wasn't him."

"No. That part's conclusive as far as I'm concerned. Where the lie comes in is that he doesn't just think he knows who killed the Parkers. He does know. Or at least that's what the charts tell me."

"So where do we go from here?"

"I'd like to run some more charts, with just two questions."

She wrote them down on a piece of paper for me:

1. Do you think you know who killed the Parkers?
2. Do you know who killed the Parkers?

"It's kind of a fine line," I said. "But you might as well try it. If you don't mind, I'll just wait right here."

She said that was fine, and I opened the book as soon as she left the room.

This time she came back more quickly.

"According to the charts I've run," she said, "he's not being truthful about the murders. He knows who killed them, or believes he does, but he says he only *thinks* he knows. We can safely say that he didn't kill the Parkers. I think he's told you the truth about Wetsel, too, but he's lying about everything else."

I thought back to what Gann had told me in the jail, that Stanford Parker had committed the murders. But Parker had an alibi. Not that I believed it. "Did he have anything else to say?"

"Just that he wants to get out of here and go back to jail."

"Well, I can sure accommodate him on that request," I told her.

Gann refused to talk to me on the ride back to the jail, even when I asked him if he'd like for me to stop and buy him a candy bar or some cheese crackers.

The next day Bolce called me to his office to tell me I was off the case.

"I'm putting you back in the rotation," he said. "We're not getting anywhere on this one, and the papers have plenty of other stuff to write about, what with the war and the moon walk."

"If this one goes cold, we might never solve it," I said. "I'd like to keep on with it."

"I'd like that, too," Bolce said, "but it's just not in the cards. We have too many cases for you to spend any more time on this one. I have two that you can start on tomorrow."

"Maybe I could break Stanford Parker's alibi," I said.

"The Jackson girl has disappeared. McGuire's been looking for her, and he can't find her. Her mother claims not to know where she is."

It figured. All we were left with was her statement exonerating Stanford Parker.

There was no need to argue with Bolce about my reassignment. It wouldn't do any good, and it would just make Bolce angry.

So I laid the Parker case down, even though I knew I wouldn't stop thinking about it for a long time to come.

Chapter 29

A month went by. In Houston, in the summer, a month can seem like quite a while. The hot, muggy days drag on, and the sun goes down late. The heat and humidity linger long after the nightfall. In fact, they never go away, and the middle of the night is often as hot as many places are during the day. The absence of the sun helps a little, but sometimes even that doesn't mean it's comfortable.

Things between me and Sarah continued to improve. There was one bad stretch of about a week when she started acting suspicious of me again, and I found out that she'd stopped taking her medication.

"I was so much better," she said. "I thought I didn't need it anymore."

Of course she was better because of the medication. I got her to Dr. Coffee, and they worked things out. She'd done fine ever since, and so had I.

I worked on my assigned cases, all of them simple enough to solve within a couple of days. Nothing nearly as interesting as the Parker case came along, and whenever there was a lull, I'd get out my reports and read them again.

As much as I hated to admit it, all my work had uncovered nothing conclusive.

I knew that Elmer Gann wasn't the killer but that he was lying to me about something. Unfortunately, I didn't know what it was.

213

I couldn't come up with a motive for the murder that would tie anyone to them. The most likely killer was clearly Stanford Parker, though I didn't want to admit it, mainly because that had been Wetsel's theory from the beginning. And besides, Parker had an alibi. It wasn't much of one, and the person who'd given it to him had disappeared. But it was an alibi, nevertheless.

As for Wetsel, he was still on suspension, but things weren't going at all well for him. I had a feeling he'd be off the force for good as soon as the Internal Affairs investigation was completed.

At least, I thought, some good would come of my investigation even if the Parker case was never solved, as I was beginning to think was likely.

And then one day I got a call from Clive Watson.

"Steve," he said, sounding unreasonably pleased with himself, "I have something new on the Parker murders."

"Is it good enough to get Bolce to make it active again?"

"You're damned right. You remember Stanford Parker's girlfriend?"

"Emily Jackson," I said, thinking of the frail young woman with the dirty blonde hair. "Parker's alibi. She disappeared. McGuire looked for her, but he couldn't find her."

"Maybe he couldn't," Clive said. "But I did. She O.D.'ed on drugs at Parker's house more than a month ago, just before you got taken off the case."

"So she's dead?"

"Did I say she was dead? Gene Moore got to her in time to save her life."

"I thought he was staying away from Parker."

"He was. That's why he found her. He'd left some of his clothes at Parker's house. He still had a key, so he went by one day when he thought Parker would be gone. He found the Jackson girl lying on the floor, about half dead. He managed to get her to the E.R. at St. Joseph's Hospital in time for them to save her."

"I'm glad he did," I said. "But how does that help the case?"

"I'm coming to that," Clive said. One thing about Clive, he knew when he had a good story, and he always told it his way. "She was in a coma for a while, and when she came out if it, she claimed she'd had a vision of the Blessed Virgin. She's going to become a nun."

"Clive, you're as full of shit as Tony Antonelli. What you need is one of those ice-water enemas. How is Tony, by the way?"

"He's fully recovered and back at work, if the Texas Rangers haven't nabbed him by now. But you've hurt my feelings, Steve. I ought not to tell you the rest of what I know."

"You mean you weren't putting me on? Emily Jackson is going to become a nun?"

"A Dominican sister. She's talked to the Mother Superior and taken the name Teresa."

We live in a strange world. About the last thing I would have expected was that Emily Jackson would enter a convent. But if you were going to disappear, a convent was as good a way as any and better than most.

"She also confessed to a priest," Clive continued, "and evidently she had a lot to say. He told her that she should go to the police with what she knew. She didn't want to do that, but she asked the Mother Superior if she could talk to Gene Moore, since he'd saved her life. So Gene went to see her."

"And then he came to see you," I said.

"You're damned right he did. After all, he works for me from time to time, and he knew the information would be valuable to me."

I had a feeling that we were getting to the part of the story that I wanted to hear. "So what did he tell you?"

"Plenty. He's sitting right here in the office, though, if you want to hear it for yourself. Can you come out here?"

"That's my car door you hear slamming out front," I said.

Moore was still a flashy dresser. He had on flared slacks with a wild pattern in green and brown, his Beatle boots, and a bright yellow shirt. He and Clive were, of course, smoking up a storm.

We said our hellos, and Clive asked Moore to tell his story. It was a good one, even better than I'd hoped.

Emily Jackson, or Sister Teresa as she now called herself, had been with Stanford Parker on the night his family had been killed, just as she'd said. But at that point the story took a new turn.

"She was stoned out of her gourd," Moore said, blowing a big plume of smoke. "But she remembers that she went with Stan to the Parker house in his car."

I sat forward on my chair. This was what I'd been waiting to hear: something that put Stanford Parker at the crime scene on the night of the murders.

"She was lying down in the back seat," Gene said. "She was pretty much out of it, I think, but she says she heard shots being fired. She was so zonked that she didn't know what that might mean."

"That's not going to help much," I said.

"Oh, it gets better," Gene said. "Earlier that day, she'd gone to the house with Stan, who told her that he wanted her to unlock the bedroom window while he kept his father occupied. He was planning to come back that night and rob his grandmother."

"Did she do it?"

"She says she did."

Here was the motive we'd been looking for. "Did the grandmother keep money in the house?"

"Stan told her that a lawyer named Elmer Gann had told

him that his grandmother had collected a big gambling debt. Gann knew about it because she'd asked him to collect it, along with some others, but this one gambler had paid the money directly to her. Gann was chapped, since he'd managed to cheat her out of a pretty good sum already, and he'd thought he could get more. Stan was supposed to give him a cut in payment for the information." Gene exhaled smoke. "And you're going to like this part a lot. Elmer Gann was there when the murders happened. He'd followed them to the house in his car to wait for his cut of the money."

More good news. If I could get both Gann and Emily Jackson to swear to all this, then Stanford Parker was as good as indicted.

And it also explained the problems with the polygraph test. Gann had been telling the truth to me at the jail, then lying about it to Mary Barclay.

"Do you think Gann knows what happened in the house?" I said.

"He must know," Gene said. "Emily says that Stan came running to the car yelling, 'Oh, shit! Oh, shit!' That's all she remembers. But the next day, when she asked him what had happened, he said that his father had sat up in the bed and he'd shot him. His mother woke up, and he shot her, too. Then he ran down to get the money from his grandmother's room, but she was awake, and he shot her. All three of them, just like that. He said he didn't have any choice."

"But he took the time to wipe the place down," I said. "And to pick up his brass."

"He's a cold-blooded son of a bitch," Gene said. "Did Clive tell you about the animals?"

I nodded.

"Then you know. I don't doubt that he wiped the place down. He also told Emily that if she ever breathed a word of what he'd said, he'd kill her, too. She believed him. I know I would have, in her place."

I was thinking about how I was going to handle all this when Clive spoke up, saying that he'd sent his son, Tom, to the convent to take a statement from Emily. Tom had worked for the agency for a while, and he was a good investigator, with good instincts. Still, I had to ask if he'd gotten what he wanted.

Clive gave me a how could you doubt it look and said, "He not only got the statement, but it was witnessed by the Mother Superior."

"Well," I said, "that ought to hold up. Did he find out anything that Gene here didn't?"

"He asked her about the gun Parker used. She said it was a dark-colored automatic, almost black. She didn't know anything about make or caliber, but she said Parker keeps it in his top dresser drawer."

"Is that the same gun he shot the animals with?" I asked Gene.

"Sure sounds like it. I never checked to see where he kept it. As soon as I knew he had it, I split the scene."

"According to Tom," Clive said, "the nuns don't know quite what to think of Emily. She's taking instruction in the Catholic faith, and she says she's determined to give her life to God. Tom believes she's sincere."

"Do you think I could talk to her?" I said.

"I'll have to find out if she'll talk to you. She didn't want to go to the police herself. She just wanted to make sure they got the information."

"She's going to have to see me or somebody from the police sooner or later. I'd prefer that it be me. And sooner."

"I'll call the convent and see what arrangements I can make," Clive said. "How soon?"

"I'll have to talk to Bolce and get him to assign my current cases to somebody else. But he'll do it. This will break the Par-ker case for sure. So I'll be ready anytime after I talk to him."

"Do you need me anymore?" Gene asked, and Clive told him he could go.

We shook hands before he left, and I thanked him for getting in touch with Clive with the information.

"Hell, if I hadn't, and he'd found out about this, he'd have skinned me alive."

We both laughed. So did Clive, mainly because he knew it was the truth.

After Gene left, Clive asked me about the case against Gann and Wetsel.

"The D.A.'s working on it. Gann never gave me the name of the county lawyer who was slipping him the information, but the D.A.'s investigator ferreted it out. Now the grand jury's looking into the whole thing. Gann's already been subpoenaed. He's still in jail, as a matter of fact. He pled guilty on the hot-check charges, and he'll have to serve nine months."

"And make restitution," Clive said. "Not that I'm counting on ever seeing my money."

I'd forgotten that he was part of the hot-check case and would know about Gann's current situation.

"He might get indicted on the Wetsel case, too," I said. "They got all the paperwork on every house Wetsel bought, and it looks like Wetsel was making more money on the real estate he was buying and reselling than he was making as a cop."

"That wouldn't be hard. When are you going to see the light and come to work for me?"

"Get thee behind me," I said, and Clive laughed again.

It was the first time I'd seen him laugh so much since Anna's death. And it was the first time he hadn't mentioned her. He was definitely getting better, so I decided not to mention her, either.

"You'll call me after you talk to the Mother Superior, right?"

"I'll call," Clive said. "Trust me."

"Right," I said.

Bolce's smile was so wide I thought his face might crack in half.

"This is great news," he said when he finally stopped smiling. "And it means that you wrap up the Parker case. I'll reassign your other cases, and you can work on it exclusively until you do."

I called Clive to give him the news, and he said, "That's great. You have an appointment at the convent tomorrow morning at ten o'clock with the Mother Superior and Teresa. Don't miss it."

As if there was any chance of that.

CHAPTER 30

The Dominican sisters came to Texas in 1882 and to Houston in 1925 when they established a mother house on Almeda Road about where it crosses Holcombe, not far from the V.A. Hospital. There's a college on the grounds, and I wondered if Emily, or Teresa, would get her degree while she was there.

The Mother Superior met me at the door. She was tall, thin, and severe. She didn't smile, but she was friendly enough. She offered me coffee, which I declined, and said that she hoped my visit with Teresa would be of some help to me.

"I'm sure it will," I told her. "I'll be as gentle with her as I can."

For the fraction of a second I thought she might smile. She didn't, though. She said, "That won't be necessary. She isn't exactly fragile, as you'll see. She really feels that she had a vision of the Blessed Mother, and it's given her great inner strength. Whether she had a genuine vision or not, I can't say. But I do know that whatever happened to her has changed her life."

About that time "Teresa" walked in. She wasn't the person I expected. If I hadn't known who she was, I don't think I'd have recognized her. She was standing straight and had on a grey outfit that I think the apprentice nuns wear. Her hair was hidden by the traditional nun's covering. Her eyes were bright and shining, and she had a small smile on her face. She looked at peace with the world, completely composed and at ease.

I introduced myself and began telling her what Clive had told me about her statement. She interrupted me and said, "Sergeant, I told Tom Watson the truth about what I know. Would you like for me to repeat it for you?"

She spoke slowly, but not because she was afraid. She didn't ask if anything would happen to her, and she didn't even seem to care. She was simply self-assured. I hadn't thought of her as attractive when I met her at her home, but now she was almost beautiful in the way she carried herself and talked.

"Tell me everything you can remember that happened on the night of the Parker murders," I said. "That should do for a start."

"You have to understand that I didn't see anyone shoot the Parkers. I think that Stanford did it, and he told me that he did, but that's all. I don't have any knowledge of what happened in the house other than that. He went into the house with a gun to rob them, and I heard shots. Not long after that, he came running out of the house. Later he told me that he'd shot them but that he didn't rob them because he got worried that he'd already spent too much time there cleaning up the scene."

She went on to tell me about going over to the house with Stanford the day before the murders and about unlocking the window while Stanford distracted his father.

"What about Elmer Gann?" I asked.

"He followed Stanford and me over to the house. He was driving a Chevrolet two-door. I don't know the model. I think the shots scared him away, because I don't remember seeing the car when Stanford came out of the house."

"And you were in the car the whole time."

"Yes. I would never have had anything to do with any of it at all if it hadn't been for drugs. I'd like to believe that if I'd known Stanford was going to kill them, I'd never have gone with him. But he gave me drugs, and I couldn't resist them. I don't mean to excuse myself, though. Whatever happens to me is God's will, and I'm ready to accept it."

She smiled at me and looked at the Mother Superior. The Mother Superior told her to please sit down as she'd been standing the entire time she had been talking to me.

"Thank you, Mother," she said, "but I have to finish helping Sister Catherine bake bread."

She looked again at me and said, "If that's all, Sergeant, I'll be in the kitchen. Unless you have to arrest me."

I opened my mouth, and for a second the words wouldn't come out. There was something about her that was almost mystical. I could barely believe that at one time she'd been Emily Jackson because she wasn't, not anymore.

"I'm not going to arrest you," I said when I could talk. "But I do have one more question. Do you know a Detective named Wetsel?"

She shook her head, and I thanked her for talking to me. The Mother Superior looked at me as Teresa left the room. I didn't know what to say. The Emily Jackson I'd met no longer existed. The girl who'd once been so desperate that she'd traded sex for drugs was now calm, unworried, at peace with the world.

As I was leaving the room, the Mother Superior asked me what I thought would happen to Teresa.

"I don't think anything will happen to her," I said. "She's a completely changed person."

"That's true. She almost died from the overdose. She came out of the coma totally different. Whatever happened to her during that time, it was very real to her."

"I can see that," I said, and I thought about it all the way back downtown.

When I wrote up my reports that day, I referred to Teresa only as a confidential informant. I didn't mention her name at all.

Bolce looked in while I was working, so I told him the whole story. The only question he had wasn't about the murders. It was about Teresa. He said, "Steve, do you really think she has found God?"

"Something happened to her, that's for sure. And whatever it was, it was for the good. I have to admit that I was impressed with her."

Bolce just shook his head, walked off, then stopped and turned around. He said, "Go to the D.A. and see if you have enough for a warrant. Then check Missing Persons to see if anyone is trying to locate your C.I. It could be that Parker or her mother might be looking for her. Or do you think they know where she is?"

"If they do, they didn't tell McGuire."

Bolce shook his head. "That doesn't mean anything. Nobody trusts the cops anymore. They call us pigs. It's a damned shame."

I finished the reports and called Clive.

"Did Gene Moore tell anybody about Emily Jackson?" I asked.

"You mean anybody but me, you, and Tom?"

He was just being a smart-ass, so I didn't bother to answer. After a couple of seconds of silence, Clive said, "Gene found her and took her to the hospital. Nobody was at the house except her. Gene didn't tell Stanford or her mother where she was. I don't think he even told them what had happened to her."

"Good. I don't think they need to know."

"There's something you need to know, though."

"And I'll bet you're just the guy who'll tell me."

"That's right. Gene Moore called me this morning while you were at the convent. Stanford Parker got in touch with him and asked him to go to dinner tonight."

"I hope you told him to accept."

"I still have a client who's paying for things," Clive said. "Of course I told him to accept. And I told him to suggest that it might be fun to drive around and shoot a few squirrels."

"Why the hell did you do that?"

"Well," Clive said, "that's where you come in."

I might have sighed, but I don't think I did. "What sort of scheme do you have cooked up, Clive?"

"I'm going to get Moore's written permission to put a tracer on his car. That way we'll know where they are. When they get to the restaurant, Moore will tell Parker that he has to call his boss. He won't mention that I'm his boss, and he'll let me know if Parker has his pistol with him."

"And my part is?"

"You'll come to my office at five tomorrow and bring along a couple of uniformed officers with you. If Parker has the pistol, they can stop the car when they start cruising for squirrels and arrest him."

"And Moore, most likely," I said.

"Yeah, but you'll make sure Moore's released when he gets to the station."

"Sounds like a plan to me," I said.

After Clive and I chatted for a while, I hung up. He hadn't gotten weepy, and he hadn't mentioned Anna. I was glad the old guy was finally recovering. Maybe talking with the priests and the minister had helped.

I called Missing Persons to see if anyone was interested in finding Emily Jackson. The answer was no. It seemed as though nobody cared enough about her to look for her.

Evidently God had found her, however.

I finished my reports and was feeling pretty good about things. But the good feeling completely disappeared when I looked up and saw two detectives from Internal Affairs standing in front of my desk.

CHAPTER 31

One of the detectives was Raul Perez. He was short, compact, and handsome, with black eyes, black hair, and a black moustache.

The other detective was taller, an Anglo with short cropped hair so blond that it was nearly white. I could see his pink scalp. I didn't know his name, and he didn't say.

There was hardly room for both of them in my little office, but they didn't seem to mind. Perez sat in the only chair I had for visitors. The Anglo leaned against the wall, got out a toothpick, and inserted it in his mouth between his teeth.

"What can I do for you fellas," I said.

Most cops aren't overly fond of the guys who work in Internal Affairs, and I'm no exception. It seems to me that they're suspicious of everyone. Maybe their job makes them that way. I know I wouldn't want to do what they did, so I was determined to be pleasant to them if I could.

"How long have you known Lou Wetsel?" Perez asked.

He leaned back in the chair and crossed his legs with his ankle on his knee. He shook out his pants leg with one hand so the crease would fall right.

"Ever since he came to Homicide," I said. "We work together some. We don't hang out, though. He goes to cop bars. I don't."

"What about Elmer Gann?"

If I wanted to be a smart-ass, I'd have pretended I didn't

know what he meant. But I was going to cooperate if it killed me.

"I met him in the course of an investigation," I said. "He was a suspect in a murder case I was working. Before that I'd never heard of him."

"Do you know how Wetsel met him?"

I shook my head. "No idea."

"But you talked to him about Wetsel, right?"

"Sure. He gave me some information."

"What kind of information?"

Perez was starting to piss me off. I said, "It's all in my report, which I'm sure you've read. I put every single thing I know in that report."

"We don't want to mess up your homicide case. Would it be all right with you if we talked to Gann?"

That was better. Perez was being polite. His partner was doing nothing at all, aside from chewing on his toothpick. Maybe he'd recently quit smoking.

"Talk to Gann all you want to," I said. "It won't hurt my case."

Perez tapped his fingers on his leg. "You know, Steve, I've heard that you don't get along well with your fellow officers. Why is that, I wonder? Do you think you're better than they are?"

That question had absolutely nothing to do with his investigation. So I decided I didn't have to be pleasant anymore. I stood up and said, "I'm out of here. You guys do what you have to do. You have any more questions for me, go through my Lieutenant."

The tall Anglo detective looked at me. He took the toothpick out of his mouth and smiled. But he didn't say a thing.

"You have a bad attitude, Steve," Perez said. "We can always haul you before a grand jury, put you under oath and ask our questions."

"Do it, then. But until you get me in front of the grand jury, you can kiss my ass."

I went past Perez, brushed by the Anglo, and walked out. I went straight to Bolce's office and said, "I want to talk to you and the Captain both. Right now."

Bolce got up. "Let's go, then," he said.

We went right to the Captain's office, went in, and closed the door. The Captain told us to sit down, which we both did. "What's the problem?" he said.

I told him about my visit with the two men from Internal Affairs. I said, "I didn't like Perez's questions. I think he was out of line, and I'm mad as hell about it. Do either of you think I don't get along with my fellow workers?"

The Captain smiled and said, "I've never heard anything like that. I wonder why Perez would mention it. Do you want to file a complaint against him?"

"No, but he gives me a severe case of the red ass."

Bolce laughed and said, "I don't blame you, Steve. But you shouldn't take it so hard. I think they were trying to get you upset to see what would shake out."

"Dammit, I'm not a suspect in the Wetsel case. I just gave you the facts as I got them, and they're all in my reports. What the hell more does Perez want from me?"

"That's just the way I.A. operates," the Captain said. "Bolce's right. Don't take it so hard. We know you're clean in all this. You don't have to worry about it."

I thought it over and realized that he had a point. The men in I.A. had dealt with so many crooked cops that they thought everybody was bent.

"You're right," I said. "I'm sorry I bothered both of you."

"You're a good cop, Steve," Bolce said. "And you get along

with everybody. Hell, you even get along with Wetsel."

"I wouldn't go that far," I said.

Later that afternoon I called Clive to see if the plans for that evening had been completed.

"I just got off the phone with Gene," Clive said. "It's no go. Parker claims he has the flu."

"Damn."

"Don't worry. We'll get him eventually."

"I was hoping we'd get him tonight."

"Not possible. But I have Tom running a complete background check on him. Maybe it'll turn something up."

"I doubt it," I said. "I've already done a criminal history check and come up with nothing."

"We have resources you don't have."

"I know. But I don't think you'll find anything on Parker."

"I'm also going to talk to Teresa."

"What's the matter? Don't you trust me and Tom?"

He laughed. "Okay. I get the point. Anyway, I just want to see if she has anything to add to what she's already told us."

"If she does, be sure to let me know."

"I'll give you a call."

"You'll have to call me at home. I'm leaving."

"It's a little early, isn't it?"

"I've had a bad day," I said.

The phone was ringing when I walked in the door at home. Sarah answered, and from the way she was laughing as she talked, I knew the caller must be Clive. He's one of the few people who can make her laugh like that.

Sure enough, after a couple of minutes she said, "Steve, this is for you. It's Clive."

I took the phone from her, and she gave me a kiss on the

cheek. At least things were going well at home.

"What's up, Clive?" I said into the phone.

"I'm looking into a new case," Clive said. "It involves our boy Stanford Parker."

"You're jerking my chain."

"I never kid around about a case. I got a call a little while ago from a man named Walter Jones down in Galveston County, a little town called Lake City. His wife, Melanie, disappeared about a month ago, and he thinks Parker's involved. From what little he's been able to find out from the police, Parker was the last person to see her."

That was certainly interesting information.

"How'd Jones get your name?" I asked.

"From some article in the paper. He wants me to investigate, and he's going to pay me a retainer. He says the cops didn't do squat to find his wife, and they don't even seem to care that she's missing."

I knew nothing about Lake City except that it was down near Galveston Island and that it had a population of about twelve hundred. I had a feeling that the police department wouldn't be exactly like McGarrett and the boys at Five-O.

"What was Parker doing in Galveston County?" I said.

"He was working on a roofing crew. Roofers will hire anybody that knows how to hold a hammer when they're looking for help. This was after the murders, and Parker must have needed the money."

I kept thinking we were going to get a break, but it seemed that everything fizzled out. But maybe this time things were going to work out. And if not, I had the testimony of Gann and Teresa.

"What are you going to do?" I said.

"I don't know yet, but I'll figure something out. Probably I'll send Tom down to Galveston County tomorrow. I'll keep you posted."

"You do that," I told him.

The next morning I went to the District Attorney's office and met with the D.A. in the Intake Division. He was about forty years old, with sharp eyes, a slash of a mouth, and the tenacity of a bulldog. I outlined what I had, and he looked over my reports.

"I'd like to see what Parker has to say before I issue an arrest warrant," he said. "We could go with what you have here, but we'd need testimony from both your C.I. and Elmer Gann. From what you've said in the reports, Gann doesn't seem likely to cooperate."

"I could try him again," I said, wondering if it would do any good, as Gann wasn't likely to think he owed me any favors. On the other hand, there was always the chance I could buy him with a couple of packages of cheese crackers.

I thought about mentioning Clive's Galveston case to the D.A., but I didn't. It was far from a sure thing, and it didn't have any direct bearing on the murders of the Parker family.

"I think you should give Gann a try," the D.A. said. "We can't go with just one person's word, especially the word of a confidential informant."

I started to tell him that my informant was a little bit different from the usual sort, but I thought better of it. Even if she was, Gann's testimony might prove to be the clincher.

"I'll go see him as soon as I can," I said.

Clive called not long after I got back to my office. He sounded more excited and alive than I'd heard him in months.

"Did you tell Teresa that Anna had died?" he said.

"I don't think so. Her name never came up. Yours didn't either."

"Well, she knew about Anna. She came into the Mother Superior's office, and practically the first thing she said after we were introduced was, 'I'm sorry you lost your wife, Mr. Watson.' "

"How did she know that?"

"I have no idea. And she didn't either. When I asked her, she said, 'I just know.' "

I was as amazed as Clive must have been. How could she possibly have known?

"She told me that God had taken Anna but that he'd left me here for a purpose," Clive continued. "She didn't say what the purpose was, but that it might just be so that I could ask God to forgive me of my sins."

"Would that take a lot of forgiving?"

"You're damned right," Clive said. "But I had to stop talking about it. I was afraid I'd break down and cry and embarrass myself. So I started asking her about Parker and if he was the kind of person who might abuse women. She told me that he's abused her."

"Did you get any specifics?"

"Some. It was a little embarrassing for me. I don't know why. I've heard it all."

"Maybe not from a nun," I said.

"She's not a nun yet."

"I know. What did she say?"

"She said that Parker occasionally accepted oral sex from her, but no other kind, and he didn't even seem to like what she did for him very much. One night she was addled by drugs and tried to get him aroused for straight sex. He hit her."

Clive rarely got outraged at any kind of behavior. As he said, he'd heard it all, and probably he'd heard it all two or three times. Or more. But there was outrage in his voice now.

"He knocked her down and kicked her," Clive went on. "She thought he was going to kill her. He went to get his pistol, and while he was looking for it, she managed to get up and get out of the house."

"She should never have gone back."

"Drugs," Clive said. "That's why she went back. They had a hold on her. She said she wanted to leave, but she couldn't. She always went back. She thought she could do it, once, but she didn't make it. Parker caught up with her and took her back." He paused. "She told me about killing the animals, too. She went out with him a couple of times. She felt really bad about that."

We'd already heard about the animals from Gene Watson, but Teresa's statement was at least corroboration.

"Tom's down in Lake City," Clive said. "He's going to see what he can come up with. If he finds anything, I'll send him after Parker. Maybe Tom could convince him to come to the office and talk to us."

"Parker has the flu," I said.

"Flu or no flu, he'll come in and talk to us. You know Tom."

I did know Tom. He was a damned good convincer.

"I'll let you know what happens," Clive said, and then I told him about Gann.

"He's soft. He'll talk if you work him right."

"Maybe I should get Tom to come with me."

"You don't need Tom. You'll do just fine on your own. You always do."

I thanked him for the thought, but I wasn't so sure he was right.

Chapter 32

I decided that I might as well talk to Gann as soon as possible, so I called the county jail. They put me through to Major Henslowe, who told me to come right ahead.

"Gann's not going anywhere," he said. "He still hasn't made his bond."

"And he's not likely to," I told him. "I'm on my way."

When I got to the jail, I checked my sidearm at the desk and saw that the Major was waiting for me.

"Hi, Steve," he said. "Gann's waiting for you."

"Considerate of him," I said, and the Major led me to the same room I always seemed to use when I talked to Gann.

When I came through the door, Gann looked up and said, "You again. I might have known it. Now that I'm in jail I don't hear from anyone else. Even my ex-wives won't visit me. The only person who has come to see me is you."

He didn't sound like seeing me was much of a treat, and I reminded him that he'd had another visitor.

"Stanford Parker dropped by," I said.

"Yeah. I forgot about him. The bastard. Can I smoke?"

"Go ahead," I told him, and he lit up.

"So why are you here?" he said after he'd had a deep drag.

"I have a little bad news for you, Gann. I've come to tell you that you're a suspect in the murders of the Parkers."

"You're kidding me. You know I didn't kill them."

"What I know doesn't matter. Let me read you your rights

under the Miranda decision."

"People keep doing that. I'm a lawyer. I know, already."

"Doesn't matter. The Supreme Court says I have to do it." I read off his rights and said, "We have a witness who's willing to swear that you were at the Parkers' house the night they were murdered."

"Bullshit. You don't scare me." He flicked ashes on the floor to show how much I didn't scare him. "I've already pled guilty on my hot-check charges, but that's the only thing I'm guilty of. I'm going to serve six months and get out, and you won't be able to touch me."

"Are you denying you were at the house when the Parkers were killed?"

"Listen to what I'm telling you," Gann said. "I took a polygraph test that was administered by a person of your choosing. It proved I didn't kill the Parkers. Remember?"

Typical lawyer weasel talk.

"I remember the test," I said. "Now you listen. I didn't say you killed them. I said you were there when it happened. Were you?"

"I'm not going to answer that. Screw you. I don't want to talk to you anymore."

I didn't want him to stop talking, so I changed the subject. "Let's forget about the murders for a minute. What can you tell me about Emily Jackson?"

"Parker's girlfriend? She was a real weirdo. She was supposed to go to work for him as his housekeeper. Just for a place to live and get something to eat."

"And drugs," I said.

"Well, yeah. And drugs. But I didn't have anything to do with that."

"Right," I said.

"Damn right. I know better than that. I might pass a hot

check now and then, but I don't have anything to do with drugs. Not ever. But she did. I never saw her when she wasn't stoned."

"What about sex? Did Parker have sex with her?"

"Parker's as queer as a three-dollar bill. He might have let her give him a little oral, but he probably did it just to humiliate her. He didn't like women, not one little bit. Some woman in a bar came on to him one time, and he slapped the shit out of her."

Parker was sounding more and more like a psycho. I hoped we'd be able to nail him soon.

"Once when Parker couldn't get any money for drugs, the girl tried to leave," Gann said. "He caught up with her at a church about a block from his house. She was about to go in, but he dragged her back home."

That must have been the time Clive had mentioned to me.

"Parker treated her rough," I said.

"You don't know the half of it. She didn't mean anything to him, but he thought having her around made people think he was straight. It's not easy in this town if you're not. I don't know if it worked, but she didn't get any thanks for it if it did. She was just dirt to him, and that's the way he treated her. Like dirt. The drugs gave him control of her, and he liked that. He liked that a lot."

Gann seemed to have forgotten that he didn't want to talk to me. He seemed very serious, and I thought that he was telling me the truth. Maybe something about Emily had gotten his sympathy. I thought this might be the time to try him on the big question again.

"Gann," I said, "were you at the house the night the Parkers were killed?"

"What if I was?" he said, and I knew I had him.

"It depends on what you did."

"I didn't do a damned thing. Okay, I was there, like you said.

But I never got out of my car."

"What were you doing there?"

"Listen carefully: I didn't do a thing. I didn't get out of my car."

"No," I said. I was getting a little tired of Gann's telling me to listen. "You listen carefully. I'm going to ask you one more time, and you're going to answer me. What were you there at the Parkers' house for? Why did you even go there at all? Who was there with you?"

Gann smoked and stared at the gray walls for a while. Then he said, "Okay. Here's the deal. I went there in my car. I followed Stanford Parker and the girl. I'd told Parker that his grandmother had collected a lot of cash, and he said he was going to get some of that money for himself."

"That still doesn't explain why you were there."

I thought for a second that I'd pushed a little too hard, that Gann would stop talking, but he fooled me. He said, "I asked Parker for a cut. For telling him the money was there. He was supposed to give it to me that night. But when I heard shots in the house, I got out of there."

"Would you be willing to swear to all that?"

Gann actually smiled. "You have that notary waiting outside the door again?"

"No, but I can send for her."

"Any chance you could get me a couple of beers and some of those cheese crackers?"

I thought about it. Gann might be a little more tractable if I did him a favor, so I said, "Why not? I'll tell them here that I need to take you to my office to get the statement. We'll pick up the beers on the way."

"That's the best offer I've had in a month," Gann said.

I spoke to the Major and explained that I wanted to take Gann to my office so he could give his statement. The Major didn't question me. He said, "I'll get a sheriff's deputy to ride along with you."

By the time I'd signed Gann out to the Homicide Office, the deputy was waiting for me. His name was Larry Follett. He was a skinny, easy-going type with big ears and a wide grin. I knew he wouldn't object if I stopped to buy Gann a beer. He went to the interview room, handcuffed Gann, and brought him out to my car.

I stopped at the first convenience store we came to and told Larry what I was going to do.

"You want a beer?" I said.

He laughed. "You know better than that, Steve. I'd eat a package of those cheese crackers, though."

I went inside and came back with a couple of cans of Bud for Gann, along with a package of crackers for him and one for Larry.

"I can't eat with these cuffs on," Gann said.

"Sure you can," Larry said. "I can't take them off until we get to the HPD."

We all knew that Gann wouldn't have any trouble, except maybe with the beer. I popped the tab, and beer fizzed out. I liked the smell, but I didn't like the product.

"Have at it," I said.

Gann set the beer between his legs, and took his crackers. The cellophane crackled as he unwrapped them.

"Don't get any crumbs on the floor," I said, and even Gann had to laugh.

Larry opened his crackers, too. I sort of wished I'd bought some for myself, but I hadn't, so I started the car and drove out of the parking lot.

Gann took a swallow of his beer and said, "Man, that's good. If there's anything I miss in jail, it's food and drink."

"You get plenty of food and drink," Larry said.

"Yeah. One bite of the crap they serve is plenty," Gann told him.

Larry laughed and said that was probably true, but Gann didn't respond. He was too busy with his beer and crackers. I hoped they'd put him in a good mood for the statement he was going to give me. I was sure that if he told the truth, we'd have what we needed to get a warrant from the D.A. And after that, we'd arrest Parker for the murders.

It would be about time.

We took Gann to an interrogation room since my little office was really too small for all three of us. Larry took off Gann's handcuffs, and Gann sat at the table.

As soon as he'd gotten comfortable, or as comfortable as you could get in that situation, I turned on a tape recorder. I stated my name and the date, and then I read him his rights again.

This time Gann admitted right away that he'd been at the Parker house on the night the family was killed.

"I followed Stanford Parker there," he said, "but I didn't know he was going to kill anybody."

"Did you see how he got into the house?" I asked.

"No. I was parked too far away, and it was too dark."

"Did you hear gunshots?"

"Yeah. And that's when I took off. I didn't stay around to see what happened. I just got out of there as fast as I could."

"Have you seen Stanford Parker since that night?"

"Just once. He came to the jail to see if I'd give him some money. He wouldn't even go my bond. He said he couldn't afford it."

I asked a few more questions, but they didn't really matter. With Gann agreeing with Teresa's statement that Parker had been at the murder scene, the D.A. would surely issue an arrest warrant. We finished things up, and I took Gann and Deputy Follett back to the county jail.

Before I left, I stopped to thank the Major for his help, and while we were talking, Sheriff Thompson's secretary came down the hall to tell me that I had a phone call.

Naturally, it was Clive.

"I've been calling all over for you," he said. "What's going on?"

I told him that I'd been taking Gann's statement.

"We've got plenty on Parker now," I said. "All I have to do is find him."

"That shouldn't be too tough," Clive said. "He's sitting right here in my office."

CHAPTER 33

"He's listening to you right now?" I said.

"Well," Clive said, "I might have exaggerated a little bit. He's here, but he's in another room. I wouldn't want him to hear what I'm saying to you. Want me to bring you up to date?"

"Do you have to ask?"

"I should know better. All right, here's the deal. I called the Chief of Police in Lake City. He didn't want to talk to me, mainly because he didn't do shit about Melanie Jones's disappearance. He's dumb as a doorknob, and he's lazy. There hadn't been a murder there in years, if ever, and he just kind of half-assed it. Didn't do any kind of real investigation at all. He said the gossip was that Melanie had fooled around with other men on occasion, so he checked into that and found out that it's true. She messed around a lot, so that's it as far as he's concerned. She ran off with somebody."

The police chief sounded like Wetsel. But somehow I couldn't get rid of the nagging notion that Wetsel had been right about the Parker case all along.

"What does Melanie's husband think about that?" I said.

"He thinks it's bullshit. Well, not the part about her messing around. He admits she's had problems along those lines. In fact, they're separated and living in different houses because of her roving eye. But she's never gone off before, and he doesn't think she did this time, either. Her car's still in the driveway, and all her clothes are in the closet. Her makeup's still in the bathroom."

"What about the county sheriff?" I said. "Couldn't the chief have called him in for help?"

"He could have, but he didn't. I talked to the sheriff, too. He said he didn't want to get involved in things without the chief's permission and start some kind of turf war."

"Sounds like a real cluster-fuck to me," I said. "No wonder Walter Jones hired you."

"You got that right. I had Tom go down there to Lake City. He had Jones's permission to search Melanie's house, and he found all kinds of evidence, stuff a ten-year-old wouldn't have missed."

"Such as?"

"A Marlboro cigarette butt on the bedroom floor, an empty wine bottle in the kitchen. And the bedroom was all messed up. Tom took all the sheets and blankets and put them in a plastic bag. He put the wine bottle and the cigarette butt in separate bags, too."

"What kind of cigarettes does Parker smoke?"

"Marlboros. He was smoking one when Tom found him."

"Where did he find him, by the way?"

"He called the roofer. Parker was working on another roof for him."

"And he just came along without a fight?"

"You know Tom, and you've seen Parker."

"Right. Has Parker said anything yet?"

"I don't know. Mary brought her equipment over here, and she and Tom have him hooked up to the lie box right now. They should have something by the time you get here."

"They'll have to hurry, then," I said.

Mary had already run two charts on Parker by the time I got

there. She was convinced by the results that Parker had killed his parents and Melanie Jones as well.

"The charts are clear-cut," she said, "but he won't admit anything directly. He thinks he's smarter than we are and that he can beat the machine. I've seen guys like that before. They feel superior to the whole world and think they can fool anybody. Tom's doing the interrogation now. He'll probably get more out of him."

We waited about an hour for Tom to finish. Clive smoked so many cigarettes that he had to open the door and let the smoke out of his office again.

Tom came in looking frustrated. He said, "The son of a bitch is guilty as hell, and I know it. But I can't get him to admit it."

"Mary says he thinks he can beat the machine," Clive told him.

"It might be possible to beat the machine, but not for somebody like Parker. He doesn't care what the charts show, though. When I point out what they show, he just laughs it off."

"He knows the charts aren't any good in court," I said. "They're not evidence."

"Even if he'd confessed and signed a statement, we'd be in trouble," Clive said. "We can't put him under arrest, and we haven't read him his rights. Steve, you'd better go in there and do that."

"Arrest him?" I said.

"That's not funny," Clive said.

"Neither is Parker," I said, "but he thinks he is. Let me read him his rights and see if I can get anything out of him."

Tom took me to the room where the polygraph was set up and introduced me to Parker. He looked pretty much as he had at the funeral, except that now he was dressed in rough working clothes instead of a suit, and he could have used a haircut and a shave. He looked relaxed and comfortable, even though he was sitting next to a polygraph machine.

"How are you today, Sergeant?" he said when Tom told him who I was. He had a light, high-pitched voice and sounded perfectly calm.

"I'm fine, Stanford. How are you?"

"I'm fine, too. We've been doing a lie-detector test. It was pretty interesting."

I could tell by his tone that he found the whole thing amusing. He was confident that he wasn't going to get caught, not for the murder in Galveston or anything else. He was so far superior to us that he couldn't imagine how we could trap him.

"I'll bet it was interesting," I said. "And because of that, I think I'd better read you your rights before we do any more talking."

"That's fine with me," he said. "You can do it if you want to, but I don't see why you have to bother. I'm not guilty of anything."

"It's not my idea," I told him. "Take it up with the Supreme Court."

"I don't have the time. I have a steady job now."

"I'm happy for you," I said, and I read him the Miranda rights.

Parker leaned forward to listen, much more interested in hearing them than Elmer Gann had been.

"If I were a criminal, I wouldn't have to talk to you anymore," he said. "Is that right?"

"That's right."

"And I sure wouldn't have to put up with any polygraph test."

"That's right, too."

"Then I must not be guilty. I don't see the point of continuing this."

"Well," I said, "I haven't talked to you. I'd like to hear what you have to say in person instead of relying on other people."

Tom took that as his cue to leave the room.

"I'll just leave you two alone," Tom said. "If you need me, I'll be just outside the door."

I was pretty sure I wouldn't need him, but you never know with somebody like Parker.

"Stanford," I said when Tom had closed the door, "the way I understand things, you've refused to admit any involvement in the murders of your parents and of Melanie Jones, even though the charts show that you're guilty."

Parker smiled lazily and fished a package of Marlboros from the pocket of his blue work shirt. "Mind if I smoke?"

I minded, but I told him to go ahead. He lit up and said, "I don't care what this machine says." He reached over with his left hand and tapped the polygraph. "It's not proof of anything. And it's wrong. I didn't do anything. Nothing at all."

"Sure you did, and we'll prove it eventually. The machine doesn't make mistakes. You could save us a lot of trouble if you'd just admit that the machine's got you nailed."

Parker smoked and smiled. I wanted to slap the smile off his face, but that wouldn't have been a good idea. I thought back over everything I'd heard about him, trying to come up with something to knock the smugness out of him.

"Let's talk about Melanie Jones," I said.

"I don't have anything to say about her. I worked on her roof, and that's it."

"I don't think so. Tom found one of your cigarette butts in her bedroom, and he found a wine bottle with your fingerprints and hers on it."

I had no idea if that was true. But maybe Parker didn't either. Whether he did or not, he didn't seem bothered. He just smoked and smirked.

Suddenly, I thought I knew what might have happened to

Melanie Jones. It wasn't a certainty, but it was a damned good bet. I said, "Melanie Jones came onto you, didn't she, Stanford? She had a habit of getting involved with other men, and there you were, the handsome roofer, maybe with your sleeves rolled up and your shirt open because of the heat, and she asked you to stick around after the others had left or on their lunch break. Maybe have a little wine with her. Nothing wrong with that. Just a man and a woman, getting close. You had a few drinks, and she started kissing and hugging you. She got you into the bedroom, the dirty bitch. She took off her clothes, and started pulling at yours."

I'd gotten myself pretty worked up, and by that time I was practically in his face, bracing myself with one hand on the table. He leaned back to avoid me and what I was saying. His eyes were wild, and his mouth twisted in disgust.

"She was naked, wasn't she, Stanford? She pulled your face down to her tits, she—"

That was as far as I got before Stanford jammed the glowing tip of his cigarette into the back of my hand.

"Jesus Christ!" I said, jerking my hand away from the table.

Parker pushed back his chair and started to get to his feet. I put my unburned hand against his chest and shoved him back down. The chair skidded on the floor but didn't tip over.

"You son of a bitch," he said.

He looked as if he wanted to come after me, but I pushed him in the chest again to make sure he stayed in the chair.

"You killed her, didn't you, Stanford? The dirty bitch wanted to fuck you, and you killed her."

"It was her fault! My God, it was awful." His disgust was palpable. "I had to get away from her. She grabbed at my arms, and I hit her. I hit her a lot. I couldn't stop hitting her."

"And you killed her."

"Yes, goddammit, yes! I killed her!"

CHAPTER 34

Tom was in the room by then, but I sent him back out.

"And get me some antibiotic ointment if there's any around here," I said. My hand was hurting like hell.

Tom nodded, but he didn't look hopeful.

Stanford was regaining his composure. I said, "Everything that happens in here is recorded, Stanford. There's a microphone hidden in the light fixture, so your confession is on record."

I didn't know if that was true, either. I had a feeling that Clive hadn't had time to set it up, but Stanford wouldn't know that.

"You're going down, Stanford," I said. "There's no way you can deny the confession."

"Yes I can. You hit me, forced me to say things I didn't mean."

"That shit won't do you any good. Clive and his daughter were listening, and they'll swear it was you. So will I. That ought to do it."

He reached in his shirt pocket and brought out the Marlboros. His hand was shaking.

I slapped the package away from him. It flew across the room, hit the wall, and bounced off.

I stuck my hand in front of his face and said, "Look at that, Stanford. You don't even remember that you burned a hole in my hand, do you? You were too pissed off, and that's probably what happened with Melanie Jones. You just lost it."

He slumped in the chair. "That's right. I lost it. I'm not

responsible."

"What a bunch of happy horseshit. You didn't lose it with your family. You shot them because you wanted to, because you hated them. Isn't that right?"

"I didn't hate them, not all of them. My father was a bastard, but not my mother, not my grandmother."

This was the breakthrough I'd been looking for. It had cost me a burned hand, but it was worth it. "Then why did you kill them?"

"I had to. I killed my father, so they had to die, too. I couldn't leave any witnesses."

"You didn't kill the kids."

"They didn't see me. They didn't know."

"Your grandmother wouldn't have seen you if you hadn't gone in her room."

"She had the money. She could have given it to me, but she wouldn't."

"There was no money in the house, Stanford. If your grandmother got payment for a gambling debt, she'd already deposited the money in the bank."

For the first time Parker looked a little disconcerted. "The money was there. I'd been told she just got it that day. She hadn't had time to get to the bank. But I didn't have time to look for it. I panicked and ran."

"But you shot her."

"Yeah, I shot her. And then I got out of there."

"No, Stanford, that's not quite true. You wiped down the window that Emily had opened. And everything else."

"I was wearing gloves. I rubbed them over the window lock, and that's all."

"You picked up your brass."

"Yeah. I knew better than to leave that lying around."

"Where's the gun you used?"

"It's at home. In a dresser drawer."

Which proved how stupid he was. He should have gotten rid of the pistol immediately. But I was glad he hadn't. Now I didn't need a confession, not with the murder weapon. Stanford was done for.

"What about Elmer Gann?" I said. "He was there that night."

"Gann's a total dumb-ass," Parker said. "He didn't have a clue. He's the one who told me about the money, and he was there hoping to get some of it. He never would have, though."

"Why? Were you going to shoot him, too?"

Parker didn't answer that one. He just sat there and looked at the floor. He wasn't smiling anymore. I hoped he wouldn't be smiling for a long time.

"Are you willing to give us a statement now?" I said.

"Hell, no," he said, but I thought he was weakening. He just needed the right kind of treatment.

Tom came back then, with a tube of triple-antibiotic ointment. I took it from him, squeezed some out, and put it on the burn. It didn't cool it much, but it helped a little.

"Where did you find that?" I asked.

"Jane had it in her desk. She says you have to be prepared for anything around this place. You need any help in here?"

"I believe it's time for Clive to come in and have a talk with Stanford," I said. "I think he can get the statement we've been looking for."

"I'll go get him," Tom said.

"Do you think Clive can get Parker to confess?" Mary said.

We were in Clive's smoky-smelling office drinking coffee. As it happened Jane had a small first-aid supply box in her desk, and she'd fixed up a gauze bandage for the back of my hand. The burn still hurt, but I didn't think it was too bad. It would be fine in a day or so. I hoped.

"You know Clive better than I do," I said. "What about it, Tom?"

Tom laughed. "He'll get it. I've seen him work plenty of times. First he'll tell Parker how we can make the case with the cigarette butt and the wine bottle, not to mention that confession you got out of him. Then Clive will start telling Parker that he thinks what Parker really needs is to confess his sins and ask God to forgive him to keep from spending eternity burning in the fiery pit of Hell. You might be surprised at how well that technique works. Clive's usually pretty successful with it. He's actually had some suspects cry when he preaches to them."

"What if none of that works?"

"Then he beats the crap out of them," Tom said, and I couldn't tell if he was kidding or not.

"What's your next step, Steve?" Mary said. "After Dad gets the signed confession, I mean?"

"I'll get a search warrant for Parker's house," I said. "Find the murder weapon and have it checked by Ballistics. And I'll file murder charges on Stanford for the deaths of his parents and grandmother. After that, it'll be up to the courts."

"And if Clive doesn't get the confession?"

"That's the least of my worries," I said.

Clive came into his office after about an hour and asked Tom to go sit with Parker.

"And take him some coffee," Clive said.

Tom filled up a clean cup and went away with it, and Clive sat down behind his desk.

"Well?" I said.

"Well, what?"

"Well, did you get the confession?" Mary said.

Clive grinned widely. "Sure." He showed us several sheets of paper torn from a yellow legal pad. "All written out in his own hand and signed."

"Did you preach to him?" I said.

"Maybe a little."

"Give us a sample."

Clive turned serious. "This isn't a joke, Steve," he said.

"I never thought it was. I was just interested."

"All right. I told him that I thought the devil had taken possession of his soul and that I thought he knew it. I told him that the only way he could ever get rid of the devil inside himself was to confess and get his business straight with God."

"What did he say?" Mary asked.

"He said he was going to pray about it and that he was going to ask God's forgiveness. I told him that was all he needed to do."

"And you really believe that?" I said.

Clive nodded. "I really do, Steve. I think Parker does, too. Why? Don't you?"

CHAPTER 35

The next day we had the gun to go along with the confession. It had been in the drawer right where Teresa and Parker had said. I knew the ballistics would check out, and I knew that Stanford Parker was going to be in prison for a long time, if he didn't get the death penalty.

Bolce was happy, the D.A. was happy, and I was feeling pretty good myself. Sarah was doing fine, and she was making plans for starting her teaching job again in the fall. She was enthusiastic about all sorts of projects that she had in mind for her classes. We still ate out a lot, but there was nothing wrong with that. We both enjoyed it.

So my life was going well.

But a couple of things about the Parker case still worried me.

I didn't know what charges we could file against Gann for his part in things. According to Parker, Gann was just a dumb-ass, out for a quick buck, and I believed that was true. What worried me was that if we filed on Gann, Teresa might have to testify, and I didn't want that. She was getting her life in order, and she wasn't even the same person who'd been with Parker on the night he murdered his family. I decided to let the D.A. make the decision without any comment from me. I just hoped he'd do the right thing.

And he did. After a few days he called to say that he figured the hot-check charges would keep Gann off the streets for a while, and that was good enough. I agreed with him. That was one worry I wouldn't have to deal with.

Which left me with Wetsel. He was still on suspension and not likely ever to get back on the force, not after the courts got through with him. He'd be lucky if he didn't wind up in jail, and in fact I thought he would. But it wasn't just his crooked real estate dealings that bothered me.

He caught me as I was leaving the department one afternoon. He'd been waiting in the parking lot, and before he'd come there he'd been drinking beer. I could smell it on him, along with the odor of sweat and cigarette smoke. He wouldn't be drinking in cop bars these days. Hardly anybody on the force would want to be seen within a mile of him, not while he was under suspicion and being investigated.

He appeared out of nowhere as I was opening the door of my car and pushed the door shut, jerking it out of my hand. The late afternoon was still stifling hot, and the swampy smell of Buffalo Bayou hung in the air.

"You son of a bitch," Wetsel said. "You cost me my job."

"You haven't lost your job yet," I said. "And I didn't do a thing. You're the one who had the illegal deals working."

He poked me in the chest with his finger. "There wasn't a thing illegal about those deals. They were all on the up-and-up, and that'll come out in court. And that's not all. I was right about Stanford Parker from the get-go. If you hadn't stolen my case, if we'd pulled him in and sweated him when I said to, that woman in Galveston would still be alive."

Wetsel had been talking to someone. Maybe McGuire was still taking his calls. And the hell of it was that he had a point.

"I didn't steal your case," I said. "Bolce took you off it. We couldn't pull Parker in because we didn't have any evidence, we didn't have any motive, and Parker had an alibi."

"We could've broken the alibi. If I'd been left in charge that woman wouldn't have died, and I'd still be on the job."

mentioned, but nothing was said about the confession being given in his office, much less about what Clive had said to Parker to get it or what Parker had said afterward.

"Did you tell her that?" I asked Clive.

"Not me." He looked at Teresa. "How did you know?"

She smiled. "I just know. Has Stanford asked God to forgive him?"

Clive looked at a loss for words, an unusual condition for him. He thought for a minute, and then said, "Yes, Stanford asked God to forgive him. He knows he might get the death penalty, but he seems prepared for it."

I wasn't sure that Stanford had been that forthcoming after his confession to Clive, but maybe he had. I didn't think Clive would lie about it, not to Teresa.

"I wish you could tell us how you know this stuff," Clive said. "There's something mysterious going on."

She gave him a wan smile. "It is a mystery. I really don't know how I know. I just knew somehow that Stanford had made things right between himself and God." Her voice, which hadn't been strong in the beginning became even softer. "I think I'd like to sleep now, Mother Superior. Remember that I love all of you. If you see Stanford tell him to remember what Jesus said to one of the thieves on the Cross: 'You will be with me this day in paradise.' "

We started out of the room, and Teresa lay back on her pillow. She was asleep by the time the door had closed.

Clive and I left the convent, neither of us saying a word to the other, both of us lost in our own thoughts. Finally I turned to Clive and said, "I don't think she'll be with us much longer."

"I doubt it myself," was all Clive said.

We rode along for a few blocks in silence. Then Clive turned to me and said, "Mother Superior told me that the doctor said that Teresa must be in a lot of pain, but she smiled for us."

I nodded. The memory would stick with me for a long time, I knew.

A month or so after that I was in the office on a Saturday. I was doing paperwork. If I ever left the police and took a job with Clive, the reason would be paperwork. I had a feeling that Clive didn't do nearly as much as I did.

When the phone rang, I thought it would be Sarah, but it was Clive.

"What the hell are you doing at work on a Saturday afternoon?" he said.

"I have to pull rotation, Clive, just like everybody else, and this is my Saturday to work. What's up?"

"I wanted to catch you up on a few things. I got a call from a psychiatric clinic the other day, and the doctor told me that Gene Moore had checked himself in. He wanted to know if I'd send Gene a couple of pairs of pajamas, a toothbrush, some toothpaste, and an electric razor."

"What's he in the clinic for?"

"Alcoholism," Clive said.

"I didn't know he had a problem."

"It's gotten worse since the Parker business. I think seeing Parker kill those animals really shook him up."

"I hope he'll be all right."

"The place he went to is one of the best," Clive said. "I also wanted to tell you that I sent some fruit and flowers to Teresa. I signed your name, too."

"Thanks. I appreciate that. How's she doing?"

"Are you sitting down?"

"You think I do paperwork standing up?" I said, though I wasn't in a joking mood. The news about Moore hadn't been good, and now I was afraid he was going to tell me that Teresa had died.

"I don't know how you do paperwork," Clive said. "And I don't care. Are you sitting down?"

"Yes, dammit. Now tell me the news."

"Mother Superior called me this morning," he said. "Teresa went in for a check-up yesterday, and the doctor said that the cancer was in remission, or going into remission. The tumor is a lot smaller."

I felt the tension going out of me.

"Teresa told the doctor that she wanted to start working again, mopping the floors, but he said that it wasn't time for that yet. Mother Superior said that Teresa had been in the chapel all morning, down on her knees, praying."

"Clive, I'm not sure I believe in miracles."

"I'm not sure I do, either. All I'm telling you is what I've heard. And you know the doctor wouldn't lie to them." Clive's voice softened. "I just wish that God had used a miracle for Anna and let her stay here a little longer. But I'm not questioning him."

I didn't know what to say to that, so I kept quiet, and after a second or two of silence Clive hung up.

I thought about what he'd told me for the rest of the afternoon, and I didn't get much paperwork done.

I didn't come to any real conclusions about miracles, either, but I did know one thing: on Sunday morning, Sarah and I would be going to church.

ABOUT THE AUTHORS

Bill Crider is the multiple Anthony-award–winning author of the Sheriff Dan Rhodes series. He has published more than fifty mystery, western, and horror novels under his own and other names.

Clyde Wilson is a former Houston, Texas, private eye whose cases have involved the rich and powerful, the famous and the infamous. He is now retired and is at work on a second novel.